CUSHING'S CRUSADE

Cushing's Crusade

TIM JEAL

faber and faber

This edition first published in 2013
by Faber and Faber Ltd
Bloomsbury House, 74–77 Great Russell Street
London WC1B 3DA

Printed and bound by CPI Group (UK) Ltd, Croydon, CRO 4YY

A CIP record for this book is available from the British Library

ISBN 978-0-571-30391-5

Preface to the 2013 Edition

I wrote *Cushing's Crusade* when I was twenty-eight, immediately after completing an extensively researched life of David Livingstone. So my choice of an impoverished archivist as my fictional protagonist owed much to my pursuit of documents in a number of small colonial and African-orientated archives. I had left the BBC three years earlier to become a full-time author and was already keenly aware of the difficulties of earning a living though my writing. Archivists, like most writers, earned very little, but had to be intelligent and hard-working to do their job effectively. People in the wider world of work, with less intelligence and dedication than scholars or writers, seemed to earn more than them and to be on secure career paths enabling them to support themselves with a lot less difficulty. It occurred to me that this gulf might be fertile ground for a novel.

So my hero, Derek Cushing, would be painfully aware of his wife's disappointment with him for earning so little and for doing a type of work which few people knew about or respected. Diana needles Derek the whole time in the hope that she will one day prod him into being more assertive, but he is determined not to oblige her with the show of manly indignation he believes she is inviting. Instead he fights back using calculated acquiescence and appeasement as his weapons. Why should he do the obvious and emulate well-off and self-satisfied people whom he has no respect for?

An old university friend, Charles, is affable and rich and

working (in Diana's eyes) in a far more interesting field than her husband's. He owns a modern art gallery. Derek suspects Diana is having an affair with Charles, but he does not allow even this to goad him into raging at her. 'The sheer dedication, almost passion, of his ineffectuality soon win us over,' wrote the *Guardian*'s critic to my relief. I had been determined that Derek, with his disaster-prone tendencies, should not be seen merely as a down-beat loser, but rather as someone who, though doing himself no favours, could still hold his own in challenging circumstances. With his lunatic jealousies, and his civilised self-lacerating jokes, there's no denying that he *can* be a figure of fun. Yet he is never that to his thirteen-year-old son, who laughs at all his jokes, even when they aren't funny. In return Derek does his best never to let the boy down – which he manages, until an astonishingly vexatious series of events unfold from the dunking of his watch in seawater, causing him, at the end of a disastrous afternoon, to miss a train, find 'slippery solace' in a field, and afterwards to confess his misbehaviour to his son and then to his wife, fatally alienating both of them *and* his new girlfriend too.

Only at the point of losing everything does Derek finally acknowledge that moderation has let him down badly and that anger and selfishness will be needed urgently if he is to reclaim even part of his family and his self-respect too. By ditching his habitual view of himself as a non-combatant in his marital war, at the eleventh hour he prevents comedy turning into tragedy.

Most reviewers thought that the book was funny and moving and my best to date. But though it won a national prize in Britain, the Americans found it too British to publish. The supportive New York editor who had published my first two novels had just killed himself and no new publisher had stepped forward to take his place. My agent tried to persuade Heinemann to give me a generous two-book contract, but he got nowhere. This was before prizes had much impact on sales. I was married by now, and Joyce and I had a child and hoped to have more, though I could not see how (even with Joyce working) I could afford to write literary fiction for a while. Perhaps I should have been braver. Anyway, I signed up to write two historical novels and then a biography, and then another biography, and more historical novels and a memoir, and somehow the moment never came when I could spare the time to write another contemporary novel. Nearly forty years have passed and at last the moment may have come.

Tim Jeal
April 2013

Chapter 1

On a fourth-floor balcony of Abercorn Mansions Diana Cushing lay flat on her face with her breasts flattened under her; the ornamented railings cast a pattern of regularly spaced stripes across her bare back. Her husband Derek squatted beside her, rubbing sun-oil into her tanned and slightly perspiring skin; absently he rolled the balls of his fingers back and forth along her vertebrae. A faint smell of melting tar and petrol fumes rose from the street below. Derek could feel the top of his head smarting; the sun had caught his bald patch. He got up quietly and stood watching his wife for several moments, until satisfied that her deep and regular breathing did undoubtedly mean that she had fallen asleep. Then he slipped through the french windows into the flat. This was an excellent opportunity to wash the kitchen floor.

Five weeks before, Diana had unexpectedly sacked their cleaning woman and, since then, had done no dusting or cleaning herself. On his return from work every day Derek had washed up the dishes, emptied his wife's ashtrays, done a little hoovering, attended to the cat's tray and thrown out the kitchen garbage; but none of this had significantly arrested the general deterioration of the flat. To start with, partly because Diana's behaviour was often unpredictable, and partly because he had always made strenuous efforts to avoid arguments of any sort, Derek had been content to say and do nothing. But then, when Diana's inactivity continued into its fourth week, and she not only rejected his suggestion that they should employ another cleaner, but also told him that he was to stop all forms of cleaning himself, Derek realized that he was

1

involved. By then the dust on the table-tops was thick enough to write legible words in.

Derek was aware that continued avoidance of a serious discussion of the situation was behaviour which might justifiably strike an outsider as insane indifference. Well-balanced people do not as a rule pretend that serious disturbances do not exist; and yet he had discovered with a sense of shock that he had no intention of bringing matters to a head. He was convinced that Diana's lethargy, far from being a cry for help or the result of some psychological disorder, was a calculated assault on him; a plot to make him assert himself and act positively, to force him out of his usual acquiescence to her moods and wishes. The challenge was equivalent to a command to change his character. So why not acquiesce again and do what she wanted? Why not end the idiotic impasse and please her with a sudden burst of explosive male dominance? Why creep into the kitchen like a criminal and furtively clean the kitchen floor, instead of demanding that she, or somebody else, do it?

Derek's answer was simple: by refusing to be assertive, he was *really* asserting himself. By rejecting her challenge, he was preserving his true persona. Not only that, he was saving her from self-deception and the mistaken belief that a display of decisive and authoritative behaviour on his part would reflect a real change of heart rather than a piece of enforced acting. He was not and never had been strong-willed and positive, and, at thirty-eight, he felt no obligation to attempt to be so. Moderation, compromise, humility and an honest desire to fall in with what other people wanted, were qualities to be cherished rather than reviled.

Derek squeezed out his mop and looked at the results of his efforts on the kitchen floor. The dirt had become so ingrained that a scrubbing-brush was called for. He was working on all fours when Diana came into the room some ten minutes later. Derek remained on his knees.

Diana was three years younger than Derek and, as he freely and often admitted, had weathered the years considerably better than himself. Her long auburn hair was still untinted, and although her cheekbones had become more pronounced, Derek thought this a distinction rather than an imperfection. Nor did he consider the faint crow's-feet at the corners of her eyes or the few delicate lines traced across her high forehead in any way detrimental. She was a little heavier around the hips than when they had met fourteen years before, but since Derek had then thought her a little thin, this was simply an improvement. And her slightly slanting eyes, which he had always thought her greatest asset, were just as enigmatic with their subtle colour which changed in certain lights from honeycomb-flecked brown to yellowish green.

Since Diana remained silent, Derek went on scrubbing, expecting at any moment to be attacked; but when she spoke it was quietly.

'What's this?'

Derek's gaze moved obediently upwards from her knees, past her floral pants and still-bare stomach and breasts, to her upheld right arm. In her hand was a small green card.

'A hospital appointments card,' answered Derek, scrubbing with less vigour.

'Yours?' she went on lightly.

'You found it in my jacket pocket.'

Diana smiled pleasantly and let the card fall on to the wet floor.

'Cancer? A kidney transplant? A ruptured artery?'

'Piles,' murmured Derek, getting up with slow dignity.

'Didn't you think it worth telling me about?' she snapped with sudden ferocity. Derek explained that he had undergone a series of rectal injections which were meant to shrink the offending veins, and that he had not wanted to cause distress before the results were known, and that although he now suspected that an operation was probable it was not certain, and that he was sorry if his well-intentioned silence had proved counter-productive and caused annoyance.

'You mean you forgot to tell me,' said Diana, making for the door.

'What would you like for supper?' Derek called after her.

She turned in the doorway and looked at him sadly. 'Why do

3

you always have to make your conciliatory gestures so obvious?'

Derek picked up the bucket of dirty water and poured it down the sink. 'I suppose,' he said, 'because if you didn't notice them, they wouldn't conciliate.' He tossed the scrubbing-brush into the cupboard under the sink and added, 'But if you do notice, they become obvious. It's a bit of a problem,' he ended lamely.

Diana made a plopping noise with her tongue, and said with a toss of her head, 'I'll have what *you* want for supper, if that small decision doesn't prove too much for you.'

She was about to go again when Derek put in, 'I didn't forget about the injections. It isn't the sort of thing one forgets; especially when there are a dozen students peering up one.'

'You just forgot to *tell* me,' she replied, leaving the room.

Derek was getting supper ready when his son Giles came in. He looked flushed and angry.

'She's lolling about on the balcony with her bosoms bare. Anybody could see her.'

Giles was thirteen, but small for his age. For the last six months he had been wearing glasses. Derek finished scraping the last of the carrots.

'She *can't* sit out there like that,' went on an outraged Giles.

Derek came and rested a hand on his son's shoulder.

'She can, I'm afraid; not that there's anything wrong with her breasts or breasts in general. In Africa . . .'

'We're not in Africa,' the boy cut in furiously. 'I might have come back with some friends.'

'What would they have said?' asked Derek with genuine interest.

Giles shrugged his shoulders and looked away.

' "Never knew your mum was a nudist." Stuff like that. "Went to tea with Cushing and his mum showed us her tits." ' Giles picked up a carrot and took a large bite. The week before, Diana had laughed at her son for locking the bathroom door. He wasn't ashamed of his first pubic hair, was he? With his mouth full of carrot, Giles muttered, 'Not that I'd want to bring anybody back with the flat like this.'

'She'll soon snap out of it,' said Derek soothingly.

'Will she?' Giles looked almost tearful. 'It's not as though she's writing any articles or anything. I lent her two of my geology books but she hasn't read a word.'

Knowing Diana's lack of enthusiasm for Giles's passionate interest in stones and fossils, Derek was not surprised. 'Give her a bit more time,' he said. 'She's been depressed. Nobody likes doing anything when they're depressed.'

Giles looked at his father derisively. 'If she hit you over the head with a frying-pan, you'd say she couldn't help it because she was depressed.'

'A bit of an exaggeration,' laughed Derek.

'Is it?' asked Giles.

'I do know what I'm doing,' replied Derek with apparent assurance.

'Everything,' came back Giles. 'And you'll go on doing everything till you tell her where to get off.'

'We'll see about that,' replied Derek as lightly as he could manage.

'Nobody else's father would stand for it,' the boy threw out scornfully as he walked out of the room.

Derek started to peel the outer skins off the onions. Soon tears were running freely down his cheeks.

The following afternoon Derek was sitting at his desk in the manuscript room of the Afro-Asian Institute, where he had been the archivist for the past eleven years. An extraordinarily idle man would not have considered the job demanding. There had been few major additions to the manuscript collection during the past decade, and the routine task of maintaining the catalogue of printed books occupied little time. Apart from answering the occasional queries of historians and biographers and helping readers to locate material, Derek was free to pursue his own research on European expansion in East Africa between 1870 and 1900.

An hour earlier Derek had had to shut every window in the room to reduce the noise of the relentless pile-driver on the building-site across the street. Now the place was like a greenhouse and Derek felt no inclination to work. Instead he idly watched Professor Elkin, one of the only two readers working in the room, take off his jacket and roll up his shirtsleeves as though preparing himself for some formidable manual task. The professor's arms were impressively hairy; the backs of his hands, even the backs of his fingers up to the knuckles, were covered with thick black hair. Derek speculated whether he had hairs all the way up his back; there was no doubt that naked he would make an imposing spectacle. In buses, tubes and shops Derek beguiled tedious moments by seeing people as animals. Red-haired people with their white eyebrows and eyelashes were pigs, small boys with large front teeth were rabbits, and Professor Elkin was undoubtedly a large lowland gorilla. Gorillas came in the main from western equatorial Africa. The professor's interests lay on the other side of that continent. With exaggerated care his hairy hands were opening another manuscript box and soon his learned eyes were scanning the contents of Folder 'A': 'Thirty-Seven Letters from Sir Harry Johnston to the Colonial Office'. Derek began to doze in the afternoon heat; inside the professor's skull the events following the annexation of Nyasaland flickered into fitful life; in the far corner of the room a small Kenyan thumbed his way through page after page of agricultural statistics to find details about the migrant cocoa farmers of southern Ghana. For Derek it was a fairly typical working afternoon.

Most of Derek's marital problems stemmed from Diana's youthful admiration for academics. In the days of their courtship he had capitalized on this, making sure, whenever they had gone together to a museum or art gallery, that he had previously read up on what they would see. He had thus been able to appear far better informed than he really was; well informed moreover on a wide range of subjects; not simply a narrow specialist scholar. He had not told Diana a great deal about his work since he had felt sure than an air of mystery would lend it a greater dignity than any detailed exposition. So Diana, who had been reading a great many Russian novels at the time, had mistakenly supposed that

6

Derek's research, even though in a confined field, would throw light on universal matters: objective reality, the nature of truth and similarly exalted concepts. Diana had married her scholar before the publication of his first two books: *Economic Imperialism and Cultural Relativism,* and *Economic Imperialism: A Reassessment.* Her disillusion with scholars and scholarship dated from her reading of these books, both of which she found turgid, wordy and narrow.

For a while, by flogging his rapidly tiring intellect into bursts of energy that left him nervous and exhausted, Derek had managed to preserve a little of his wife's former admiration for the variety of his knowledge and interests. But this could not, did not last. He needed time to take on new ideas, but since he was with Diana all the time he never had a chance. Her demands increased; like an eager oil magnate she tapped her husband's head, without restraint or an eye to the future; soon she had sucked his resources dry. Once she had seen businessmen, lawyers and scientists as men pursuing mundane and trivial objects in comparison with the scholar's elevated pursuit of pure knowledge. Now she could not conceal from Derek that, in her opinion, to be an academic was to be an emotional and mental bankrupt: a man who had never had the courage to take his chances in the real world.

At half-past four Derek woke with a start, his shirt soaked with sweat; somebody was telling him something. He recognized Diana's voice and sat up abruptly.

'Another arduous day in the archives,' she said, looking down at him.

'Must have dropped off,' he muttered. Since Diana had not been out of the flat for over a month, he suspected she had come to cause a scene. He braced himself for the coming onslaught. But she seemed unnaturally cheerful and amiable.

'Time we went shopping together. You need some new clothes.'

'Do I?' asked Derek hesitantly.

'I'll meet you outside the tube station at half-past five.' She had not bothered to lower her voice and Professor Elkin was looking at her disapprovingly. She gave him a friendly wave as she went out. Derek was still trying to work out what her evident change of mood meant when five o'clock came.

Having politely ejected Elkin and the Kenyan, Derek locked all the manuscript boxes used by readers during the day into the safe upstairs. Security arrangements at the Institute amused him. He liked to imagine a small band of historians with masks, sticks of gelignite and metal-cutting-gear, blasting their way into the main archives and making away with everything. But scholarly thieves, he reflected bitterly, were rather less spectacular than bank robbers in the manner of their operations: a letter furtively slipped into a briefcase or casually folded between innocent pages of notes, all under the archivist's eye—that was their cowardly way. That was how almost the entire Raffles collection had disappeared two years before.

Outside in the evening sunlight Derek started walking towards his rendezvous with Diana. Across the road on the building-site the pile-driver thumped out a brisk marching rhythm. Buses, cars, motor-bicycles, taxis, even the occasional invalid-carriage swept by as the heart of the city pumped men and metal outwards towards far-flung suburbs. The sun glittered on office windows and secretaries hurried home on high heels. Cotton frocks and flimsy underwear. Women wear less in summer. To rub genitals against the thighs or buttocks of strangers in the tube is called 'frotteurism' and is an offence: technically an assault. It is virtually impossible not to assault people in the tube. Fascinus was a classical god whose image was the erect male organ. Virgins celebrated his festival with ceremonies of public defloration; their implement was a suitably sized replica of the god. The useless verbal lumber in Derek's head was extensive, and growing year by year; the thought did not displease him; words to replace dying brain cells. A losing battle but life was that anyway, little man against an unfathomable universe. Libraries and archives were arsenals for the battle against time, voices for the dead, and archivists pursued the noble cause of guarding the produce of brains long since decomposed. There were other ways to look at it, and Derek often looked at it in other ways. Libraries were vomitoriums, places for storing gobbets of half-digested matter for living men to feed upon, escapist palaces where past regurgitations could make the present palatable.

Some distance from the tube station Derek could see a gradually increasing traffic jam. The cause of it seemed to be an untidily parked car not unlike the Cushing family saloon; inside it was a woman not unlike Mrs Cushing. The resemblance was too great for coincidence. Derek started to run towards the offending vehicle. Diana flung open the passenger-seat door and motioned him to get in. From the direction she drove off in, Derek assumed that they were on their way to the crowded chaos of Oxford Street.

They had blundered through the semi-darkness of five boutiques before reaching the one where Diana spotted what she thought Derek could do with for the summer: a light cotton suit in a delicate pale-blue material, with a battledress-style jacket and breast pockets picked out with darker blue thread at the edges. Derek was so delighted with his wife's apparent recovery that he did not feel able to suggest that brown, green or even mustard versions of the same would have looked less overtly homosexual. Struggling into the light blue hipster trousers behind a flimsy curtain, he found that their figure-hugging cut was such that if he wore them regularly, his testicles would be forced into his lower abdomen. Armed with this certainty he objected, making sure to look disappointed rather than relieved. In the end Diana chose him a blue-and-white-striped jacket and an innocuous pair of beige flared trousers.

Before her recent malaise Diana had always decided what clothes he should buy, so Derek saw her resumption of this habit as a sign that all would now be well. Incredibly he appeared to have won a significant marital victory. He had never minded Diana's desire to dress him up in clothes more suitable for men ten years younger, and today he minded still less. She had often told him that he was burnt-out and dull, so he had never resented her attempt to make him look more vital and alive. It was rather like the macabre habit of some undertakers who put rouge on the cheeks of corpses to make them more life-like, but there was no

9

sense in getting worked up, even though he could not share the spurious sense of individuality experienced by many who bought fashionable clothes. But better to adopt off-the-peg fashion than off-the-peg ideas. Whatever indignities his acquiescence inflicted on his appearance, his mental clothing, he hoped, remained his own.

The sitting-room in the Cushings' flat was a large room with a high ceiling and french windows leading out on to the narrow balcony. They had inherited half the furniture from the previous tenants, whose taste had been unusual. There was a terrible standard lamp with peculiar fluted swellings carved at intervals on the wooden column, a large reproduction Jacobean table and an equally dark and heavy-looking sideboard. Diana had tried to brighten up the flat by putting down a red carpet but this had merely emphasized the sombreness of the furniture. Two modern chairs, with metal frames and canvas seats, also tended to accentuate the bulk of the large Victorian sofa with its ornate wooden scrolls on the arms. Diana particularly liked ferns, palms and other rubbery dark-leaved plants, which, Derek thought, gave the room an unnatural underwater look. Diana tossed him his parcel of clothes.

'Don't just stand there. Take off your trousers.'

Derek did as he was asked and then slipped on his new garments. Diana watched him critically. She had often told him that his legs were short and stubby, quite wrong for his long torso, and that his head was too large for the width of his shoulders. Derek had always admitted she was right. She looked him up and down for a few moments and smiled.

'You'll do,' she said generously.

Derek stood awkwardly in the middle of the room.

'All dressed up and nowhere to go,' he said.

'I wouldn't say that,' she replied after a pause. 'The jacket looks just right for the sea.'

Since they rarely went to the sea, Derek decided she was being sarcastic. He was mistaken.

'Charles rang up this afternoon,' she went on. 'He's bought a house on a Cornish estuary; wants us to stay there for a couple of weeks.'

Diana's evident excitement made Derek cautious. He hated sitting on beaches and swimming.

'That's jolly good of him,' he said. 'Of course there shouldn't be any problem about getting time off. When does he want us to go?'

'Last week in July and the first in August.'

Derek sank down on to the Victorian sofa.

'I see,' he replied quietly. How could she possibly have forgotten that he had arranged to spend those very weeks in Edinburgh at the National Library of Scotland going through the Macnair papers: documents vital to his East African research. So that was her game. She'd clean up the house and stop messing him around if he gave up his crucial research trip. Diana was going on about how much Giles would enjoy himself. He could even learn to sail, and the opportunity for looking for his precious rocks along the sea shore could scarcely be bettered. Derek had a very fair idea of how Diana would respond if he said he intended going on with his research. What sort of a man could put a load of yellowing papers before a child's enjoyment? If his research actually had any importance she might feel differently, but what was it except a dead-end subject about dead people? A convenient escape from the real world and real people.

'Those were the only dates?' he asked helplessly.

Diana nodded. 'So I can let him know it's all right?'

He took a deep breath and prepared himself for the worst. 'I'm going to Scotland then.'

'Doing what?' said Diana, as though he had just made a uniquely disgusting proposition. 'You can't intend to prevent us going.'

Derek put his head in his hands. Dear God, to think that he'd thought he had won a victory over the flat and her lethargy; if he had, she was going to make him pay for it all right. She wasn't even remotely aware of the ludicrous irony that all her efforts of the last six weeks had been designed to make him assert himself, and now, when he did so, she wanted him to revert to his old

11

obsequiousness. Suddenly the solution came to him.

'You go,' he exclaimed triumphantly, as though announcing an idea of amazing brilliance. 'You and Giles go to Cornwall and I'll go to Scotland.' He smiled at her and started laughing. 'That's the answer.'

To his surprise Diana did not argue with him. He had been sure he would have to deliver a lengthy monologue on his personal feelings in order to convince her that he would ruin the holiday rather than contribute to it, but now, mercifully, there was no need.

A few moments later Diana said, 'Apart from my wanting you to come, don't you think Charles is going to find your refusal rather peculiar?'

Derek laughed. 'He only likes me because he thinks I'm peculiar.'

Diana laughed too and asked no further questions. Derek had known Charles Lamont for almost twenty years, but did not exactly like him. Yet Charles went on asking him to dinner parties and he went on accepting because he didn't dislike the man either. Derek certainly wasn't jealous of Charles's wealth or his successful art gallery, nor did he feel hurt by his near-certainty that Charles only enjoyed producing him at dinner parties to demonstrate the wide range of his acquaintance. You see, I don't just meet people in the art and business worlds, and here to prove it from the eccentric world of scholarship is Derek Cushing, the unassuming archivist. Ever been to the Afro-Asian Institute, by the way? No? I'm not surprised at all; it's the sort of place one thought had died with the Empire. Straight out of the Victorian era: masses of pictures of Empire builders and elephants all jumbled up with Rhodes's inkwell and Livingstone's toe, and thousands of books which nobody reads. Yes, it is a funny sort of job, but he doesn't seem to mind. Lives in a dark and cavernous flat near Kilburn. It's in one of those mock Tudor monstrosities; all white plasterwork and fake beams. Strange thing is he's got a rather good-looking wife. That's her over there; the bored one with that slightly embittered look. I was at university with Derek, same college; the dons all said he was

12

brilliant. And today . . . well, look at him. But there's something rather attractive about lost causes and wasted opportunities. Derek's the best example of it I know. I'm thinking of having him stuffed actually; something for my private collection. I wouldn't be able to sell him in my gallery, but at home he'll look rather fine with the Etruscan statuary. Of course it was just possible, Derek conceded, that he had misjudged Charles, but he didn't think so.

So he had saved his research and Giles and Diana would get a good holiday in Cornwall; for the first time in weeks Derek felt happy. To think how narrowly he had escaped the tedium of lying for hours on some nasty beach with his stubby legs burning, and the top of his head going redder and redder and starting to peel, and suffering the enforced bonhomie and the drinking, and the walks in the rain, to show that one was determined to make the most of every situation, and the conversations about plays and films and art and life and above all the gratitude for what we have received at your lovely house in such lovely country and, yes, how incredibly clever of you to have got it all for only seventy thousand and . . .

'I'll ring him and explain,' offered Derek magnanimously.

'I'd be much happier if you came,' murmured Diana.

But Derek was already dialling Charles's number.

Chapter 2

Shortly after 4.00 p.m. on July 13, ten days before his scheduled departure for Scotland, Derek Cushing lifted the receiver of his phone in the Afro-Asian Institute and dialled his dentist's number. Derek was not worried about his teeth but wished to leave a message for his wife, who had informed him that morning that she had a dental appointment for four o'clock. The receptionist was apologetic and regretted that she could not give Mrs Cushing a message, since to her certain knowledge no Mrs Cushing had an appointment that afternoon. Did Mrs Cushing have an appointment on any other day that week? The receptionist denied knowledge of any such appointment. Derek thanked her and rang off. He had simply wished to let Diana know that he intended going straight from work to the address where they were having dinner and would not go home first.

Diana could be absent-minded and mistake a day, but to mistake the week of a dental appointment was taking absentmindedness further than Derek thought probable. She had lied to him on occasions in the past and he had been known to lie to her and perhaps there was nothing in it, and if there was something in it perhaps it didn't matter anyway. If she felt like telling him that she had gone to the dentist and had instead spent the afternoon in a sauna bath, that was her business. Derek was irritated only because he now felt impelled to go back to the flat before going on to the dinner party.

At breakfast the following day, after eating an all but hard-boiled egg without complaint, Derek cleared a visual path between the three large packets of cereal on the table and said, 'I

14

really am a selfish sod. I forgot to ask how you got on at the dentist.'

'Better late than never,' replied Diana. 'A couple of fillings; that was all. I've got to go back on Friday to let the hygienist have a go at my gums. Hygienist, my foot; it's as bad as calling dustmen "disposal operatives".'

So she had added another lie. If one lie was innocuous, were two lies rather different?

'Why did you change dentists?' Derek asked abruptly.

She was buttering some toast. He watched carefully to see whether her knife stopped dead or whether she seemed put out in any less obvious way.

'Christ, how awful. You didn't go to meet me at Gilchrist's, did you?'

'I phoned and you didn't have an appointment.'

'I'm surprised I didn't tell you. I've got a new man.'

'What was wrong with Gilchrist?'

There was no sign of embarrassment, no surprise, no evidence of quick thinking. Diana took a sip of coffee and smiled.

'I didn't like Gilchrist's eyes. I don't suppose you've noticed, but they're yellow, not the pupils but the whites. They're usually bloodshot too. They made me feel ill, the way he used to peer into my mouth with his eyeballs brushing my cheeks.'

'And the new dentist has white whites?'

'Very white. He's an Indian so I suppose that might make them seem whiter than they are.'

'Should I go to him too?'

'If you don't like Gilchrist's eyes, it mightn't be a bad idea.'

Could anybody possibly leave a dentist because of the whites of their eyes? Derek pondered the question for a few moments before conceding that Diana was capable of it. Or had she just thought of it there and then? Suddenly he felt irritated. Nobody ought to leave dentists because of their eyeballs. That might be a reason to leave an oculist. The only physical defect that could possibly justify leaving a dentist was a mouthful of bad teeth; no, delirium tremens and Parkinson's disease should be added.

'I've never heard such a lousy reason for leaving a dentist,' he said. Diana was looking at him with unfeigned surprise. He was being assertive, which was unusual enough, but, more unusual still, he was being assertive at breakfast. 'What I mean is,' he went on, 'I don't understand such a reason.'

Diana lit a cigarette and exhaled twintusks of smoke from her nostrils. She seemed amused now.

'I would have thought I'd made it pretty clear. Anyway, why should you understand? Is my one aim and object in life meant to be making myself comprehensible to you?' she paused and then added, 'There's no reason to look so persecuted. You've as good as said you don't believe me. Fine. If you don't, it's your tough titty.'

'Thank you for being so explicit.'

'Pleasure,' she replied.

Diana had started to read the paper, and since Derek could think of nothing else to say he left for work.

For Derek the morning rush-hour was a special violation. He was convinced that people who worked in shops or other crowded places did not detest the shoulder-to-shoulder pressure and the constant buffeting as he did. How could they know the agony of the timid archivist, accustomed only to the womb-like security of his library, when he was plunged into the alien maelstrom of the commuters' cauldron? On some mornings Derek managed to establish a scholarly distance to the whole sub-human business by making classical comparisons: Charon the ticket-office clerk to whom he gave his coin, the lift Charon's boat, the doors of the train the gates of Hades, and Pluto himself the power of money that sucked all men into the bowels of the earth. But on this particular morning such thoughts held no consolation. In the tube, just as the train was leaving Baker Street, it came to Derek that Diana had been lying to him. Since she lied to him quite often, it was not the lying itself that alarmed him, but the conclusion that on this particular occasion it might matter that she had lied. Although he mistrusted intuition he could not escape this feeling. My wife, Mrs Cushing, has this morning attempted to persuade me that she spent the greater part of Wednesday afternoon at the premises of an Indian dentist. If she lied to me what am I to understand? Derek was now on the escalator, gliding upwards past many underwear advertisements. Dear Mr Cuckold, if you are so blindly and wilfully stupid, is it surprising that your wife is deceiving you, deceiving you furthermore with grotesque and improbable stories? Can you think of any reason except the most obvious one why your wife should have lied to you? Pure bloody-mindedness is admittedly a possibility, and a desire to tease, irritate and wound should not automatically be ruled out; but since your wife has recently started an afternoon course in antique furniture restoration, and has during the last four months purchased as much clothing as in the past four years, can you reasonably suggest that such arguments hold water?

During the morning, to try to take his mind off his wife, Derek retreated to the basement archive room. Having locked himself in, he went behind the stacks containing the Institute's Far Eastern Missionary Correspondence and opened a carefully concealed tin chest. Inside was the private correspondence of the Imperial British East Africa Company for the years 1879 to 1901. Since the donation of these documents, by an elderly Scottish widow, at the beginning of March, Derek had known that he would be able to write a far more comprehensive account of the British intervention in East Africa than Professor Elkin, who was writing a book on the same subject. All Derek had to do was to refrain from cataloguing the chest's contents till the professor's finished manuscript was with his publisher. Normally, reading these previously unpublished letters, written by Lugard, Mackinnon and Kirk, banished all other thoughts from Derek's mind, but this morning their usual magic failed. His thoughts repeatedly returned to Diana.

For some reason he kept on imagining himself in his bedroom at the flat; but the room had changed dramatically. Gone from the dressing table was the clutter of pots of cosmetics, scraps of cotton wool, spilt powder and hair-rollers, usually left by Diana; gone too were her clothes and the two Indian rugs on the floor. No trace of her remained. The emptiness of the room struck him so forcibly that for a moment he had to hold on to the tin chest to remind himself where he was. A sudden stab of panic under the diaphragm made it hard for him to breathe for several seconds. This was not grief, not self-pity, but naked fear. Fourteen years suddenly dismissed; the safety net of habit gone, his assumptions and expectations splintering like glass. When he had recovered sufficiently he returned to the manuscript room, where he was immediately accosted by a scholarly Asian wishing to know about population figures for Perak in the 1790s.

Only when most of the readers had gone out to lunch was Derek able to think about his panic in the archives. Any decent man would surely not have trembled in such circumstances. Rage, jealousy, sorrow, reproach would have been more appropriate than fear. Would a normal red-blooded male sit helplessly on a tin chest and suffer without disgust or distress the idea of a strange tongue stroking his wife's nipples? Would he not roar out in savage abandonment: 'Some scheming bastard has besmirched my wife!'? Yet no biblical denunciations had formed in his brain; instead, under his diaphragm, tremors of panic still quivered. What really puzzled and distressed him was the certainty that although he thought he loved Diana, separation from her did not in itself terrify him. His fear had been far more personal and overwhelming. He had not been so much afraid for his marriage as afraid for himself.

Early in the afternoon Derek went home, leaving the Institute in the hands of his assistant Miss Prideaux. An hour later he was sitting in the bedroom which he had imagined stripped of all traces of Diana; around him the evidence of her continued residence was plentiful and reassuringly real. Yet he was far from happy. His panic had shaken him so badly that he felt impelled to discover the precise reasons for his fear or, if that were impossible, at least find some formula that made it seem less frighteningly irrational. Certainly the simple loss of having her around was not in itself alarming; the real change would be the absence of her decision-making. He tried to envisage a life with no Diana to organize his social life, no Diana to choose his clothes, decide about holidays, or about new chair covers, or a room to be painted, a meal to be bought, a present to be given, a film to be seen. She always knew what she wanted, but did he? Again slight tremors of panic troubled him. For so long he had persuaded himself that his acquiescence was a defence, a way to protect himself from her disappointment in him; an infallible method to stave off quarrels and stop real clashes; a protective wall around the real Derek. Yet what if the wall had enclosed nothing? What if he had deferred to her wishes for so long that he no longer had any wishes and preferences of his own? If that had happened, her desires had defined and even constituted his existence, and without her all orientation would disappear. He fought against the idea, accusing himself of crass amateur psychology. Every married person had to defer to the wishes of his partner almost every day. Nothing extraordinary in that. He had just taken surrender a bit further. Nothing to be alarmed about. In any case he wasn't really sure that she was having an affair. Her fit of clothes-buying earlier in the year, her lies about the dentist and the furniture course, were not in themselves proof of anything. Her long period of inactivity in the flat and her refusal to go out hardly indicated the existence of a lover, although it was just possible that he had jilted her before her decline and then taken her back, thus causing her recovery. But even if there was a lover, this didn't mean that she would leave her husband. Derek got up from the bed and walked over to the window. An ordinary summer day. The radio told of no disasters, natural or otherwise; cars passed and people went about their business as usual. There were leaves on the trees, clouds in the sky, glass in the window frames. Everywhere he looked, normality. Traffic lights functioning normally; the Thames, although he could not see it, was doubtless flowing calmly along its usual course. All was well. He tried a laugh, and when that sounded rather hollow he smiled to himself. Then he felt the panic again; not overwhelmingly, but fluttering disconcertingly in his stomach; a slight but unmistakable reminder that it might take a lot more than logic to solve his problem.

A scene of tranquil amity and calm repose. Midnight and the Cushings are in bed. She is reading, and he stares thoughtfully at the ceiling, as his mind unwinds after a rich and varied day. Her face is glistening with moisture cream, which, according to the advertisers, will keep her skin younger longer and help build new cells during the night. His face is solemn and a little strained, as though he needed some relaxing evening beverage to pave the way for a profound and untroubled sleep.

Diana had put down her book and was reaching for the light-switch when Derek said, unexpectedly, 'Tell me about your furniture course.'

'Now?' She turned round to make sure he was being serious. 'You've never shown the least interest before.'

'What sort of things do you learn?' he asked innocently.

'How to tell a Sheraton chest from a Victorian copy, when a Hepplewhite tallboy isn't what one thinks it is. Satisfied?' She reached for the switch again.

Derek said hastily, 'How *does* one tell a Sheraton chest from a copy?'

'I want to go to sleep.'

Derek's heart was thumping. She was trying to get out of it because she didn't know; because the whole course was an invention. 'Tell me,' he murmured.

Diana sighed and shut her eyes. Then she opened them reluctantly and replied in a distinct emphatic voice, as though he were deaf or cretinous, 'The keyholes will be different, the back will have been hacked about, and the curved front will have been cut through in the middle. All right?' She snapped off the light and curled up with her back to him. Of course she could have read it all in a book, or might even have invented it on the spur of the moment.

'What got you interested in antique furniture?'

'Boredom,' she came back at once. 'Now go to sleep.'

'That new dentist of yours,' whispered Derek, after a short silence. A loud sigh from Diana. 'I think I've got a loose filling. Do you think he'd suit me?'

She jerked into a sitting position and turned on the light. 'Do you have to settle your dental problems in the middle of the night?'

Her exasperation could be genuine, or again she could be trying to put him off.

'I want to change my dentist,' Derek said.

'Are Gilchrist's eyes getting you down too?' she asked with feigned incredulity.

'He's too far from my work. Where's your Indian bloke?'

'South Ken,' she replied without hesitation.

'Would you make me an appointment?'

'I'll ring him tomorrow.'

'You won't need to,' he came back quietly. 'You're seeing him tomorrow.'

'Thank God you reminded me. That bloody hygienist. I'll ask him in person.' She reached out for the switch. 'Can I?' she asked imploringly. Derek nodded assent. Darkness again. Diana said, 'Of course he may not be able to take on any more National Health patients. I was lucky he took me on.'

It was then that Derek was finally convinced that the Indian dentist did not exist. A little later he knew that he would have to follow her in the morning; wherever she was planning to go, it would certainly have nothing to do with her teeth.

Chapter 3

Derek left the flat shortly after half-past nine and made his way to the telephone box on the opposite side of Fitzsimmons Avenue. After his early departure from the Institute the previous afternoon, his assistant was not surprised to hear that he felt unwell, and did not intend coming in to work that day. After finishing his call, Derek stayed in the phone box for a further quarter of an hour, holding the receiver and pretending to talk. In this way he felt less conspicuous observing the entrance of the flats; but the arrival of two women, both eager to use the phone, forced him from his concealment. Later he might be able to go back but in the meantime somewhere else had to be found. It was not very likely that Diana would see him from the window but it was just possible, and Derek was unwilling to take any chances.

Fifty yards to the right of the phone box was a group of shops and beyond them a couple of plane trees with a seat under them. On his way to this new vantage point Derek went into a news-agent and bought a paper as quickly as he could. The seat, placed almost opposite Abercorn Mansions by a considerate council, was black with dirt and haphazardly patterned with bird droppings. Derek dropped a page from his paper onto the bench and sat down, holding the rest of the paper up in front of him. Every few seconds he glanced over the top of the paper, but, a little later, feeling that this was overdoing caution, he laid the paper on his lap. Her appointment was likely to be between ten-thirty and noon. It might be a long wait. The sun was climbing in a cloudless sky and already it was hot. A slight breeze stirred the dust and the paper in the gutter.

Derek had already given some thought to the method he would

use in following Diana, but he had only solved the problems posed if she should take the tube. At the opposite end of a long platform she would be unlikely to see him, but if she chose to go by bus things would be very different. He would not be able to wait in the queue with her, and if he jumped on after her she might very well see him. In films there would be a conveniently placed taxi with an obliging driver quite willing to 'follow that bus' without questions. Derek imagined himself perfectly disguised with a false beard and a wig. Would anything fool her? Certainly not dark glasses. He had a vision of Diana sweeping along the gangway of the bus and, to the amazement of the other passengers, snatching off his dark glasses. Any sensible man would have let well alone or gone to a private detective. She might go shopping on her way to South Kensington and that would mean every kind of difficulty; he would have to dart in and out of shop doorways, stop abruptly, pretend to look at pairs of shoes, watches, second-hand books or travel posters. Very possibly he might lose her. If she went into a department store and got into a lift, he wouldn't have a hope.

A hundred yards away Derek could see a policeman coming towards him. Nothing wrong with sitting on a bench; people sat on benches every day. But if the policeman saw him on the same bench an hour later mightn't he suspect something? Suspect that Derek was watching the movements of residents of the flats with a view to burglary. If the policeman saw him farther along the street later on in the day, he might be accused of loitering with intent, which in a sense was a very apt description of what he was doing. At least there was no school so he wouldn't be suspected of trying to molest minors. The policeman passed by.

Shortly after ten-thirty Derek left the bench and walked along the street to a bus shelter. Nothing strange about a man waiting there. Four buses called at this particular stop, so he would be able to remain there for at least half-an-hour without drawing attention to himself. If Diana was going to come out, she would probably do so fairly soon. Derek smiled to himself. This idea that he was conspicuous was madness. In London one could wander about in one's underwear without getting a glance. Nobody would notice if he spent the whole day at the bus-stop. There had been a piece in the papers several days before about a man who had fallen in a river and drowned. His corpse had floated twenty miles downstream, past people fishing, past picnicking families and couples walking along the banks. Several had seen the body but had thought nothing of it. One woman had supposed the drowned man to be a swimmer who liked letting the current do the work for him. He had only been found to be dead when his corpse had floated into a lock.

Two buses called at the stop within ten minutes: the 158 followed by the 42. Derek was feeling considerably more relaxed when he saw a potentially alarming situation developing. On the other side of the street Mrs Harvey, who lived in a flat on the second floor of Abercorn Mansions, was heading straight for the bus-stop.

Mrs Harvey and Derek talked about the beauty of the day and the unpredictability of the bus service. Then came the question Derek was dreading. 'Which bus are you catching, Mr Cushing?'

Derek hedged. 'Which bus are *you* catching?' he asked archly and then added, 'Perhaps we'll be getting the same bus.'

Mrs Harvey said the 42 was her bus and in return Derek told her his was the 158. Although Derek had survived the danger of a journey on the same bus as Mrs Harvey he was still extremely worried. If the buses were running to schedule it was more than likely that the 158 would come before the next 42; Derek was trapped and knew it. The 27 came and then the 158. As it approached Derek went through a pantomime of fumbling in his pockets. He swore aloud and, after a few inarticulate words about having forgotten his money, dashed across the road to Abercorn Mansions.

Please God don't let Diana come out now. Derek stopped in the hall of the flats and tried to think quickly. Since it was possible that another 158 might come before Mrs Harvey's 42, there was no question of returning to the stop while she was still there. But since the woman had just missed a 42, she might have to wait for fifteen minutes. Derek realized that he could not stay in the hall for that length of time.

In front of Abercorn Mansions was a low privet hedge. Derek made up his mind what he had to do. He would slip out of the entrance and hide behind the hedge. There was a chance that Major Smythe in the front ground-floor flat might see him but there seemed no alternative course of action. The hedge was too low for him to stand behind, so he had to squat; a casual observer, who failed to notice that his trousers were up, would certainly think he was opening his bowels. Through the hedge it was impossible to see whether Mrs Harvey was still at the bus-stop. Derek felt that he would not be safe until another four buses had passed. If Major Smythe did see him what could he say? That he had dropped his car keys from the balcony? It wasn't very likely but would have to do if necessary. Derek remained squatting behind the hedge; already his thighs were aching. Sweat was running down his back.

There was a gap in the hedge near the doors of the flats and through it Derek watched for Diana. The gap was large enough for Diana to see him, if she should happen to look round. Derek imagined her saying: 'You're insane, completely off your trolley. You'll have to be committed.' He would leap over the hedge followed by Diana, Major Smythe, Mrs Harvey and the police-man armed with a strait-jacket. Enthusiastic passers-by would join in the chase with howls of derision. A cuckold *and* a lunatic would be an ideal subject for mockery. The hedge smelled of dogs' excrement. Gardens worthy of mansions. In my father's house are many mansions. The person who first decided to call second-rate blocks of flats 'mansions' must have had an extrava-gantly warped sense of humour. Behind Derek was a row of laurels, their leaves grey with dirt; these dismal-looking shrubs were all that had been thought necessary for the thin strip of garden.

Derek came out of his hiding-place a few minutes after eleven and headed for the phone box. He had no intention of making a call. Inside, it was as hot as a small greenhouse. Just above the phone two messages had been written: 'For a suck and a fuck ring 401-8871' and 'Mary likes being buggered 223-9364'. Most of the directories had been ripped out. When the heat got the better of him, Derek went back to his bench. Heat haze was shimmering on the road; in the distance cars seemed to float into view. How long ought he to sit on the bench? Mrs Harvey might see him on her return. 'Still there, Mr Cushing?' 'As a matter of fact I am conducting a survey on traffic flow in Fitszimmons Avenue.' 'Saw you hiding behind that hedge. Funny place to keep your money.' 'I buried it there for safe-keeping.'

By noon Derek had realized that the assumption on which he had based his vigil had been far from cast-iron. If, as he had supposed, she had no appointment, there was no reason why she should go anywhere. Only his overdramatic imagination had led him to suppose that she would pretend to go to her non-existent dentist. In fact it was far more likely that she would content herself with a straightforward lie when he came home in the evening. But that would prove the case against her just as surely as a successful pursuit. No sooner than he had begun to see the matter as a foregone conclusion, tremors of the now familiar panic returned. A few moments before, he had been sitting quite calmly on his bench, but now he could not keep still. He had to get up and pace up and down for a while to relieve his nervousness. If there was no point in waiting any longer, what ought he to do? This question had terrified him before but then he had dismissed it with phrases like 'cross your bridges when you come to them', 'find out first and then decide', 'no point in making decisions before you know the facts'. Suddenly Derek stopped dead in the middle of his pacing. He had told himself that as soon as he knew one way or the other, his panic would go. But it hadn't gone at all. Once again he found his chest tightening and his breathing laboured. He also felt slightly sick; his mouth was uncomfortably dry.

Derek forced himself to sit down again. He might go home in the evening to hear that she had put off her morning appointment and gone in the afternoon. He couldn't be sure yet. Had she really told him that she was going in the morning or had he just assumed it? The return of uncertainty calmed him at once; it was like a reprieve. Nothing would be definite until after five in the afternoon. He would have to wait on. No point in thinking about what to do until then.

It started shortly before two o'clock but, because he hadn't drunk much at breakfast and had sweated a lot during the morning, Derek at first decided that his desire to pee stemmed from his nerves rather than his bladder. Twenty minutes later this pretence was no longer tenable; he wanted to go and would have to go. His first thought was the privet hedge but that was dangerous not only because of Major Smythe; he might bump into Diana in the entrance. The nearest lavatory was at the tube station three hundred yards down the road. An athletic man would be able to run that distance in roughly forty seconds; eighty seconds there and back and forty seconds to pee. Two minutes away from his post. Well, a little over two minutes since he wasn't an athletic man. Three minutes. Not long at all. He would have to be particularly luckless for her to come out at this precise time; even more luckless if she caught a bus or a taxi at once.

Four minutes later Derek was back at his bench and feeling reasonably confident that he hadn't missed her. To make certain he decided to phone her. Naturally he would not say anything, just to check whether she answered. Back in the now familiar phone box Derek dialled the number and heard the phone ringing. Two minutes later it was still ringing. Derek rang the operator who had the line checked and confirmed that there was no fault on it. She could be in the bath, under her hair dryer, asleep; if she was going to pretend to have kept her appointment, she might be ignoring the phone deliberately. There was however another possibility; she had gone out while he was in the lavatory. Nothing to be done though.

At three o'clock Derek concluded that his persisting feeling of sickness might be hunger. One of the shops opposite Abercorn Mansions was a delicatessen. He went in and bought a couple of slices of salami, a quarter of a pound of cheddar, a carton of milk and a packet of biscuits. Having returned to the bench, Derek ate his lunch slowly and without enjoyment. He had eaten the salami, finished the milk and started on the cheese, when he saw, on the other side of the road, either Charles Lamont or his double. Lamont walked briskly past Alfriston House, past Tunstall House, past Derek's privet hedge and then, after a momentary pause, into Abercorn Mansions. Charles had never mentioned knowing anybody else in the block apart from the Cushings. The time of his visit made it equally clear that he intended to see Mrs Cushing rather than her husband.

Derek nibbled at his cheese mechanically. The idea of Lamont being Diana's lover seemed at first too grotesque to be true. Diana was certainly an unusual woman but nobody could have done what she had done. Derek recalled the way she had so convincingly attempted to force him to come to Cornwall, and how she had finally allowed him to *persuade* her to go without him. He remembered something else: she had told him, shortly after Charles's invitation, that Giles wanted to go with his school Scouts to the Peak District, instead of spending the first week of the Cornish holiday with her; he would come down to Cornwall for the last few days. At the time, Derek had thought nothing of this, but now it appeared in a very different light. Everything fitted, there was no doubt about that, and yet he could not quite face the final conclusion. Had he been so thoroughly fooled and manipulated? Had she really come to view him with such contempt that she had been happy to make him almost a conniver at her infidelity? She had never forgotten the dates of his projected trip to Scotland. She had merely used her knowledge and gambled on his natural reluctance to abandon his research.

Derek put the rest of the cheese into his mouth and chewed vigorously. From where he was sitting, he could see the front rooms of the Cushing flat, including the window of the principal bedroom. Perhaps they were in there already. Maybe Charles had hardly gone through the door before ripping off his trousers. Derek tried to whip up feelings of rage and jealousy but all he felt was chilling bitterness laced with self-pity. If *he* ever chose to race into the flat at the end of a day's work and suggest instant intercourse, she'd tell him to stop pawing her, or plead the supper to be cooked, or clothes to be ironed. But Lamont, with

28

his charm, affluence and, above all, his novelty, was another matter. The sudden production of his appendage would be enthralling, the same old blood and gristle as the archivist's apparatus, but novel nonetheless. An old play, but a new actor. So easy with an income like Charles's to be gregarious and spontaneous, since spontaneity could be manufactured with a meal in a different restaurant, an unexpected present, an invitation to a country house. Should have taken up hot-air ballooning, Derek told himself, or formed a collection of Patagonian erotica, if such things existed, or at least made a study of unusual liturgical objects. Even an archivist could have competed with conventional success and conspicuous wealth, given a burst of sudden eccentricity. Could have ridden to work on a penny-farthing, sat for hours on end with a fungus in his mouth, opened bottles with his teeth, had himself tattooed in improbable places, and been gratuitously rude to fellow-passengers in buses.

After all, what originality had Lamont ever shown? He had made his money in property and then transferred to art the safe way. Bought several Rouaults at auctions, the odd Picasso drawing, kept them a year or two, and then sold them at a profit. Like property all over again. Then he'd branched out, taken on a few youngish artists who'd already started to make it, lured them away from other galleries with larger payments and thus spared himself the trouble of helping them through the more difficult early years of their painting lives. Charles had always been good with people, expert with contacts, alive to the way critical opinion was moving; a man without taste or conviction, but with a good nose for future buying patterns. A good nose for bored wives too; flattering it must be to inject new lust into tired loins, to raise the sexual dead, so that they murmured about miracles.

By now they would be certain to be at it. Should he surprise them? Burst in and catch them moist-handed in the act, their trousers down, in flagrante delicto? All right, Lamont, get your pants on and get the hell out of here. I'll give you ten seconds. And Charles, stammering and frightened, would thrust his projection into his made-to-measure underwear, and dash for the doors, which he would promise never again to darken. Like hell.

The boots were on other feet. Deceived husbands had no magic cards to play.

Derek's first instinct had been to avoid telling her what he knew; to avoid it at all costs. Yet in such circumstances it would surely be lunacy to remain silent. After all, would telling her be so fatal? It was possible that she would feel guilty enough to promise never to see the man again; not likely but possible. Of course she might promise to give him up and then go on seeing him, taking more care not to be found out. Derek's initial assumption, that, if he told her what he knew she might feel obliged to come to a final decision, had obviously been too hasty. Other possibilities occured to him. If confronted with her affair, she might say that she had no intention of breaking up their marriage but simply needed another man as a diversion. She *could* feel forced to leave him but that was just as likely to happen if he said nothing. A long and honest talk might bring them together again, persuade her that for too long she had under-estimated him.

Only when he started to think seriously about what their long and honest talk might involve, did Derek's resolve begin to weaken. In the past Diana had made it abundantly clear that she found his work pointless and dull and considered him to be personally vacillating and ineffectual. The start of their talk might very well centre round what she would get out of staying with him. Such a discussion might pin-point and clarify dissatisfactions of which she had previously been only dimly aware. This would increase rather than diminish any desire to leave him. One question would be inevitable: What did he get out of their marriage? What did it mean to him? This would force him to go into a detailed and far from romantic explanation of his dependence and the panic he had recently experienced. It wasn't utterly inconceivable that she would listen with sympathy and tender concern but she was far more likely to be frightened and irritated. Had she really obliterated his character to that extent? Why the hell hadn't he said anything about it before? Just two of the questions she would be certain to ask. She would also accuse him of attempting to blackmail her into staying with him by threatening to go to pieces if she went off. Could she really take seriously the notion that he was unable to organize a life of his own on his own? He might have no intuition about choosing clothes or wallpaper, but that surely extended no further than a few other similarly mundane examples? If he then admitted that it extended a great deal further, he would become still more pathetic and despicable in her eyes. In fact the long and honest talk seemed pretty well guaranteed to force her out of the flat and his life.

Left to itself, the affair might die a natural death. In time Diana would find art exhibitions and private views just as boring as colonial history. Charles's anecdotes would soon be exhausted and the novel pleasures of expensive restaurants and fast cars would likewise begin to wane. She would discover that he liked certain kinds of food, disliked other kinds, changed his underwear so many times a week and picked his nose at traffic lights. With the exhaustion of novelty, boredom would get to work; boredom, acceptable in marriage but not in affairs. But if it didn't work out that way, if she left him and he had done nothing, how would he feel then?

Derek got up and started walking with no sense of purpose. He passed the phone box and stopped. He imagined the phone ringing as she reached her climax and went in with a sneaking desire to spoil pleasure, to cause anxiety. He dialled the first few digits and then put down the receiver. His eye had caught the obscenities written above the directories: 'For a suck and a fuck ring . . .' Farther down the street he stopped outside a florist's. A placard in the window posed the question: 'When did you last say it with flowers?' He went in and bought an azalea, imagining as he paid for the plant how mean and guilty she would feel as he presented it. He would follow up by telling her that he had bought tickets for the opera and had booked a table at an excellent restaurant nearby. Confronted by a new Derek, she would relent.

Back on his bench, Derek placed the plant beside him and prepared for the long wait till Charles left the flat. Occasionally his old panic distressed him with a sudden flutter, but he felt calmer than he had done at any time during the day. A decision had been made: he would attempt to keep his wife by ignoring her affair and by renewed attention to her, which would in the end convince her that she had been blind to his very real but retiring merits. He might fail, but at least he had a plan, and that was a considerable advance from his previous indecision. Derek shut his eyes and enjoyed the warmth of the sun on his closed lids. When he opened them again, he leapt to his feet.

Giles was going into Abercorn Mansions. It was the afternoon he usually went swimming, and Diana had obviously not reckoned with any change of routine. Derek was torn for a moment between racing after the boy, and phoning Diana to warn her. But warning her was impossible, for then he would have to admit that he knew. Instead he started in pursuit of his son, hoping to overtake him on the stairs. Unfortunately Giles had a start of a hundred yards, and, because of the traffic, Derek had to wait almost a minute before he could cross the road. He did not catch up with Giles, and arrived breathless and sweating at his front door. He started fumbling in his pockets and then stopped. In his excitement he had forgotten about having no key; it had been lost the week before, and, although Diana had promised to have another cut, she had not done so. Nothing for it but to ring. He took a deep breath and pressed the bell.

Giles answered the door, and, to Derek's relief and amazement, did not look shocked or grieved. Instead he said in a matter-of-fact voice, 'Charles is here,' and then walked away towards the sitting-room.

Derek followed him. Instead of the horrifying scene which Derek had imagined, all was calm when he entered the room. Charles's trousers were on, and although Diana was in her dressing-gown, she did not seem at all uneasy about it. Charles rose to greet Derek with a fine expansive smile that emphasized the whiteness of his teeth.

'And how's the Empire?' asked the genial gallery owner.

With some difficulty Derek twisted his face into an affable smile. 'Dismembered and discredited,' he replied briskly. Dear Charles, ever ready with a joke about the Institute. Derek inclined his head pedantically. 'You know George V never said that on his death bed.'

Charles looked puzzled for a moment but then realized what Derek meant.

'I know. He said: "What's on at the Empire?" or "Bugger Bognor"; humorous old goat. You must have told me.'

Derek looked at him impassively. 'I don't suppose you know William Pitt's last words. Archivists are always good on last words.'

'The suspense is killing us,' put in Diana.

' "I think I could eat one of Bellamy's veal pies," that's what he said.'

'So he died of food poisoning,' said Charles with a wink at Giles. 'Bet they never told you that at school. Your father ought to bring out a dictionary of last words with lots of scholarly notes. Call it "Having the Last Word". Ought to do very well.'

Diana laughed, Giles laughed, Derek laughed. A good-humoured little group of people all laughing happily while Charles's semen trickled down the legs of the archivist's wife.

'I don't like your title,' Derek said. ' "Death Sentence" would be better.' More laughter, mostly from Giles. Derek was always touched by his son's loyalty.

Derek looked at Diana. That dressing-gown . . . not to mention it seemed stranger than to make a pointed remark. 'Just had a bath?' he asked casually.

'My God, you've noticed. No, I've been in bed. I had a headache this morning, so I didn't get up. Charles probably thinks it's just an excuse and that I normally slouch around in my dressing-gown till after lunch.'

Derek waited patiently. Diana had done her bit and now Charles would do his.

'Of course I don't think anything of the sort,' chuckled the gallant art dealer. 'My fault for dropping in unannounced. But what are friends for if one can't drop in on them? Especially when one passes their welcoming door twice a week.'

'I didn't know you had connections in Maida Vale,' chipped in Derek, choosing his words with care.

'In Maida Vale? No connections here, and more's the pity. No, the truth is, I have business farther north in a warehouse near

Burnt Oak—heard of it?' He smiled humorously at the thought that anybody should have done so. Diana grinned back.

'I have,' cut in Derek.

'Trust you,' went on Charles, in no way put out. 'Well then, knowing it as you do, you will know that it is past Colindale and past Cricklewood and frankly past redemption.' Diana laughed delightedly.

'Aren't we all,' sighed Derek, but nobody heard. Charles was explaining the new trend for vast paintings, and how, even if he sold out every show, he would still become bankrupt if he showed such large work in the West End.

'So what could I do?' he went on, raising his arms, displaying spotless cuffs and a fine pair of platinum cuff-links. 'I could hardly disown the rising generation of British and American painters. So I bought this warehouse, filled it with outsize canvases and run a couple of chauffeur-driven cars up and down bulging with clients. None of them agree to go unless they're serious, or deranged, or both.' Another chortle from Diana. 'The long and the short of it is, that I've got round West End overheads and turned financial disaster into quite a profitable little sideline.'

Derek coughed drily: 'And on your way to Burnt Oak you pass through Maida Vale.'

'In a nutshell,' cried Charles, with a manly laugh. 'Wish I had your gift for precision and brevity.'

'No criticism intended,' replied Derek. Could jovial Derek even be suspected of being critical? A man stupid enough to listen to and believe such apparent excuses could hardly have the wit to know his way round his own flat. He smiled at Charles. 'Every word you uttered confirmed your exceptional business acumen.'

'You mean you've rarely heard a more blatant piece of self-advertisement. You really ought to be more direct, Derek. I almost took it as a compliment.'

'So instead you bluntly suggested that I was being rude,' replied Derek. Why spoil Charles's fun? The man liked verbal masturbation. Let him have what he wanted.

34

'You rude? Nothing so vulgar as that. What an idea.' Charles laughed heartily. 'You're far too subtle for that sort of crudity. That's why I like talking to you. You're so unlike the dreary people I normally deal with.'

Derek smiled. He suspected that Charles was getting considerable pleasure out of flattering him. Steal a man's wife, destroy his peace of mind and then get him to love you; like a doctor winning a patient's trust and then slowly poisoning him with arsenic.

'After the gaiety and exuberance of the art world you spend an hour or two in some stagnant backwater and find it diverting by way of a change.'

Charles shrugged his shoulders and gave Diana an apologetic look.

'Invert everything I say, twist my innocent praise. I don't know, Derek. You must think I'm incredibly dull to have to misconstrue every word I utter. In fact, come to think of it, that's probably why you prefer those letters in Scotland to coming to stay with me.'

'You'd have to buy a library to get him to change his mind,' put in Diana.

Another jocular response was expected but Derek felt too weary and sickened to go on talking. After a brief silence Diana turned to Derek and said:

'Don't mind me asking but what's that thing you're clutching?'

Derek had forgotten the azalea, concealed under light wrapping paper.

'A present for you.' He handed it to her. She unwrapped it carefully and then got up and came over and kissed him lightly on the forehead. A delightful little joke for her to share with Charles; see how pleased the old fool is by a moist peck on the forehead; little things like that convince him that I'm a dutiful wife.

'Of course you know that flowers are sexual organs on stalks,' Charles said throatily, with an arch wink at Diana. 'Saying it with flowers can be a pretty risqué business.'

Diana was examining the plant more closely. 'It wasn't like this when you bought it?' Derek noticed that it was twisted over on one side. He had obviously managed to knock it against the wall in his dash up the stairs. 'If it was,' Diana went on, 'you'd better take it back.'

'It must have happened in the tube. I'll buy another. I'm sorry.'

'No need to be sorry; isn't it the thought that counts? I expect it'll recover.'

Derek found her tone patronizing and derisive. It was as if she had assumed all along that if ever he gave her anything he would have dropped, sat on or spoilt it in some other way before making a presentation. He realized just how much it had cost him to suppress his anger earlier on when he'd listened to their exhibition of accomplished lying. His voice shook as he said, 'Of course it won't recover. Half the stems are snapped off. What are you going to do? Put them in splints or phone a tree surgeon?'

'It wouldn't have been very tactful if I'd told you I intended throwing it out. Be reasonable.'

'It would at least have been the truth. Did you think I couldn't take it?'

Charles had started laughing again. Derek realized that he must have thought his show of anger an act specifically put on for his amusement. Why not give him his money's worth? Derek took the plant from his wife and went back to his chair. For the next minute or so he snapped off all the stems and pulled off every leaf. He then gave it back again to Diana.

'Highly symbolic,' chortled Charles. 'A brief play about man's destruction of nature. You ought to submit it to a fringe theatre group.'

'Utterly puerile,' cut in Diana angrily.

'What did you think?' Derek asked Giles. 'Did it look to you like a short piece of *avant-garde* theatre or a short piece of childish petulance?'

'I couldn't see what was wrong with it to begin with. It was a bit bent but it could have been tied to a stick.'

'If you couldn't see, you need another pair of glasses,' snapped Diana.

Giles blushed deeply. 'I got this pair last month. I may be

blind but not that blind.' For a moment Derek wondered whether the boy was going to cry, but instead he went on, 'I thought it was ungrateful, if you want to know.' Before anybody could say anything he had jumped up and left the room.

'He's a bit self-conscious about his glasses,' Derek said for Charles's benefit. 'Hasn't been wearing them for long.' Derek smiled wanly at Diana, who scowled back at him.

'You forced him to take sides, so don't pretend I did the damage,' she came back at him.

As soon as Derek could see that his wife was giving Charles such a fine exhibition of the worst side of her nature, he felt better and his own anger ebbed away. He decided to try and make her look still more unreasonable. He turned to Charles with a rueful smile.

'Give your wife a plant and see what happens. It wasn't even a very good plant either; just a cheap azalea.' He paused. 'Did you read about the children who swallowed laburnum seeds and had to have their stomachs pumped? The average English garden's a death trap for the incautious.'

'Belt up, can't you?' Diana exploded.

'Then there's giant hog-weed,' Derek went on affably, 'and stinking hellebores, deadly nightshade and numerous toadstools, not to mention a wide variety of poisonous fungi, roots and berries.' Charles was studying his expensive, well-polished shoes, Diana was clutching the arms of her chair. Derek looked at them both with something approaching satisfaction. It came to him that Charles might like to hear about his anal affliction; people did not talk about things like that. Diseases and infections had definite categories of acceptability; some were even glamorous, but piles were undoubtedly unmentionable: a sign of senility, an affliction as graceless as bad breath. His tone was confidential and hushed as he continued, 'I don't know if Diana told you but most of my bad behaviour has a fundamental cause. My bowels hurt me. I'm suffering from piles; she's absolutely right, I ought to belt up but my piles make me irrational.'

'I've heard it can be bloody painful,' Charles replied.

'Bloody's the word, not much more than a teaspoonful with each movement—lovely the way they talk about moving the bowels, like moving mountains or moving house. Evacuation's not much better, although it does sound rather noble, a monumental movement or even movements.'

Diana got up and walked out of the room.

After a pause Charles said quietly, 'Do you often annoy her like that?'

'Hardly ever. I usually get down on my knees rather than irritate her. Didn't she ever tell you, I'm a case of chronic acquiescence? It's unconditional surrender every day of the week in Abercorn Mansions.'

'What happened today?'

'She hasn't got a headache.'

'She says she has,' replied Charles, unable to hide his confusion, which increased when Derek started to laugh. 'I'm sorry but I don't get it.' Charles's mystification was giving way to irritation.

'Maybe that's just as well. Just a little joke of mine, something personal.' Derek got up and held out a hand to Charles. 'You mustn't let me keep you. You're a busy man and unless I go and take my beating soon, Diana may burst a blood vessel.' He paused and stared hard at Charles, who was now looking at him with concern. 'Charles, I've been thinking about Cornwall; to be precise I'm still thinking about Cornwall. I've come to no decision yet but I may do, if you get my drift.'

'Well, give me a ring when you have.' Charles walked to the door, the same look of concern on his face. 'Are you all right? It sounds a bit funny asking but . . .'

'Are you as mad as a hatter?'

'I was going to say worried.'

'Anything on the mind?'

'Is there?' put in Charles.

'Nothing a lobotomy wouldn't cure,' he replied feeling a sudden surge of anger; wanting to take Charles by the throat and shake him. Instead he opened the door and said with forced calmness, 'Let me know when you're going to Burnt Oak again. Pure luck I came back early today. I wouldn't want to miss you.'

As soon as Charles had gone, all Derek's sense of mastery and control left him with the same speed that it took his nervous energy to drain away. He had intended to be charming, affectionate and guileless; the ideal husband whose simple goodness wins back an erring wife. Instead he had given way to obtuseness and a display of facetious malevolence that amazed him in retrospect. A few more efforts like it and she *would* leave him. He paused in the corridor outside the bedroom door.

Humility, diffidence, even self-contempt would all be needed, coupled with acceptance of each and every criticism she threw at him, however unreasonable. Derek tried to imagine that he had committed a terrible crime: something in the order of infanticide. How would he confront the parents? That was the required attitude. Forgive me, for I knew not what I did.

Diana was lying on the bed staring at the ceiling when Derek came in and closed the door behind him. Derek put down her refusal to notice his entrance to utter indifference, or possibly a feeling that he was too vile to look at. Fearing that she might walk out if he sat on the bed, he lowered himself onto the floor; on thy belly shalt thou go. Silence. Derek recalled Giles saying that even if Diana battered him with a frying-pan, he would still apologize. Would he, if quite suddenly she produced a pan from under the bedclothes and belted him? My head got in the way; I'm sorry if I dented it; I'll buy another. Tremors of anger made him clench his fists. Charles had just dropped by and she'd been in bed with a headache; how lucky that some sixth sense had told her to put make-up on her face just in case.

'I'm afraid I behaved very badly,' he murmured.

To his amazement Diana leant over and kissed him. She drew back and looked at him with something approaching tenderness. Then she whispered, 'You shouldn't be apologizing at all.'

Was she going to confess it all? He must stop her at once. He blurted out, 'I deliberately tried to annoy you.'

Diana laughed and ruffled his hair playfully.

'I deserved it for being rude and childish.' She got up and put her arms round him. Her dressing-gown had come open. She started to undo his shirt buttons. Derek shut his eyes. Was her appetite insatiable? She had started to stroke the hairs on his chest. A moment later she leant forward so that her breasts brushed his face. Derek got up and walked towards the window.

'Didn't you want me?' she asked, with, what seemed to Derek, a horrifyingly convincing show of disappointment. He was now certain that she had thought his earlier aggression stemmed from suspicion about what she had been up to with Charles. But get him to bed and he'll think himself a fool ever to have doubted her.

'I'm afraid I can't change my moods as quickly as you.'

Diana didn't seem cross, as he had expected her to be; instead she laughed, threw off her dressing-gown and started to dress.

'What about your headache?' asked Derek.

'Gone.' She noticed his doubtful expression and smiled. 'Aren't you pleased?' Derek made no reply, but she didn't seem to notice. After slipping on an old pair of slacks and a loose sweater, she brushed her hair rapidly and turned to face him. 'I'd better get some supper before the delicatessen shuts.' Before he could ask her not to buy any salami, she had gone.

'Won't be long,' she called from the hall. Her sudden energy left Derek feeling exhausted. He imagined her tripping gaily across the road, smiling at the man in the delicatessen, treading lightly as she walked and breathing in the cooler evening air appreciatively. Derek lay down on the bed. Possibly she was in love with the man; that would account for her light-hearted mood. He turned over and buried his head in the pillow. A few minutes later he thought of getting up and talking to Giles but his limbs felt too heavy. Why not just lie there for hours, days, years, surfacing only for food and trips to the lavatory? Or would it be better to go to the bathroom now and slit his wrists; die a Roman death? She would shout: 'Supper's ready!' and he would hardly hear it as he watched the blood leaping from his wrists like little red dolphins. A closed account at the blood bank, no more to withdraw. A white corpse, only the slight drip of a tap, as the last corpuscles drained away. At first the final tranquillity of the image pleased him, but then, quite unexpectedly, he felt angry. Wasn't the 'wait and see' policy he had proposed not much better than being a corpse? Diana had always wanted him to be assertive;

perhaps she ought to have her way. Derek sat up abruptly. The discovery that he intended to fight to keep his wife came to him almost with the force and suddenness of a revelation. How he would set about it, or even when or where, he was uncertain; but set about it, he was sure he would.

Chapter 4

Once a month Derek visited his father at his Bayswater flat. Unlike many former colonial administrators, Gilbert Cushing had not brought back and cherished much local furniture and bric-à-brac; one small Malayan teak table, a solitary parang and a large bronze incense burner were the only major relics of his twenty years in the East. Apart from these there was a framed photograph in the lavatory of the Government Offices in Kuala Lumpur—the Saracenic style had always amused Gilbert—and, hanging in the hall, a portrait of himself, dressed in a fur-lined Chinese coat, painted in 1932, and exhibited the following year at the Academy entitled 'The Sinologist'. At that time he had been Protector of Chinese, Malacca.

As Derek helped his father pour the tea and watched his fingers busy with cups and saucers, he wondered whether his own hands would one day be as skeletal. He would lose all his hair, as Gilbert had done, but would his bald skull be so peculiarly wrinkled and framed by such a pathetic little fringe of white hair? Only the old man's eyes had retained their sparkle and alertness. Gilbert had been working at a cluttered desk by the window, and, having taken a few sips of tea, he went over to it and returned with a yellowing photograph of a cheerful-looking man wearing a bow-tie. He showed it to Derek.

'Remember him?'

Somebody from Malaya. Derek pretended to be deep in thought before finally shaking his head.

'I was seven when I came home,' he muttered apologetically.

'Some of us didn't come home. We left it,' replied Gilbert with the hint of a smile. He tapped the photograph with a mottled finger and said, 'Bill used to take quite an interest in you.'

'Bill Eggars?'

'Poor Bill,' sighed Gilbert, sitting down and spilling tea in his saucer. Derek had heard the story of Bill's death many times. He'd done it in Room 37 of Raffles Hotel: trouble with his wife, no promotion in sight and none of his painstaking work acknowledged by the head of the Monopolies Department. A very methodical suicide; he had torn up a few private letters and had then carefully sorted his official papers. Having locked all the doors and fastened the blinds, he had stood in front of the mirror and shot himself in the left eye. The coroner had intelligently surmised that one shot had been insufficient because a second had been fired into the mouth. Before summoning the hotel management the room boy had taken the opportunity to steal all the dead man's personal effects. A meditative look absorbed Gilbert's face.

'The Government analyst shot himself at the opium factory the following week.' Derek watched his father take a bite from a stale biscuit. The old man turned to him and asked. 'How many suicides have you known? In this country, I mean.'

'Two or three.'

'I knew almost twenty in Malaya; knew them well too. The heat, monotony, lack of seasons, drink, of course. There was a lot of drinking. Knew a Chief Justice and a Senior Inspector of Schools and they both became alcoholics.'

'Those were the days,' put in Derek with a smile.

'We were happy enough in Malacca.' Gilbert's nostalgic expression faded. 'For a while at any rate,' he added quietly.

Since the death of his second wife at the end of the previous year, Derek's father had been thinking far more about the distant rather than the immediate past.

On 14 February 1942 Derek's mother and eleven other survivors were landed from their torpedoed ship on a deserted beach in Sumatra and shot by their Japanese captors. A week before, Derek, then a boy of seven, had sailed for India from a beleaguered Singapore and his ship had successfully evaded the Japanese navy. His mother had stayed on after her son's departure solely to try to get her parents a passage to Java. She had left Malaya with them three days before Singapore fell. Now over thirty years later Gilbert was making a final effort to clear his conscience. For some months he had been working with letters, diaries and newspaper cuttings to put together a precise chronological account of the year leading up to February 1942. Derek considered his behaviour unbalanced and unnecessary. He was quite satisfied that his father had had every reason to suppose that Malaya in 1940 was a safer place than London in the 'blitz'. Gilbert himself had been invalided out of the Malayan Civil Service and had returned to England the same year: 1938. When war was declared with Germany he had sent his wife and son back to Malaya for safety while he himself took a job in the Colonial Office. In September 1941 when events in the East had started to look menacing, Gilbert had trusted the personal assurances of the Commander in Chief Far East that Japan was not preparing any immediate aggression. In any case he had been frightened at the thought of his wife and child making a seven-thousand-mile sea journey at the height of the U-boat onslaught.

'Do you have to go through it all again?' asked Derek, gesturing in the direction of his father's writing-desk.

'It's got to be done, and when you're my age it's as well to finish things sooner rather than later.' Gilbert noticed Derek's look of weary and exasperated concern. 'I think I may surprise you, Derek,' he murmured and then smiled. 'Anyway it keeps me off the streets, and stops me taking up painting on porcelain or wood engraving.'

A little later, when Derek was leaving, his father took him by the arm and said, 'You won't be offended by a bit of paternal advice?' Derek smiled. 'Your clothes—' he paused and looked his son up and down—'wouldn't they look better on a younger man?'

Derek, who was wearing the striped jacket Diana had recently bought for him, nodded agreement and then burst out laughing. He liked the way his father always said what he thought and resented the fact that Diana disliked Gilbert to the extent of refusing to ask him round for a meal or even a drink. Perhaps the time had come to redress matters. So rare were Derek's genuinely impulsive ideas that when they came he found them all but irresistible. With a sense of shock he heard himself saying, 'Doing anything at the end of July?'

'I'm rushed off my feet these days,' Gilbert replied with heavy irony.

'I'm thinking of going to Cornwall. Like to come?' Derek's tone was light.

'If you want me to,' his father returned gruffly.

'Spoken like a Cushing,' laughed Derek. 'Right. I'll ring you about the exact date.'

From the moment Derek had made up his mind to take active steps to keep Diana he had considered abandoning his research and going to Cornwall, but until he actually framed the invitation it had never occurred to him to take his father with him.

On the pavement outside his father's block of flats, Derek's excitement quickly subsided. With a sharp stab of apprehension he realized that, without having deliberately planned it, he was now committed to no less than an all-or-nothing attempt to destroy his wife's affair. The full implications of this terrified him. If he pressed her too hard, mightn't she feel forced to take drastic counter measures? Would he find, even if he succeeded, that his very success had destroyed any hope of any future with her? Panic again, and an attack of it quite as powerful as the one he had experienced in the archive room at the Institute. He stood motionless in the middle of the pavement while people jostled past him. An empty taxi was passing; he ran out into the road and hailed it. Safe inside he breathed more easily. The repetition of his terror was enough to convince him that however distressing and distasteful were the steps he might have to take, they were essential. He *had* to keep her; and from the moment he had decided that action was more likely to achieve this than inaction, he had without fully realizing it cut out the possibility of any half-measures.

As the taxi reached Marble Arch it started to rain. Derek watched the drops gathering on the glass and smiled to himself. It was not hard to imagine how Charles was going to take the news; not only was he going to have to put up with Diana's husband, he was also going to have to suffer her obsessive and unpredictable father-in-law. As time passed the art dealer would become more and more irritated and resentful, and Diana would be the only person on whom he could vent his displeasure. A successful man like Charles would be used to getting his own way and would find it very hard to tolerate such spectacularly bungled plans. Diana had probably boasted about how easy it had been to fix up a time when they could be alone together. When he got back to the flat Derek intended to write to Giles's scout master telling him that G. A. Cushing would not after all be going with the school party to the Peak District but would instead be going to Cornwall for a family holiday.

Derek's only remaining problem would then be to choose the ideal time and place to inform Diana and Giles of the change of plan. He would contact Charles after that. The later they were all told, the less chance they would have of doing anything about it; the nearer Derek could make it a *fait accompli*, the happier he would be. Ideally Diana should be confronted with the news on an occasion which would make it very hard for her to start a violent argument. If he could survive her first reaction, Derek was confident that he would not weaken or back down. The right setting for his disclosures was clearly of vital importance.

Chapter 5

The Cushings turned into the narrow drive; ahead of them, sandwiched awkwardly in a small triangle of grass between two railway lines, the school buildings rose up with all the imposing grandeur of a badly designed Victorian hospital. In front of the main block, a boy with a white arm-band directed Derek to the end of a line of parked cars.

Open Day for parents of boys at Linacre High, Wandsworth, took place on the last Friday of each summer term and was, according to the headmaster, 'an opportunity for parents to see some of the extra-curricular activities of the boys'. Dotted around the grounds were a number of outdoor stands: Rowing Club appeal stand, Gliding Club, Archery Club and so on. Derek glanced at his wife and saw her sour and disapproving look. Diana's educational views had been that if Giles could not go to one of the half-dozen academically orientated public schools, and Derek's salary had ruled this out, the boy ought to have attended the local comprehensive. Giles had not done so because the science side had been so bad there. Instead he had been sent to Linacre, a direct-grant establishment with minor-public-school pretensions that made Diana cringe.

Giles's contribution to Open Day was the Geology Exhibition, which he had set up with the help of two other boys. His parents found him in an almost deserted prefabricated classroom tacked onto the back of the main block. The contents of the exhibition were ranged on tables pushed back against the walls of the room. Giles handed Derek a typed description of the various displays. 'TABLE 1 Devoted to hardness of rocks. TABLE 2 Streak, specific gravity and amber test. TABLE 3 Lustre and crystal systems.'

A table on mining, another on volcanoes with models, types of synthetic minerals, polishing, mounting and displaying of stones. Derek and Diana wandered from table to table, admiring their son's professionalism. Giles was only thirteen and yet half the exhibits were incomprehensible to his parents; both pretended to find the exhibition exciting; Derek did better than Diana, partly because for the past two years he had tried to keep up with his son's hobby, and partly because adrenalin was lapping in his stomach and he found enthusiasm relieved his inner tension.

They had arranged to meet later for tea in the school cafeteria. Arriving before Giles, Derek and Diana queued for a cup of tea and went and sat down at a table in the far corner of the room. No long oak tables and minstrel's gallery in the Linacre dining hall. A modern cafeteria, self-service, strip lighting and tables with blue, pink and green formica tops. The Victorian dining-hall had long since been split up to make more classrooms. Derek's hand shook as he lifted his cup. Diana was looking round glumly at other parents sitting with their sons. The atmosphere was hushed, as though nobody wished the people at the adjacent tables to overhear what they were saying. Derek's nervousness had increased, but the time, he told himself, had undoubtedly come. He pushed back his chair. 'Just going to get something from the car.' Before Diana could object he was threading his way across the room towards the door.

When he returned, Derek was clutching a long cardboard box; from a distance he saw that Giles was now sitting beside his mother. Derek sat down and smiled at them both, then, without saying anything, he unwrapped the package and produced a large pair of green flippers and a matching face-mask and snorkel. A short silence and then Giles leaned across the table and grasped his father's hand.

'That's fantastic.' The boy examined his mask more closely and fiddled with the adjustable strap. 'I can't wait to use them.'

'You won't have to,' Derek replied, smiling at Diana, who was looking puzzled and put out. He breathed deeply and held onto the edge of the table. 'We're all going to Cornwall,' he said, in a tone that a man might have used in telling his family that he had won the pools or been made managing director of his company. Silence. Derek smiled nervously and gave a little cough. 'Well, aren't you pleased?'

Giles looked confused and embarrassed. 'But I'm going to scout camp.'

Derek shook his head.

'I'd rather you came with mummy and me,' he replied gently. 'I've written to the scout master.'

'But your research,' cut in Diana with unconcealed amazement.

Derek studied the formica table top and sighed.

'There are more important things in life than research,' he murmured, and then, with a slight tremor in his voice, 'You said that yourself and you were right. Of course you both come first.'

Diana, who had been frowning to herself, suddenly took Derek's hand and smiled.

'It's not that I'm not pleased; of course I am. But it is rather short notice. Have you told Charles yet?'

'No,' admitted Derek. 'But he won't mind. You heard him yourself the other day, telling us how disappointed he was that I wasn't coming. He'll be pleased too.'

Derek felt less nervous already; perhaps he had underestimated himself to imagine that there could be any difficulties. After all what possible objections could Diana have raised to his changing his mind? She had pretended to be disappointed when he had stuck to his research. She could hardly go back on that now. A moment of doubt recurred when he heard her ask Giles whether he would mind missing his scout camp, but it was over the moment he heard the boy say, 'I can always go next year.'

'So it's all fixed,' cried Derek, clapping his hands and smiling broadly. He sipped his tea thoughtfully and then put down the cup with a clatter. His father. So intent had he been on judging her reactions to the news that he himself would be coming, he had briefly forgotten the deadlier bit of information he had to impart. He toyed with and then dismissed the idea of telling his father that it was all off. The problem was whether to tell her now while she was still shocked and surprised by his first revelation, or whether to wait till another occasion. Derek tried to think logically but without success. Better get it over with quickly.

'I know the idea won't immediately appeal to you,' he said to Diana, 'so please don't jump at me.' He took a bite from a chocolate biscuit and chewed, giving himself time to think. 'I saw my father the other day and I hinted, no more than hinted, mind you, that there was a faint chance that he might come to Cornwall with us.' He smiled apologetically. Diana was looking at him as though he had just confessed to a particularly abhorrent perversion.

'You mean you've asked him,' said Diana in a chillingly level voice.

'No, I don't mean that,' returned Derek, passing the back of his hand over his sweating forehead. 'I simply told him that there was a possibility of his coming. I did go on to say that I couldn't see any immediate reason why he shouldn't come, but I left the matter open.'

'You asked him,' repeated Diana in the same flat cold voice.

'All right. I asked him conditionally.' Derek smiled and dabbed at his forehead again. Diana's face was flushed and her eyes narrowed with anger.

'You'd better un-ask him—' she paused slightly—'unconditionally.'

'Isn't that being a bit unfair? He won't get in anyone's way. There must be a good many pubs in the area. He can stay at one of them or at a bed and breakfast.' He lowered his voice a little. 'Quite honestly the only reason I suggested he might like a holiday is this whole Malayan business. I thought a few weeks away would give his obsession a rest; take him out of himself. You surely can't disagree with that?'

'You don't suppose that when Charles realizes your father's staying in the local pub he might feel obliged to ask him to stay at the house?'

The savage tone of sarcasm was worse than Derek had expected. With as much calmness as he could manage, he said,

'I'll tell Charles that my father's a recluse and that he only wants to see us once or twice every couple of days. He'd honestly be happier in a pub.'

Diana looked him in the eye and said quietly, 'If he comes, I don't.'

'You can't begrudge an old man a chance to get away for a bit. You'll hardly see him. How can it affect you?'

In any other circumstances Derek was certain that she would have thrown something at him, but the other people around them prevented her. He could see from the way she was breathing that the effort not to scream at him was almost unendurable. She twisted her mouth into a bright social smile.

'Oh Charles, something I didn't tell you; my father's been a bit odd lately so I've brought him along. He's at the local pub down the road. No, he's not a lunatic, just rather unbalanced. I'm sure you wouldn't mind having him to lunch every other day.' She threw up her hands suddenly, and, abandoning any attempt to keep her voice down, went on, 'Why not have a mad wife as well? Two for the price of one.'

Giles was looking around with acute embarrassment. He could see several members of his form sitting three tables away with their parents.

'I suppose Giles and I could go on our own,' Derek said, 'but it obviously wouldn't be the same.'

'Blame yourself,' snarled Diana, pushing back her chair with a loud scraping sound.

Giles got up and blurted out imploringly, 'Can't you talk somewhere else?'

Diana looked at him coldly and said, 'As far as I'm concerned there's nothing more to talk about.' Giles picked up his mask and flippers and fled. Diana stared furiously at Derek.

'That was your fault,' she forced out between clenched teeth.

Derek didn't reply but started to eat a nasty-looking piece of pink cake.

'Hadn't you better sit down?' he muttered.

Diana was fumbling in her bag.

'Give me the car keys,' she said, holding out a hand. Derek

shook his head. 'All right; let me have some money for a taxi.'
She was swaying slightly as she held on to the back of the chair. It would not altogether have surprised Derek if she had started ripping off her clothes and throwing them at amazed parents.

'Let's go outside and talk,' he said, taking her arm.

'Will you give me some bloody money?' she shouted.

'Later.'

Heads all over the room had turned to look at them. For Giles's sake it was just as well it was the end of term, reflected Derek. Observers might well imagine that he was a prostitute's client who had just refused to pay. Diana turned on her heel and headed for the door. Derek followed at a distance.

When she reached the main entrance to the building, Derek was relieved to see that Diana started walking towards the cricket field and not towards the drive. He caught her up on the far side of the ground in front of the sight-screen. The scoreboard opposite showed that the fathers had bowled out the boys for 137 and were now 36 for 4 in reply. A boundary was greeted with a thin round of clapping from the small pavilion. She stared straight ahead of her, ignoring him.

'If you cared a damn about my coming,' he said quietly, 'my father wouldn't bother you at all. He'll go for walks on his own, look at plants; he used to collect butterflies.' He suddenly saw his father blundering along a cliff path brandishing a large net. He hoped that Diana had not had the same vision. A boy using a loud-hailer was exhorting fathers to enter for a tug of war against the school's rugger fifteen. Her silence was unnerving Derek. She *had* to come; he had not even guessed at the possibility that she might pull out altogether.

'I really will go with Giles if you refuse to come. I won't be blackmailed.'

She turned to him wearily and let her hands drop to her sides. Her anger had clearly burned out.

'Not wanting your father to come may be selfish, but it isn't blackmail. So stop being so melodramatic.'

Derek studied the grass and tried to think of what to say. A ragged shout from the distant cricketers announced the fall of a wicket. The fathers were in danger of collapse. Diana lit a cigarette and tossed away the spent match.

'All right; I'll come,' she said suddenly. 'Now let's go home.'

'We'd better check up on Giles on the way.'

She nodded agreement. Derek's relief was such that he slipped an arm round her waist. She didn't disengage herself.

A little later she said, 'You've been incredibly thoughtless even for you; but it still wouldn't be fair if I refused to come.' She stopped and took both Derek's hands in hers. 'I was so delighted when you told me you were coming. Then you sprang your father on me. Surely you can see why I was so upset?'

Derek's confidence wavered for a moment but no longer. Her contrition was proof of her guilt. In any other circumstances an invitation to his father would not have been forgiven for several months. In silence they followed the boundary rope back towards the school.

Chapter 6

During the two days remaining before their departure, Derek was fully occupied making arrangements, so he had little time to brood over the outcome of the next two weeks. The car had to be taken in for a service, its first in eight months; there were various items of clothing to be bought, including a new pair of swimming-trunks. He liked the idea of a striped pair in violently contrasting colours. There should be nothing drab on this particular holiday. Then Mr Cushing senior had to be accommodated. Derek spent the best part of a morning on the phone before finding his father a room in the *Three Pilchards*, a village pub five miles from Charles's house.

Now that he was committed to going to Cornwall, Derek felt a sense of relief so great that, in spite of continuing fears for the future, he was still able to enjoy the immediate preparations and was even capable of relishing their hidden ironies. He had discovered from a book called *Cornish Rivers and Estuaries* that they would be staying barely two miles from a famous prawn breeding-ground. Prawning would be an excellent family activity, so he bought three large nets. In the same shop he also acquired some mackerel spinners. Since Diana had attacked him for failing to provide a real family holiday the year before, Derek was determined that this time she should not be disappointed: there would be bags of fun for all the family with prawning, fishing, beach cricket, picnics and numerous outings to places of interest. Derek made his preparations with the hearty bonhomie he felt sure a good-natured and happily married paterfamilias ought to display on such occasions. Giles, who had evidently forgiven his mother for her outburst on Open Day, was equally enthusiastic, and Diana, Derek noted with ironic pleasure, also felt obliged to enter into the holiday spirit.

It was not until the eve of their departure that Derek remembered the cat. When Derek and Diana went away, their black cat, Kalulu, was usually looked after by the couple in the flat above, but unfortunately on this occasion their holiday coincided with the Cushings'. Derek suggested that rather than spend hours the following morning trying to get the animal into a cat's boarding-house, they should take him with them. Diana remonstrated briefly but then gave in. Derek was not really surprised at her uncharacteristic surrender. After all, if you tell your lover you'll come alone and then turn up with your husband, son and father-in-law, the addition of a cat doesn't make much difference.

By half-past eight the following morning they were passing through that no man's land between city and country; the tree-lined avenues of semis and the palatial factories lay behind them; now houses gave way to scarred open spaces, car dumps, reservoirs, shunting-yards and gasometers. A sunny day, and ahead of them the holiday traffic thick on the roads. For a while country, but not for long: the green belt, followed by the stockbroker belt, followed by cummuter-belt Camberley and after the belts the M3 and overspill Basingstoke. A long way to the real country and all the way Kalulu in his basket howling with fear and indignation. The car's service had not cured the steering-wheel judder, nor the curious whine that came from the region of the back axle. So many new cars on the road, their paintwork shining, bumpers undented, engines energetic and responsive, their owners all better paid than archivists. Diana was driving; in the back Giles was reading a thriller. Derek sat beside his wife with the cat basket on his knee; above him the shrimping-nets beat out a regular tattoo on the roof. Derek smiled to himself.

Take the average holiday-maker speeding towards the sands in his metal box, is his life, happiness and security not at risk? Apart from the fear of a fatal crash, what economic, social and moral pressures act upon him unawares as he rushes so blithely upon his way? What lewd memories of infant sexuality shape his sub-conscious mind and afflict his wife with lascivious dreams? A horrifying thought, and yet in one family car, one family man is aware of all the snares and hazards faced by married couples in a competitive and commercially distorted society, and furthermore this man has pledged himself, within the limited ambit of his own family, to do battle with these disruptive forces. *Cushing's Crusade*, a modern morality play, with Charles epitomizing the power of wealth and lust, and Diana representing human weakness in the face of avarice and envy. The archivist himself is reason, moderation and decency. It had been some time, Derek reflected, since he had allowed himself the pleasant fatuity of such idly self-indulgent fantasies.

The heat in the car was increasing. In front of them the road floated in the rising waves of warm air; patches of melting tar made dark smudges. Kalulu was panting. The windscreen was now splattered with insect corpses, their body secretions smeared dribbles of yellow, red and brown. They intended to have lunch just outside Shaftesbury and already Derek was thinking with pleasure of liver sausage sandwiches, apples, plums and a cup of coffee from the thermos. Cold consommé would have been nice, followed perhaps by a light salmon soufflé. He must have started to doze because by the time he realized that Kalulu was retching it was too late to take evasive action. The cat had eaten half a tin of reddish-coloured meat early that morning, and now a thin greasy mess of roughly that colour was seeping into the fabric of Derek's trousers. Several delicate strands of vomit and saliva hung from the corners of Kalulu's mouth. Gone were all thoughts of food; Derek swallowed hard to banish the spasms of nausea he felt at the back of his throat.

'We'd better stop,' he murmured faintly.

'Christ what a pong,' Giles exclaimed, putting down his thriller for the first time on the journey. 'Only another two hundred miles,' he added considerately.

By late afternoon they had left the main road, and were threading their way through a network of Cornish lanes; tall hedges rose up on each side and long grass and cow-parsley brushed the sides of the car. For several hundred yards at a time the interlacing boughs of low stunted oaks formed a canopy overhead and shut out the sky. Through the open windows of the car Derek could smell the honeysuckle in the banks and hedges. A few more miles and the road dipped down from the plateau of hedged fields into dense woods of hazel, oak and holly.

A few miles farther on Derek, who had taken over the driving, stopped on a small stone bridge spanning a narrow creek. Away to their left they could see the main arm of the river winding in a deep, twisting channel through shimmering banks of mud. In the distance a group of gulls rose from the mud and wheeled high above the river: tiny white specks against the sombre green woods on the opposite shore. Beyond the bridge the road curved upwards into the woods, leaving the river for a while.

Nearer the sea, the mudflats and the narrow channel of brown-green water had vanished. A very different river now, and the woods had given way to fields once more. Between the granite pillars flanking farm gates they glimpsed shimmering blue water in V-shaped clefts where steeply sloping hills met. Across the wide estuary the evening sun caught the windows of a group of grey stone cottages and warmed the ochre lichen on the squat tower of a nearby church. A patchwork of cornfields and stony grassland sloped down to small shingle beaches and rocky inlets. Away to their right between two bracken-covered headlands was the sea, throwing a thin white ribbon along the rocks. Near the horizon a long bar of darker blue faded imperceptibly into grey where sea and sky met.

Charles's directions for locating the house had been precise: 'At the crossroads just before you get to Tregeare village, turn left; go on past the Wesleyan chapel and a white farmhouse and the drive is another 200 yards on the right just beyond a group of firs.' There were no gates, just two stone piers surmounted by carved pineapples. Ahead of them, at the end of a short drive, flanked by rhododendrons, stood the house. Derek had expected something more imposing: Tudor, Carolean or Georgian, but what he saw was a rambling late Victorian house built around three sides of a slate-paved courtyard. To the right across rough grass was an overgrown tennis court and dilapidated summer house and beyond that a thicket of giant bamboos. Derek pulled up opposite the front door and switched off the engine. He smiled experimentally. Not a bad journey, traffic could have been worse. The cat was sick but apart from that we managed very well. I'm told that the prawning in these parts is quite exceptional. . . . Charles had appeared in the doorway. Derek threw open the door and jumped out energetically.

'Dear God, it's good to feel the ground under one's feet after a long voyage,' he shouted, as he leapt round to the other side of the car and opened Diana's door with an excess of gallantry. 'Step ashore, my lovely.' Diana smiled wanly as Charles came up to them.

'Come in and have a drink, or for Derek's nautical benefit we might splice the mainbrace.'

'The sun's got to be below the yardarm,' returned Derek in the gruff tone of a ham actor auditioning for the part of Long John Silver or Captain Hook. His opening line had been a joke that couldn't be sustained and now almost in spite of himself he was bludgeoning it to death. 'No drinks until the ship's cat's been watered. Giles, un-hatch the hold and fetch his tray and litter.'

A few sentences and already Diana was embarrassed by his heartiness. She always disparaged people who allowed pets to dictate routines. She hadn't wanted the animal to come and would therefore hate him underlining the cat's presence immediately on arriving. Better forget Kalulu and have a drink straight away, Derek told himself. Stupid to begin with such obvious wrecking; greater subtlety was required. But Giles had already extricated the tray and cat litter from the boot.

'Can't the cat wait?' asked Diana.

'He's waited for nine hours,' Giles countered. 'You wouldn't like to hold on that long. He must be bursting.'

Derek turned to Charles.

'Is there a box-room or somewhere he can go for the time being?'

They followed Charles into the house; Giles lugging the sack of cat litter and Derek carrying the frenzied cat. Charles led them into a small unused conservatory tacked onto the side of the house.

'This do?' asked Charles.

'It'll need sweeping out and he'll have to have a carpet and a bed.... No, it's fine, perfect. He was sick all over me on the way so maybe food wouldn't be a good idea.'

As soon as Giles had closed the door, Derek bent down and gingerly undid the leather straps of the basket. He had opened the lid barely six inches when Kalulu sprang out like a jack-in-a-box and backed away spitting defiantly.

'Friendly little soul,' Charles remarked with a forced smile.

'He'll be all right in the morning,' replied Derek. The best thing would be to fill the tray at once and leave the room as quickly as possible. To delay would merely irritate Diana more. Derek's plan had been to disarm through charm, to be so friendly, so likeable and good-natured that they would both feel ashamed to be deceiving such a good and pleasant man, and yet little flickers of anger like acid in the stomach wrecked his intentions. Why had he been fool enough to presume that he could muster sufficient self-control to play such a game? Better to have gone to Scotland and let them fuck freely until boredom brought an inevitable end. As he started to shake cat litter into the plastic tray he saw Diana's disapproving expression, the slight puckering of her brow. As though his little sin in bringing the animal could compare remotely with her guilt. How dared she condemn anything he did, when his offences were so trivial? He pushed the tray over into a corner. Kalulu sidled up to it and started scratching at the litter sending handfuls onto the floor. Diana had moved towards the door. What delicacy. She was eager to leave before the animal urinated, before a dark stain formed in the tray. Derek began a monologue to detain her.

'His name's Kalulu which is a bit ironic really; the first Kalulu, you see, being a born traveller and our Kalulu hating journeys as he does. Kalulu was a young African boy adopted by Henry Stanley: not adopted as a child but as a pet: a delightful piccaninny to produce as an exhibit on lecture tours, all kitted out in Eton jacket, starched shirt and shiny black shoes. He was drowned in the end when Stanley was tracing the Congo to the sea; attempted to shoot some rapids and disappeared for good. He's called Kalulu because of his black fur, not that there's anything racist about it.'

Kalulu, who had produced two turds as well as a bladderful of urine, was covering up his doings with showers of litter. Derek smiled at everyone.

'Shall we have that drink now?' he asked.

Charles ushered them out into a short corridor that led into the hall and from there into the sitting-room, which overlooked the garden and the estuary. Derek had supposed that Charles would have transformed the interior of the house with hidden lighting, whitewashed rough brick walls and modern pictures and furniture, but his guess had been entirely wrong. Charles had evidently bought the house and its contents with the intention of keeping the place as it was. The sitting-room, like the hall and the main staircase, was panelled in oak and only saved from gloominess by wide french windows. Charles described it as Jacobean with a touch of Hollywood baronial. He was planning to get some antlers, a few Gothic armchairs and several highland scenes by Landseer. Diana laughed and suggested an Etty nude as well; Charles promised to get one when the opportunity arose. Derek imagined himself coming home from work and calling to Diana: Got your Etty, darling. Only a couple of thousand.

When Charles had poured drinks for all of them, he led the way out onto the lawn, which was bordered on both sides by a fuchsia hedge. At the end of the lawn a large rockery dropped away towards a tangle of shrubs and bushes which skirted a strip of woodland. Through a gap in the trees Derek could see the estuary.

'What a heavenly place,' murmured Diana. She sipped her drink elegantly and asked, 'How far is it to the nearest beach?'

'Just through those woods,' replied Charles pointing. 'There's a path of sorts.'

'So you've got a private beach?' she came back with a mixture of surprise and pleasure. Derek felt his bitterness stirring again.

As though the man hadn't already told her. Perhaps they were enjoying the mutual joke of her girlish admiration. How clever to have a private beach; did you make it yourself or have it built by a firm? Starfish and rock pools optional extras. So much better than a swimming-pool somehow, more natural and so few people have them. Giles nudged his father and whispered, 'There's no such thing as a private beach, not below the tide-mark anyway.'

'If you can keep people off there is,' Derek replied quietly and then, turning to Charles, 'What do you do when people land from boats?'

'They very rarely do, so there's no problem.'

'You could put down a boom like they did in the war to keep enemy submarines out of harbours,' Giles suggested.

'I don't think I'd go that far,' laughed Charles.

But if they came in a small armada of pleasure boats, what would you do? If they spread out their plastic forks and plastic knives, their plastic chairs and plastic wives would you let them? But of course they wouldn't come because *they* don't like solitude and empty beaches, *they* like crowds, beach shops, caravan parks and seaside amenities. Trippers are bored by beauty; only we, who spend weekends in comfortable houses and cottages, really appreciate the country and an isolated coast, and there are so few of us, we like to think.

'I'd put down mines,' said Derek with conviction, but Charles couldn't have heard because he was on his way back to the house to bring out more drinks.

'Do you imagine you're being funny?' Diana blurted out. 'You've been behaving like an imbecile ever since we arrived. One minute you're like an idiotic buffoon and the next making some snide and vicious remark. Are you jealous or something?'

'I am utterly consumed; I covet most excessively but will not openly admire what I cannot have.' See my horns, madam, am I not a jealous fool? Derek expected her to continue but instead she walked away towards the rockery.

'I'm jealous too,' said Giles. 'Imagine having a house like this and masses of money. Did you see his car in the garage? He really must be loaded.'

'I wasn't being entirely serious,' Derek replied.

'You were being snide?'

'Does it matter?'

'Mummy thought so.'

'That's her affair. Now stop badgering me.'

'Just because I said it's nice here, and it *is* nice.' Giles gave Derek a wounded look. 'I'm going to walk down to the beach.'

Charles came out again with a tray of drinks and Diana rejoined them.

'Where's he off to?' Charles asked, pointing at Giles, who was jumping down the rockery.

'The private beach,' Derek replied.

'Why not call it the beach?'

'It's shorter,' Derek conceded, as Charles poured him another drink.

'And I prefer it,' Charles added.

'Fine; it's shorter and preferable and it's where Giles has gone, is going.'

Charles was looking at Derek quizzically.

'Why did you change your mind about coming?' he asked.

To stop you fucking my wife, to keep at bay feelings which some days ago seemed to threaten my personal equilibrium, to . . .

'Diana,' he said abruptly; the truth, no doubt about it. Charles was looking puzzled rather than alarmed. Diana glared menacingly at her husband.

'Diana?' Charles repeated.

'Yes, Diana. She went on at me so much that I had no choice; she used everything but the thumbscrews. But being a firm believer in family holidays, I finally allowed myself to be persuaded.'

'Absolute rubbish,' cut in Diana, trying to cover her anger with a light bantering tone. 'He realized what a fool he was being and changed his mind. Nothing to do with me.'

Charles looked disconcerted and slightly embarrassed.

'I shouldn't like to think you felt obliged to come.'

'Please,' implored Derek. 'No really, I'm going to enjoy myself,

62

I assure you. I haven't brought my shrimping-nets for nothing, you know. Wait till you see me in my striped bathing-trunks.'

Charles forced his mouth into a smile and took Derek's arm.

'Quite right; the main thing is that you're here. I've been a bit strained recently. You understand how it is?'

'Perfectly,' answered Derek.

Charles clapped him on the shoulder and looked at his watch.

'I'm going to have to check our supper. The woman who comes in is as bright as a spent match.' Diana laughed loudly and Derek accompanied her in a lower key. The Cushing family's famous laughing duet. Charles was momentarily taken aback, but, not to be left out, he joined in too.

'Bright as a spent match,' chuckled Derek. 'Tries to cook things in the fridge, I suppose.' The trouble one has with staff these days. Take our butler for instance. . . .

Half-an-hour before supper: Diana in the bath, Giles still down on the beach and Derek wandering in the rough grass near the tennis court. Looking back towards the house he could see Charles glancing along the side of the house and then walking to the beginning of the drive. For a second Derek contemplated hiding behind the summer house, but, before he had time to do so, Charles had spotted him.

'There you are. What on earth are you doing?' he shouted.

'Looking for phantom balls,' Derek yelled back.

'I know what you mean,' said the approaching Charles, nodding towards the tangle of tall grass and weeds in the court. 'They never played on it after the eldest son died in the trenches.'

'Really?'

'I meant that's what it looks like.'

'I'll watch for ghostly players gliding through the grass.'

Charles was smiling sadly.

'Derek, Derek,' he said affectionately, 'you didn't think I expected you to give me the usual sycophantic balls about what a gorgeous house and all that. You're one of the only people I know who's honest with me.'

'Tennis with sycophantic balls. That's rather nice.'

'I meant what I said,' Charles replied reprovingly. 'If I'd wanted some showplace to impress fools I wouldn't have bought this. Just look at the garden!' He threw up his hands. 'But who wants beautifully manicured lawns with sprinklers spurting day and night and chauffeurs polishing cars in the drive?'

'You sound like that song *Who wants to be a Millionaire?*'

'All right, I'll spare you any more.' A brief silence before Charles continued. 'I was annoyed but not for any reason you imagine. Do you want to hear?'

Derek felt sick. How many times would Charles treat him to *sincere* talks and man-to-man honesty?

'Tell me,' he said.

'It was what you said about family holidays; it brought home to me the fatuity of having a place like this without a family.'

Charles was separated from his wife and children. Go back if that's how you feel, Derek wanted to say.

'Won't Anne let the children come?'

'She wouldn't let them stay more than a couple of days.' Charles kicked at a tuft of grass and managed a rueful smile. 'Enough self-pity. I thought I ought to explain why I was edgy. Subject closed, all right?'

'Fine.'

'I'm afraid I've got another apology to make. I had asked Otto Meyer and his wife. Do you know his collages?' Derek shook his head emphatically. 'Anyway for various reasons he couldn't come. A pity because you'd have got on well. I tried to get several other people but no go; not surprising at this time of year.'

Derek nodded agreement. Like hell he'd asked other people.

'I don't mind if we're the only guests,' said Derek.

'I wish you were. Angela turned up out of the blue a week ago; you remember sister Angela? Who'd forget. She left her husband last year and's been sponging off me ever since. Not all the time but most of it. To crown it all she asked her new man without a word to me and had the gall to suggest that since I'd met him before I wouldn't mind. He used to come and soak up booze at my private views and then write hostile drivel in *Studio Inter-*

national. The galleries are dead, art objects are finished, that old line.'

'I see.'

'This morning I told her as tactfully as I could that he'd stayed long enough. Not a case of brilliant timing, I'm afraid.'

'What did she say?'

'She'd have to think about it.'

'Awkward.'

'I thought I'd better warn you.'

'Have you spoken to either of them since?'

'They went out early this morning, so I haven't had the chance.'

'I suppose I'd better get the stuff down from the roof of the car,' said Derek after a brief silence. Charles nodded and they walked back towards the house. While the two of them took down cases and untied ropes securing Giles's bicycle, Charles said, 'I'd much rather your father stayed here. There isn't a decent hotel in miles and the pubs are pretty terrible.'

'I'll ask him what he wants to do when he gets here.' Derek lifted down the bicycle and rested it against the side of the car. 'I've got to collect him tomorrow. Three something at Truro; I'll have to check the time. I'm grateful you've been so good about it all. Diana was dead against his coming. Perhaps I shouldn't have said that.'

'I can't see why. Say what you like.'

Derek could hear a car farther up the drive.

'Trust them. Haven't missed one meal since they've been here,' muttered Charles. Derek thought of making a joke about the Last Supper but didn't. Instead he picked up two cases and walked briskly towards the house before the car drew up.

Diana had dressed for dinner, not in her smartest clothes, it was true, but since Charles's sister Angela was wearing a man's shirt and a pair of faded jeans, Diana's green dress decorated with beads and small glass panels seemed conspicuously fashionable. Between mouthfuls of soup Derek examined Angela's friend Colin. A sallow angular face framed by long black hair; deep-set eyes with well-defined creases under them, a sign of Angela's nocturnal demands? A bright yellow T-shirt with an eagle, probably the American eagle, stamped on the chest. Three drops of blood fell from the bird's beak. Silence while they drank soup. Derek concentrated on not slurping it. Diana always accused him of doing so at home. Giles was looking at Colin's shirt.

'A boy in my form's got a shirt like that.'

'They are mass-produced,' Colin replied coolly. Derek was irritated by the slight sarcasm in his voice. At least Giles had been trying to start a conversation.

'Normally of course it's the pelican which is portrayed with a bleeding beak. I don't know the medieval fable well, but it's something about the female pelican feeding her young with blood from her breast. There's some parallel with Christ's shedding his blood for mankind.' Derek gave Colin a donnish smile and re-applied himself to his soup.

'I don't see the relevance myself,' Colin replied.

'You must be a man of few words if they're all relevant,' answered Derek.

Charles laughed loudly and Angela joined in. Colin looked at Derek angrily.

'If you mean do I bore people with academic marginalia at every possible opportunity, the answer is that I don't.'

'I didn't mean that at all, so you're the irrelevant one, old man.' Derek wasn't sure why he added the last two words; possibly an instinctive feeling that they would annoy him more. The effect was considerably more insulting than he had intended.

Angela turned to Derek and said quietly, 'I suppose Charles asked you to be rude to Colin?'

'Let him play with himself,' cut in Colin derisively.

'Are you suggesting that I ought to start masturbating?' asked Derek mildly. Giles's spoon stopped halfway between his plate and his mouth. Diana was studying the surface of the table.

'Do what you like but just leave me alone.'

Derek nearly made a joke about mutual masturbation but restrained himself. Instead he smiled blandly. 'It's strange how many aggressive people wear anti-war shirts.'

'That's a pretty cheap generalization,' said Angela in a flat matter of fact voice.

'I'm a bit mean with my expensive ones.'

Giles laughed nervously but when nobody else did he blushed and pretended to scrape a last spoonful from his already empty plate.

'Do you find it amusing to make jokes about people's beliefs?' Angela enquired with polite interest rather than anger.

'Prig,' exploded Charles. 'Haven't you ever told a joke about a Jew? Do you think Derek's a mass murderer because he hasn't got *Love* or *Peace* written on his clothes? I suppose it never occurred to Colin that Derek might feel strongly about medieval fables.'

Derek found himself grinning at Charles: an alliance of old friends. It was almost as though Charles had deliberately set up Colin as a target for a repetition of the vitriolic wit which had first drawn him to Derek when they had been at university together. And I fell for it, thought Derek with incredulity. No reason to dislike Colin. He hardly knew the man. The real reason for his irritation had had nothing to do with the wretched art critic. He had been angry because Diana had taken such trouble with her appearance. Charles and Diana should have been his targets. He ought unobtrusively to have taken Colin's side but of course that was no longer possible. Charles's cook, Mrs Hocking, had shuffled in and was removing the plates.

'What delicious soup,' said Diana brightly. 'Did you make it, Mrs Hocking?'

Before the woman could reply Angela cut in, 'Haven't you heard of Porthleven crab soup? It's tinned ten miles away. Every crab a Cornish crab, if that's any consolation.'

When Mrs Hocking had gone, Charles murmured, 'That wasn't very tactful.'

'God, how frightful of me. I'm terribly sorry.' Angela gave her brother a look of grovelling contrition and then tossed back her head and laughed. 'Tactful! I'm surprised you've got the gall to use the word.'

Up to that moment Derek had thought Angela rather glum but

her sudden animation made him wonder whether her remarks about his attack on Colin had been made tongue in cheek. The last time he had seen her she had been seventeen or eighteen, ten years ago, and she didn't look very different now. No make-up; straight blonde hair brushing her shoulders. A sprinkling of freckles across the bridge of her nose and a slight gap between her front teeth; her expression almost sulky in repose but utterly transformed when she reacted.

'Be as rude to me as you like,' said Charles, 'but don't offend Mrs Hocking.'

Angela turned to Derek and said, 'Don't be fooled by him. He doesn't care a damn for the woman's feelings. He's just scared of losing a cook and not being able to get another.'

'There's nothing wrong with that,' Diana replied.

'Perhaps you'd be less inclined to be sympathetic to my charming brother if you and your husband were suddenly asked to leave. Colin and I got our marching orders this morning.' Angela smiled pleasantly at Diana and folded her arms with complete composure.

Mrs Hocking wheeled in a trolley with their main course: chicken casserole. As Charles doled out helpings he turned to Angela and said without apparent resentment, 'If I suddenly turned up at Colin's flat and asked to stay, I wonder how he'd react.'

Angela let out a little cry of sisterly admiration. 'Isn't he just wonderful? Of course he has seven bedrooms and Colin lives in a two-room flat, and then Colin did just happen to come with me, and I am Charles's little sister, but apart from that the comparison's absolutely bang on target.'

Charles put down the serving-spoon with a clatter. 'The possession of a large house doesn't give the owner's relatives the right to come and occupy it at will.'

Angela nodded understandingly and murmured to Derek, 'In most primitive tribes generosity creates loyalty. Isn't that so?'

Before Derek could answer, Charles cut in, 'In our society it creates parasites like you, Angela.'

'What are you then?' rapped out Colin, bringing down his fist on the table. 'Art dealers are the biggest bloody parasites of all.'

'And critics?' asked Charles, as he started to pour out wine.

Colin looked as though he was about to choke. 'What did you make out of that Léger show? A hundred thousand? Two hundred?'

Charles finished pouring wine into Diana's glass and replied soothingly, 'They weren't given to me, you know. Interest rates aren't cheap these days. Shall I tell you what the overheads were on that one show?'

'Shall I tell you what my salary is for one year?' shouted Colin, pointing his fork at Charles.

'I'm sure the Inland Revenue would be more interested,' Charles came back coolly.

Colin pushed back his chair abruptly and left the table. A moment later they heard his footsteps on the stairs.

'You don't suppose he's decided to leave?' Charles asked Angela.

'What do you think?' she replied savagely.

Charles shrugged his shoulders. 'Let's say I'm hopeful.'

'If he decides to go, I still intend to stay,' Angela said quietly. 'I've no use for gestures.'

'You're making one by staying,' smiled Diana.

'If it gets on your tits, it'll have been worth it.'

Giles, who had been listening in horrified disbelief, suddenly let out a stifled sob. Derek looked round guiltily; he had been so engrossed with what was being said that he had not noticed the effect it was having on his son. Before he could intervene, Diana had helped the boy to his feet and led him from the room. As they left, Colin appeared in the doorway, holding a battered suitcase. He glared at Charles for a moment and then turned on his heel. After a short silence Charles said to Derek:

'How about some lemon meringue pie?'

Diana, Derek and Charles were drinking coffee in the sitting-room when Angela rejoined them. Without a word to Charles she opened the drinks and poured herself a brandy. She passed the glass slowly under her nose and sniffed deeply.

'What bouquet. I think that's the word.' She paused and smiled contemplatively. 'My husband loved brandy. He drank a whole bottle the day I left him. Very nearly became an alcoholic.' Charles had shut his eyes. Angela came and sat next to Derek. 'There's a happy ending, though. He's living with his switch-board operator now and doesn't touch a drop. They're thinking of getting engaged.' She nudged Derek. 'Get it? Engaged ... switch-board girl ... No? Well, never mind.' After a long silence Angela said, 'I hope the boy was all right.'

'He was sick,' said Diana softly.

'I'd better go and see him,' murmured Derek.

'He's asleep now.'

Angela seemed to be having trouble stopping herself laughing.

'I actually made him physically sick?' she asked in amazement.

Diana nodded solemnly. A moment later Angela's laughter filled the room. Diana rose with dignity and said that she was ready for bed.

'And I must feed the cat,' muttered Derek, following her out.

Diana hung up her dress carefully, took off her pants and got into bed. Derek climbed in beside her.

'Was Giles badly sick?' he asked.

Diana laughed maliciously. 'He wasn't sick at all. I said it to embarrass that ghastly girl.'

'Giles knows what you said?'

'Of course. He thought it was quite funny.' Derek said nothing. 'Don't you think so?'

Derek thought for a moment. 'No, I don't really.'

'You heard how rude she was to me,' said Diana sharply.

'Everyone was rude.'

'Let's forget it then,' she replied, turning off the light.

After the usual dull roar of traffic that permeated even the rear rooms of Abercorn Mansions, Derek found it hard to get used to the unfamiliar stillness of the countryside. The distant barking of a dog or even the sudden notes of a blackbird on the lawn sounded unnaturally loud. Derek tried to sleep but thoughts about the following day prevented him. He had imagined a very different first evening with Charles, the suave and unruffled host, effortlessly in command of everything and everybody. But after the chaos of the past hours, the arrival of his father, which Derek had envisaged as a severe blow to Charles's perfectly planned holiday arrangements, would go virtually unnoticed and might very well prove more embarrassing to Derek himself than to anybody else. Already Derek could see that his trip to collect his father from Truro would leave Charles and Diana alone for the best part of the afternoon, and the last thing he had intended to allow them was uninterrupted time together.

Other worries also distressed him. He had imagined himself easily acting the perfect husband, but all the time the corrosive acid of his bitterness ate away his capacity for good humour and bonhomie. But more alarming than this was his suspicion that affability might not be the answer anyway. If he *did* manage to be pleasant and amiable every minute of each day, they might very well think him a more gullible idiot than they had previously assumed. Don't worry, Charles, we can do it in the sitting-room in front of him; he'll think we're doing keep fit exercises or rehearsing a modern ballet.

As Derek lay in the darkness he began to doubt even his belief that his decision to come to Cornwall had been proof of his independence and newly found resolution. Why was he in Cornwall? Because of Diana. Why was his father coming? Because of Diana. Why had he forced Giles to come too? Because of Diana. Derek saw his suitcase on a chair near the foot of the bed. Why not just pack and leave? Place a note on the dining-room table: 'Have gone to Ujiji.' He imagined the stunned silence when they read the note. They would feel that he had weighed them up and found them wanting. He was thinking what a long time it would probably take them to find out where Ujiji was, when he fell asleep.

Chapter 7

A thin channel of sunlight pierced the gap between the curtains and formed a neat square of light on the pale green fitted carpet to the right of Derek's bed. He reached for his watch on the bedside table: after ten. Diana had got up without waking him, had let him lie unconscious while the early morning freshness faded with the steadily increasing heat of the day, had allowed him to miss the dew and in all likelihood his breakfast. Hurriedly he put on the clothes he had worn the day before and went downstairs.

Nobody in the dining-room; only the remnants of breakfast. The noise of a hoover came from the sitting-room. As he came in Mrs Hocking switched it off and asked what he would like for breakfast. Five minutes later when she brought him toast and coffee he asked where everybody was. Apparently Charles had taken Diana down to the village, Angela had not got up and Giles had gone off with his snorkel. So that was how they intended to deal with his intruding presence: pretend he wasn't there. Derek gulped down a cup of coffee and hastily ate a slice of toast. They wouldn't get rid of him that easily.

He thought of going to the village in the car but decided that Giles's bicycle would be more in the holiday spirit. Tregeare was only half-a-mile away and downhill all the way so it didn't take long. A small place, not much more than a cluster of cottages and a single street leading down to a narrow harbour. Considering the time of year there were surprisingly few people about. Derek had noticed Charles's silver-grey Lancia outside the village shop but they weren't inside. He propped the bicycle against the church-yard wall and walked down to the harbour. No sign of them there. Out to sea he could see a returning fishing-boat pursued by a clamouring cloud of gulls. In the harbour itself there were more yachts and motor boats than fishing-craft. He walked back up a worn flight of stone steps to the centre of the village. The pub wasn't open yet. Derek decided to try the church.

He heard their voices as soon as he entered the porch. They were obviously up at the east end because he couldn't make out what they were saying. Suddenly he had a childish urge to give them a shock. He peered round the edge of the half-open door. They were examining the carvings on the pulpit. Derek saw a small arch with stairs leading up from it, probably to the belfry. He moved quickly behind the font and managed to reach the steps without being seen. Breathing heavily, he started climbing. From an internal window in the belfry he could look down on the nave. Now he could hear them clearly. Charles was pointing to a bench-end.

'Pretty crudely done really,' he was saying.

'I think she's rather fun,' replied Diana.

'As mermaids go I suppose she's not bad,' Charles conceded.

'Are there lots of them in Cornish churches?'

'Not that I know of. No, the story is that a young choir-boy here in fifteen something had a lovely voice and used to sing down on the rocks near the harbour. Anyway this mermaid took such a fancy to his voice that she lured him into the sea and that was that. Maybe I've got it wrong. Usually mermaids are the ones with lovely voices.'

'Maybe this one liked duets,' laughed Diana.

What other fey little pieces of local information did he have up his sleeve? Something interesting in the vestry? Spread out the choir boys' cassocks on the floor and . . .

'There's a pretty good view from the tower. One can see right across the bay over the roofs. Very picturesque.'

'Lovely.'

To his right Derek could see some wooden stairs leading up-wards, doubtless to the top of the tower. Nothing for it but to announce himself before they found him spying on them. He took hold of one of the three available bell ropes and gave it a sharp tug. A feeble clang sounded somewhere above him. He tried again with a more gratifying result. Then he clambered down the stairs and gave them a cheery 'good morning'.

'We didn't see you come in,' said Charles with a smile. For a moment Derek wondered whether they might suspect him of malice but on reflection that did not seem very likely. Good old Derek sneaking up into the belfry, just the sort of idiotic, retarded adolescent joke he'd fancy to start the day.

'Didn't know I was a campanologist, I suppose? One of my many talents.' He grinned at them both and then feigned dismay. 'God, it isn't some time-honoured local way of summoning a fire engine from the nearest town?'

'Not that I know of,' Charles replied.

'What a relief.'

The view from the tower was quite as good as Charles had predicted. The sea a brilliant blue, the sky clear, the hills on the other side of the estuary a pleasing green. They would probably take it in good part if he made a desperate lunge for the parapet. Didn't know I could fly, I suppose? One of my many talents. The wind blew back Diana's hair attractively. She was wearing a very short pair of white shorts with matching socks that came up just below the knee. Derek hadn't previously seen her green singlet with a yellow stripe across it just below the breasts. It suited her; so too did her large sun glasses.

She turned to him. 'Don't you wish we had a house down here?'

Derek nodded. The archivists' strike is now into its eighth week. Angry crowds of book lovers broke windows outside several public libraries yesterday. The archivists are demanding a basic rate of ten pounds a week. Last week booksellers announced that Mr Derek Cushing's *European Expansion in East Africa: 1870–1900* has become a best-seller in Burundi. Ninety-seven per cent of the population of Burundi one thought to be illiterate. Derek could remember dozens of dinner parties, when they had entertained more frequently, and the same topic: a small weekend place in the country. Suffolk's still cheap. No, not any more. Lincolnshire then? A bit flat and dreary, isn't it?

74

Most of the participants had had no intention of buying anything anyway. I was thinking of something a little different: a semi in a dormitory suburb, a penthouse in an industrial overspill, not actually in the country but with the country not too far away. A chance to do an exciting survey of the sort of social problems that crop up where country meets town.

All three of them were silent. If I had stayed away they would be talking now, thought Derek. Charles would be pointing out interesting features of the panoramic view. How interested Diana had been by the story of the mermaid, how happy and exuberant and now his presence seemed to drain her. Once, and not so many years ago, he had told her similar anecdotes about buildings of historic interest. The piscina on the south side of the chancel —pronounced pisseena—was used by the priest to pour away the water he had used to wash the cup and his hands after communion. Strange that a small stone basin in a wall should have the name the Romans gave their fish-ponds; and so he would have talked about words and how they changed. And she had not found it dry and dull; but now my hair is falling out, and I suffer from piles and there's no denying Charles is very well-preserved and she has never had to wash and mend his underwear. They are not long the days of wine and roses. Sympathies should belong to lovers and not to thwarted husbands. They could have kissed under the bells without his intrusion. So why not leave them now? Why tag along simply to watch your own defeat in each look and word that passes between them? You suffer and achieve nothing except an increase in their desire.

Outside the church Charles suggested that they went all three to see a nearby creek which could be reached by walking through some woods; a most delightful walk, he said.

'You two go,' answered Derek.

'Are you sure? No, come on, Derek.'

'I'd rather not.'

So Charles accepted it and he and Diana got into the silver grey Lancia and drove off towards their wood. Derek mounted his son's bicycle and pedalled back to the house; a hard up-hill ride that made his thighs ache and misted his glasses with sweaty condensation.

He didn't go into the house but taking one of the prawning-nets from the garage, where he had left them the night before, he headed down to the beach.

When he reached the shore Derek realized that he had no bag to put his possible catch in. He sat down on a rock and put his head in his hands. A fine sight he would be to any observer: a balding man with his prawning-net, sitting alone by the sea like a forgotten child. What possible point could there be in catching prawns anyway? Did any sane man pursue pop-eyed crustaceans while his wife was screwed on the ferny floor of a nearby wood? Was such a pursuit reasonable or probable? Derek imagined some alternatives: a trunk call to his solicitor, a feverish bicycle ride to the nearest town to buy a camera and then a blundering lumbering run through the undergrowth to surprise them with his flash bulb. A long swim towards America, or some more bizarre form of suicide involving a deadly jelly-fish. In my position there is nothing rational to be done. Simply by coming to Cornwall I have destroyed all normal courses of action, all natural responses.

The question was whether to wade into the sea in his trousers or whether to take them off. Stupid to get them wet. In sky-blue underpants Derek wandered along the beach searching for a container. After some time he found a rusty can. The prawns could be kept down with a flat stone. The next step was to find the prawns. From childhood holidays by the sea he remembered that prawns normally liked places where there was an abundance of the kind of seaweed with bubbles that pop when trodden upon. If he could find this weed and a firm sandy bottom there was every chance of success. The tide was low and just beginning to turn. Perfect conditions and in an estuary famous for its prawns.

For fifteen minutes he was unsuccessful but then as the tide began to flow they started to come, not small and sandy-coloured like shrimps but large and clear green in the sunlit water. He had forgotten how quickly they could dart away, forwards or backwards, to hide under a ledge of rock or in a clump of weed. They needed stalking carefully; the net had to be plunged down and then retracted quickly if they were not to escape. The best way would have been to have a bag tied round his neck to drop them into, so that both hands could be free to wield the large cumbersome net, but Derek managed well enough with his one free hand and the tin clutched firmly in the other. After an hour his fingers were numbed with cold, his back ached and his legs felt weak but he had filled the tin. Elated he splashed back to the shore and lay down on the shingle, listening to the prawns rustling and flipping under the retaining stone that blocked their escape. For the first time in several weeks he felt light-hearted. In circumstances like these? He thought of his wife's white shorts discarded, her green vest tossed aside carelessly on some bush, he thought of more intimate details, but strangely his mood did not change immediately. Suffering and fear are sometimes said to give way to numbed indifference; but that wasn't it at all. The truth was that while hunting his prawns he had forgotten her. So intent had he been on the green bottom of the sea that he had barely noticed the passage of time. A brief and futile piece of self-induced forgetfulness? A temporary anaesthetic to numb the pain? But the mood persisted. He had acted by himself and for himself without any suggestion from her and not in response to something she had done.

When he got back to the house she would ask him what he had been doing and he would give her a full account and perhaps she would think: how typical of him to be so easily duped; searching for prawns while Charles and I were fucking. Maybe one day he would tell her that he had known but had gone prawning in spite of his knowledge. I enjoyed myself more because I knew, and he would laugh at her stupefaction. You see, I'm free. I let you have it away with him, not because I couldn't stop you; I could have cramped your style to the bitter end, forced you to do everything with me, subjected you to family games on the sand till you screamed with anger and frustration, but I decided not to. Ironic, isn't it, that you were bored with me because you thought you knew me through and through? Sad; because you didn't begin to understand me. You jumped to a foregone conclusion and looked for easier pleasures. I forgive you. And she would weep as she had never wept before. Derek heard footsteps crunching on the shingle. He turned to see Angela looking down at him.

'Catch anything?'

'In the can, as they say in the film world; I haven't counted them.'

'Shrimps?'

'No, prawns.'

Derek was suddenly aware that he was still trouserless. He started to reach for them but then stopped. Why bother? He laughed aloud. Angela gave him a questioning look.

'I'm sorry,' he murmured. 'Shrimps, you see. Reminded me of my favourite spoonerism. Shrotted pimps.' He looked at her expectantly. 'Potted shrimps.'

'Stupid of me,' she replied with a wry smile.

Derek tried to think of something else amusing to say but invention failed him. He very much wished to avoid a repetition of the aggression of the previous evening. Angela was still stand-ing beside him. He wanted to get up because he disliked any woman looking down at the top of his balding head, but the thought of standing up without his trousers kept him seated on the shingle. True, there was little difference between some swimming trunks and some underpants but all underwear had a greater tendency to appear soiled and stained, and Derek had not changed his pants for several days.

'Why not sit down?' he suggested.

When Angela had done so, she said, 'What'll you do with the prawns?'

'There'll be just about enough for each of us to have a couple before lunch.'

'Why not eat them now?'

'A small matter of cooking.'

'We could light a bonfire and boil them in seawater.'

'There's nothing to keep the can above a fire, unless you'd care to hold it.'

Angela shrugged her shoulders. 'I thought men were supposed to be able to solve that sort of problem.'

'And I thought independent women didn't make remarks like

that, but we can but try.' He got up and hurriedly clambered into his trousers.

'If it's all too much trouble, don't bother,' she replied.

'I said we'd try.'

So they set about making a fire. Angela had some matches and they used her cigarette packet to provide the initial flame to ignite the dead heather, dry bracken and other kindling which Derek collected from the edge of the woods. The principal fuel was driftwood. After a fair amount of experimenting they managed to balance the can over the fire using two piles of stones and two thick planks of damp wood. Their hope was that the water would boil before these wooden supports burned through.

In the bright sunshine the flames were hardly visible but appearances were deceptive for the fire was a good one and the water heated up fast. As it started to boil, the prawns changed from brownish-green to pink as though a powerful dye had suddenly been put in the water.

'What was so hard about that?' asked Angela with a smile.

As she spoke one of the supports gave way and Derek had to give the can a hefty shove with a stick to save the prawns from the flames. The can and its contents spilled out onto the beach but well clear of the fire. Having cooled the cooked prawns in the sea, they stripped them and then started to eat.

'I've never tasted better,' Derek admitted and Angela didn't argue. They ate seven and a half prawns each: the entire catch. Ahead of them the tide was slowly advancing up the beach making slight noises like a wet sheet brushing the shingle. The water sparkled, caught by the sun where the slight breeze ruffled the surface: like reflections in fragmented glass. To their left a low reef of black rocks jutted into the sea. The bonfire was dying down. Once again Derek could think of nothing to say. He prodded the fire with a stick sending a shower of sparks into the air. Angela was looking at him with undisguised curiosity.

'Why were you so nasty yesterday?' she asked pleasantly.

'Why should I tell you?'

'That's a child's evasion.'

'It was a child's question. One thing led to another as things tend to do.' He tossed a stone down the beach into the sea. 'Your friend would have said that I was temporarily overcome by the fragmentation, alienation and despair endemic in a decadent bourgeois culture.'

She lay back on the beach and shut her eyes. A long silence.

'I'm afraid I'm not much good at instant honesty,' said Derek.

'You should give it a try; it's not much harder than cooking prawns.' She sat up and grinned at him. 'Would you mind if I take off my shirt?' she asked suddenly. Derek had noticed she was wearing no bra.

'I've got to be honest?' She didn't answer. 'It's much harder than cooking prawns but I'll try.' He paused for a moment. It wasn't nervousness precisely but his heart was beating faster and his mouth felt dry. 'I do mind and I don't, or part of me does and part of me doesn't. I like looking at strange breasts ... strange in the sense of new rather than deformed or grotesque, if you get my meaning; or to be strictly honest I *think* I like looking at strange breasts. You see it's some time since I've had the chance, although there was a time when I did and enjoyed it thoroughly. I don't find nudity boring like some people do, or say they do, because working in a library I'm not in daily contact so to speak —we don't have a collection of erotica, you see—so I wouldn't mind from that point of view. But looking has other effects and although I like to think that ... no, the other effects don't need explaining. Elderly men in strip clubs often hold newspapers on their knees, or laps I should say. Then I suppose somebody, my son, for example, might come upon us as I looked at them and might draw conclusions that were incorrect; might assume that we were not merely being honest with each other but were being intimate or about to be intimate. Other considerations too. If you take your shirt off I will want to look at your breasts but won't want to be seen looking at them because that would make it appear that I'm so tit-orientated that I can't behave naturally in the face of something natural. You might want to talk to me about racial integration or a voluntary wage restraint policy and I might want to extend my hand and this might get in the way of a useful discussion of topical ... I'm afraid I find decisions rather hard to make so I usually let other people make them for me.' He smiled apologetically. 'If you want to take your shirt off you ought to.'

'I don't think so,' she replied quietly.

Derek was surprised at the extent of his disappointment. He had been certain that she would take it off whatever he said; have made the decision for him and then have asked him to be honest about his feelings. Being a blonde, her nipples would have been as pleasantly pink as the prawns they had just eaten and the skin around them pebble smooth and very white in the sun. The black rocks, the white skin, the blue sea and that single touch of pink . . . those two touches of pink. As a child he had played doctors and patients with several little girls. Hadn't there been a similar atmosphere? Playing at doctors or playing at honesty could have similar results. Is the pain there? he remembered asking, prodding a plump little stomach. Fluttering eyelids, a slight blush and the patient would say: It's lower down, doctor. There? You ought to have a proper examination. I feel better . . . No, Derek. I'm still the doctor. Anger and alarm. You're not the doctor, you're Derek and take your hand away at once. Perhaps he had completely misread Angela's mood; invested the occasion with an ambiguity it didn't possess.

'Are we still being honest?' he asked.

'If you want to be.'

'I *would* like you to take off your shirt. I wasn't being intentionally dishonest before.'

Angela took off one of her shoes and tipped some stones out of it. Then she shook her head slowly.

'You weren't being dishonest before, intentionally or unintentionally. You want me to take off my shirt because I decided not to. You're more interested in influencing me than in seeing my tits.'

'My desire to influence you goes no further than the removal of your shirt.'

Angela threw back her head and laughed until she was weak with laughing. At last she said, 'That's what all the boys say . . . the words are sometimes slightly different.'

'Haven't you broken the rules?' asked Derek.

'Sod the rules.' She winked at him. 'If I show you, promise you won't tell?'

'I think I can be honest about that.'

'Just a short look, mind. Don't go making a meal out of them.'

'I'm a little old for that.'

She was laughing again as she undid her shirt so they shook up and down. Derek started laughing too.

'It's the air down here; does something for a girl.' She paused. 'What do you think?'

'The air?'

'*Them*, you fool. John liked bigger nipples. I used to tell him it had something to do with babies.'

'I think they're very nice.'

She looked down modestly.

'They're quite convenient; not too large or anything like that. No lumps yet.'

'Like pink prawns,' he said.

'You're bloody twisted.'

'I meant the colour of your nipples.'

'I suppose they are.' She looked at him with sudden concern. 'You look sad. All that laughter and now you look sad. Why?'

'Still honest?' he asked.

'Of course,' she replied.

'Your brother is fucking my wife in a wood.' He smiled for a moment but felt tears pricking beneath his lids. 'It sounds like the first line of a bawdy poem but I'm afraid it's true.'

She had kissed him before he quite realized what had happened; not that he remembered it as rushed afterwards: the reverse in fact, for the kiss seemed to last for some seconds after she had moved away.

'Silly her,' she whispered.

'I wasn't appealing for compensation; a sort of *quid pro quo*.'

'I'm not a fool,' she said with sudden anger.

'I'm sorry.'

She buttoned her shirt and stood up.

'We were strangers all the time,' he said.

'Come on,' she replied. 'Lunch, and we can't keep Mrs Hocking waiting. We're not strangers. We're you and me, and I can't think of what to say because moods come and go like the fire we lit burned and went out.'

As they walked up the beach towards the wood she took his hand and he was sure she had made the gesture because she felt sorry for him and he cursed himself for destroying a morning he had enjoyed in spite of so much. As they walked through the wood he forgot her hand and remembered Diana. What did you do this morning, Derek? Flirted on a beach. I suppose she flirted back; as soon as one man goes she's ready for another. Like with her husband. . . .

Lunch was uneventful, although Derek could see that Angela was watching Charles and Diana with more attention than hitherto. Giles had found an underwater cave and wanted an aqua-lung so that he could explore it properly.

'You will be careful, won't you, darling?' said Diana.

'I can hold my breath for ninety seconds so I know how long I can go down for. I count under water.'

'It still sounds dangerous. Your eyes look rather bloodshot too.'

Although she was being critical and concerned, Derek knew that she felt guilty for not being with her son; guilty because she knew that she would let him go back to his cave and not even sit on the beach watching him diving.

Later Charles suggested that they went fishing in the bay during the afternoon.

'I've got a motorboat; not a speedboat, I'm afraid. We should be able to catch a few mackerel.'

'Just my luck to be going to Truro,' said Derek. 'My father's train, you see.' He caught Angela's eye and looked away. 'You'll be going, won't you?' he asked Giles.

'I haven't been asked,' the boy replied quietly.

'Of course you're coming,' came back Charles heartily.

'In case you're thinking of asking me, don't bother,' said Angela.

'You have more interesting plans, I suppose?' Charles returned.

'There are several things I want to buy in Truro. That's if Derek will take me.'

'Could I get them for you? Save you the journey?' asked Derek.

'I'll have to choose one or two things myself, but thanks for offering.'

Derek and Angela had to leave before the end of the meal. As they went out Diana was laughing at an amusing anecdote about a picture framer who had gone mad.

They drove in silence along the enclosed lanes and through the woods which led down to the head of the river. The height of the hedges and the dense canopy of trees which often blotted out the sky made Derek feel claustrophobic. He had wanted time to think before being alone with Angela again. Outside in the fields or down by the sea they could have walked and looked around and silence would not have been oppressive but in the car it weighed on Derek heavily. The sun beat down on the car and sweat started to trickle down his back sticking his shirt to the plastic seat. By contrast she seemed relaxed and cool. Nearly thirty, perhaps? Twenty-six or seven anyway, but she looked a lot younger. That slight gap between her front teeth and the lack of make-up probably accounted for it. It was a long time since he had studied a female face carefully. He liked the way little brackets formed round the edges of her mouth when she smiled and the way her cornflower-coloured eyes narrowed. Her slightly turned-up nose gave her an almost insolent look, which he had once thought sullen but now found amusing. She didn't comb her hair much but in her man's shirt and rough jeans it gave her a pleasantly windswept appearance. Not beautiful, perhaps, her cheekbones were a little too broad, but not far off it. And him? An ill-assorted couple, the two of them. From the front his hair wasn't too bad, but it was very thin at the back and another year or two and it would be worse. Until his late twenties he had never worn glasses unless he had to, for films, plays, driving a car; now he wore them all the time and had done for years. He wasn't fat and although Diana thought his legs too short for his body, it wasn't a criticism that previous girl friends had made. Two years before at the Institute a young American postgraduate had seemed interested for a few months, had offered to help him tidy up and take manuscript boxes down to the archives, but nothing had happened; there had been no furtive embraces behind the stacks of missionary correspondence, no impropriety in the archives. A perfect place which he had never thought of using. Come and see my manuscripts were words which had remained unspoken through the years.

'You didn't want me to come, did you?' she asked as they passed the reeds and mudflats at the head of the river.

'What makes you say that?'

'Come on. You wouldn't have offered to save me the trouble of coming by buying what I wanted for me.' She gave a sniff of mock grief and added, 'Now would you?'

'Do you suppose,' asked Derek, pointing at a distant bird sitting on one of the blackened ribs of a rotting boat, 'that we are looking at a lesser-spotted grebe or a crested peewit?

'My supposition is that you're changing the subject and being facetious.'

Derek felt suddenly irritated. Why should he tell her what he thought? Honesty was an amusing game for a time but making a habit of it was a different matter. Fine for her to amuse herself by cross-examining him when she was so utterly uninvolved. Up to now Derek had not taken against Angela because she was Charles's sister. Suddenly he felt irritated by this relationship.

'You wanted to come so that you could ask me more about Charles and Diana. Mind you, I don't altogether blame you; it can't be everyday that one comes across a husband who takes his holidays with his wife and her lover; and after all, you must have thought, with the vision of your delightful boobs still burning in my brain, that I would tell all without any further asking, in the hope of having another visual treat.'

'You flatter yourself. I didn't want to spend an afternoon afloat with Mrs Cushing, Master Cushing and my brother. The alternatives were loafing about on my own or coming with you. I enjoyed this morning so I opted for a trip to Truro.'

They drove on in silence and were soon on a main road driving along the barren central spine of the county. They passed a granite quarry, the ruined engine houses of several tin mines and ugly little groups of bungalows. To the south-east the sun picked out the strange white pyramids of china-clay waste, making them shine like distant snow. Since he did not wish to talk about himself, he told her about his father; a necessary chore since she would soon be meeting him. He explained briefly about his work in Malaya and then about Gilbert Cushing's current personal interest in the years immediately preceding the fall of Singapore. Since the subject would have been meaningless without it, Derek mentioned his mother's death and his own lucky escape.

'Do you remember much?' Angela asked in a hushed and gentle voice.

Derek thought she was looking at him with greater interest now that she knew he had suffered as a child. For a moment he was tempted to play along with her and paint lurid pictures of a sky black with Japanese bombers and three weeks at sea on a small life-raft waiting for rescue, but instead he said brightly, 'I was a boy hero; brought down five Jap planes with my catapult.' He smiled. 'No, I left before the last week when it all started happening. There was bombing, no worse than in London, except in Singapore people used to rush out to look at the planes. Lots of black smoke; a direct hit on the oil tanks at the harbour. The shops were open, hotels functioning normally, water in the taps. I missed the looting and the unburied corpses. The ship I was in wasn't dive-bombed. The last time I saw my mother was waiting in a mile-long queue outside the shipping manager's bungalow. She was trying to get a passage for her parents. I don't remember crying at all.' A long silence and Angela looking at him with solemn sympathy.

'Did your father remarry?' she asked at last.

'He did. She died a year ago of cancer of the colon.' Derek's tone had been detached, light and ironic. He had wanted to avoid melodrama and false emotion by being matter-of-fact, and yet the result disgusted him. He wanted to answer again and do it properly and honestly, but the time had passed. They were entering Truro.

According to Derek's watch, they were no more than ten minutes late at the station, but there was no sign of his father either in the booking-hall or on the platform. Since Gilbert often failed to keep appointments, Derek did not think it worth waiting for the next train. His father might come the following day; he might even have caught an earlier train. The only rational thing to do was to drive to the *Three Pilchards* at St Mabyn, where Derek had booked a room for his father. He could then find out if Gilbert had cancelled, and, if he hadn't, leave a note for him. St Mabyn was only five miles from Charles's house, so the detour would cause little trouble.

They were leaving the town when Angela asked him to tell her about his Malayan childhood and so Derek obligingly extracted little vignettes for her: the Tamil *ayah*, who looked after him till he was six; Ngah, the gardener, who had hated pulling up cabbages because he thought them more beautiful than other more familiar plants; and Che' Sulong, the *syce*, who drove the Humber in spite of being cross-eyed. There were animals, like his pet armadillo, the house itself with its polished teak verandah and the bamboo blinds in the nursery that rattled like castanets when a 'sumatra' was blowing. Angela seemed disappointed. Derek supposed she had wanted him to talk about his mother.

A sunny June morning in 1942. Derek and his father eating breakfast in a Battersea flat. Gilbert saying, 'Don't look so glum. The Japs aren't as bad as they're painted. Most of it's just propaganda.'

Gilbert didn't give up hope of his wife's ship having reached Java till late in August. By then the news of atrocities in Hong Kong and Singapore had been confirmed. Derek had been sent away to school in the country to be out of the bombing during term-time. One holiday his father had bought a packet of seeds of the coleus plant, Derek's mother's favourite on account of its beautifully coloured leaves. The seeds had been placed by the sunniest window in the house but had failed to germinate. No news came and letters which Gilbert had sent to Java were returned unopened. Derek imagined her being tortured; to hear she was dead would have been a relief.

Early in 1943 Gilbert had met Margaret, or that was when Derek had first seen her. One day he saw them kissing. What would happen if they fell in love? Would Derek be sent away? Fear made him conciliatory. He tried too hard to be friendly to Margaret. She found his efforts embarrassing, especially when he had tried to make her laugh. He believed she resented him being around; his relationship with her was one long apology for existing.

Three days after his tenth birthday Derek heard that his mother was dead. No tears at all; in four years she had died too many times already. Just a chill, numbed feeling, more anger than grief.

'You'll marry Margaret, I suppose,' he said to his father, more as a statement of fact than as a question. Gilbert had shaken his head and mumbled about having no plans.

'But you will, you will,' Derek had shouted. Later he apologized and tried to pretend he wanted Margaret as a step-mother. When he did finally break down and cry, it was more for himself than for his mother. She was dead, but he had to face the future. In retrospect he was sorry for his father, who had felt obliged to postpone his second marriage for almost two years.

They had been silent for half an hour when they reached the point where they had to turn off the main road and thread their way through the network of narrow lanes that led to the river. Derek felt that he ought to make conversation but couldn't think of what tone to adopt. Thinking about the past no longer pained him, but memories could still lead to depression. He could see Angela smiling at him.

'Do you know those large gorillas,' she said, 'that chatter like mad and leap about crazily for a while and then sit down for hours, without moving, looking constipated?'

'I look just like one. Many thanks. My hairy hands on the

wheel, my tiny black eyes darting back and forth and my jaws working a mouthful of orange peel.' When Angela laughed, he felt better at once. Absurd to be so easily restored by a bit of female laughter. He shook his head. 'I know what you mean but I'm more like a car with faulty plugs; sometimes I fire on all cylinders and sometimes I won't start at all.' He gave her a long mournful look. 'A man haunted at times by an inexpressible melancholy, he seemed like a prisoner trapped deep within himself in a dark region far beyond rescue.'

She was looking at him with such amused tenderness that he found it hard to believe he was the cause of it. But who else? Diana rarely laughed at or reacted to what he said.

'I was wrong about gorillas,' Angela said seriously. 'You're more like a sad teddy bear.'

Derek's elation vanished. A teddy bear. That fey toy. Could ever an animal be more impotent? More harmless and futilely good-natured? Taken to bed by children and trusted to do nothing naughty with the dolls or golliwogs. No hybrids in the nursery. A far cry from frozen pine forests. Perhaps the description was apt. Hair falling out in chunks, becoming worn and tired, far from new—definitely a used bear, ill-used.

'One glass eye and my stuffing coming out. I'd rather be a gorilla any day. Imagine being able to snarl and gnash one's teeth as they do. They look unhappy all right but I wouldn't mind being able to vent my rage like they do, hurling myself about against the walls and beating my chest.'

'I suppose it might be rather impressive.'

'Of course it would. Imagine Diana's face if I told her that I knew and then started bouncing myself off the walls and thrusting whole apples into my mouth.' Angela laughed. 'Of course I'd be put down humanely. It's one of the major evils of modern life, you see, no rituals for anger and grief. Nobody tears their hair any more or covers themselves with ashes. Once they respected that sort of thing. I haven't got a bible in the car but my memory's not too bad. "He stripped off his clothes and prophesied before Samuel and lay down naked all that day and all that night. Wherefore they say: Is Saul also among the prophets?" '

Derek pulled out to overtake a bread van and narrowly missed the travelling library coming in the opposite direction.

'Sorry about that.'

'Killed by several tons of Enid Blytons. A nice death for an archivist.'

Derek gave her a fleeting smile but did not laugh. The night before she had seen him as an aggressive pedant but now he had become the comic teddy-bear archivist whose wife mucked him around, whose father couldn't even arrive on the right train.

'You find archivists funny?' he asked.

'When they're killed by travelling libraries I might briefly enjoy the irony of it.'

'You needn't be apologetic about it. They are funny and slightly pathetic. There's very little use in guarding, sifting and cataloguing huge quantities of documents.'

Angela gave him a puzzled look. 'Historical facts aren't trivial.'

'Documents aren't facts,' he replied, recognizing and regretting his fastidious tone, but then feeling the need to justify it. 'Historians analyse a number of documents and deduce facts from them. Archivists just catalogue and describe. Documents without historians are so much lumber to stuff attics with.'

'What are historians without documents?' she asked innocently.

'Out of a job,' he conceded.

'Charles said you're doing some big research job.'

'What else did he say?'

'That you were considered brilliant when you . . .'

'When I was younger?' he cut in. 'Since I can't easily draw conclusions from the evidence of my own life, Charles is a liar.'

'Is that a fact?' she asked with a hint of a smile.

'You're making fun of me,' he replied.

They were passing the mudflats at the head of the river, but now they were almost entirely covered by the tide. The fire they had lit before lunch would be several feet under water.

'As though I need to make fun of you,' She laughed. 'I've never met anybody who makes so many jokes against himself. Give him a knife and he stabs himself in the back even when his hands are tied.' Her amusement had gone and he could sense her concern and sympathy. It made him feel angry, just as her fault-less analysis of his acquiescence and self-mockery had done a moment before. Did he make himself that obvious? As he changed down for a sharp corner, he felt her hand on his.

'I didn't mean to annoy you.'

'Are my moods so transparent?'

'No, just your efforts to conceal them.'

'Did Colin like your honesty?' he asked viciously.

'You shouldn't be unkind about him,' she replied with a frown.

'Why not? He's ten years younger than me, with no erring wife or thinning hair. I don't feel obliged to be nice.'

'No, Colin didn't care for honesty. He's rather a hypocrite.'

'Did that annoy you?'

'Hypocrisy's no worse than bad breath.'

'Bad breath isn't incurable. I had pyorrhoea, so I ought to know.'

She shook her head and smiled sadly. 'Another sharp, self-inflicted stab in the back. Why should I pay good money to be whipped when I whip myself so nicely?'

Derek tried to laugh but was surprised to feel tears coming. Tears on such a sunny afternoon? They had just passed a sign-post and he had not seen it properly. He reversed back towards it. The place indicated was called Tresithian. He started searching through his road map as though his life depended on it. 'The last village we went through was Faddon. Another couple of miles on this road and we'll be at St Mabyn. He probably won't be there, and if he ever was, he won't be still, and either way we'll have gone for nothing.'

Angela touched his cheek with the tips of her fingers and said very quietly, 'I don't care.'

Derek turned off the engine. Above them the wind sighed in the telephone wires. White wispy clouds moved across the deep blue sky, grasshoppers chirped in the hedgerows. A cow stared at them mournfully from a nearby gate. He reached for the door-handle but didn't open it. Unless I can get out ... Fear. The same tightness in his chest that he had felt with the panic but different now, mixed with the tearful yearning ache he sometimes knew when listening to music. On the brink, as they say. Have you ever been kissed? Like this? Or this? This? What is this disproportion, under my diaphragm this adrenal flutter? I want to put my arms around you—no, more—I want to *crush* you in my arms. To hell with sophisticated inhibitions and the doubtful pleasures of the mind. No strategy, no premeditation: a simple need. Your body, my body, now. He was breathing heavily, gulping air like water. Pink like prawns.

'Would you care,' he said and stopped. 'Care if . . .'

'Please do,' she whispered moving round in her seat. He breathed out with a long sigh, more like a moan. I am thirty-eight next month, moderate in my ways. Glasses. Must take them off. As he reached towards them she lifted them away for him and their faces met and more than faces for he had swung round and pressed her back against her seat; before he could think of how to perform the manoeuvre he had done it; one knee on the handbrake and the other awkwardly in mid-air. His sudden fierceness had surprised him. No cool and hesitant beginning this as he pulled open her shirt. How long? Twenty, thirty seconds before they parted and held each other's eyes as though incapable of looking away until they had kissed again.

'Not often,' he murmured, meaning never before, fearing never again the same. I have misused my life on occasions too numerous to mention, but never better.

'Perhaps another place?'

'Yes.'

The cow still observed them from the gate.

'There?' Derek pointed. She nodded and they climbed over as the cow backed away. A field of rough grass. Bees in the clover. A tractor far away. Thank God for high hedges. Improbable nude photography in rural places. The ground was hard and dry under its covering of grass. Derek laid his shirt down for her. To think he might have caught that train. Praise be to God for unreliable fathers. She took off her trousers without waiting for him to fumble with zips. He took off his own. Socks? Men look stupid just in socks. Feet look worse? He took off his socks, she her pants. Hips wider than Diana's, legs longer, hair fairer. The cow watched from a distance their proceedings. She lay down and stretched out her arms. The ground was hard under his knees and elbows but no bed could have compared. In a field! In the sun! Minutes after discussing the historian's use of facts.

'This is a fact,' he whispered as they began to move together and for answer she kissed his lips and did not move her mouth away.

Though troubled briefly by a bee searching out clover near his rump, Derek enjoyed Angela and himself without guilt, fear or foreboding. Happiness had not come often enough of late for him to risk questioning its rare appearances, however bizarre. Why complicate and explain when there can be such slippery solace in a field, such unexpected sights and sounds? Play-acting in the past; pretence, convention and reserve no more than thistledown on the breeze. Tenderness without sentimentality, lust without regret and country pleasures rediscovered in their proper setting: matter for gratitude and wonder but not for rational thought.

Afterwards they lay together awhile, but the grass tickled and the ground felt hard; lewd flies embarrassed them. They kissed briefly before dressing. Thank you for having me, thank you for being had. Faunacation with Flora. Brisk and to the point; now where were we? Two miles south east of St Mabyn in the county of Cornwall. As I was saying before my genitals interrupted me . . . Words in unsatisfactory combinations were no help to him. Unable to think of anything appropriate to say, he looked at his watch; unless time had stood still for several hours it had stopped. Angela laughed easily.

'Did you time us?'

Post-coital clichés formed in his brain: all right for you? You were marvellous. No regrets? Winding had no effect on his watch.

'I think I got water in it this morning. The prawning did for it.'

'What a bore for you. Salt water rusts terribly quickly.'

'It's not a good one.'

Derek sat down next to Angela and put an arm round her.

'You don't have to, you know,' she said.

'It meant a lot to me.'

'What did it mean a lot of?'

'A slice out of time, a moment of . . .'

She was laughing again. 'Just your watch. Other things too. A slice out of time, a magic moment. A good screw. Why dress it up? A smashing, spur-of-the-moment fuck.'

'We had a good time, we fancied each other enough and so when the opportunity arose we leapt over a gate and had a good screw, a smashing fuck.' Derek jumped up and slapped his thighs. 'Right, what's next? Let's be getting along.'

'I didn't want you to feel obliged in any way. I wasn't trying to devalue anything.'

Since there are no obligations I think I'll leave you here. You won't mind walking home. Now that I've had my bit of fun you're as much use to me as an old apple core. No point in being sentimental about simple bodily functions; people do it the whole time in many remarkable places and positions and think no more of it than slipping out a casual turd. Why, only this morning my wife, finding a convenient wood, did it just like that and will probably do it again when the opportunity offers.

'Because such things happen to me rarely,' he said, 'I like to savour the after-glow a little; I like to believe it unusual and special because it may not happen again these next few years. Because you are ten years younger, and I am not an Adonis in any conventional sense, I felt gratitude, surprise and elation. I have seen young lovers in parks going through the preliminaries and have thought: there but for my thinning hair, my wife and child and thirty-eight years would I be still, but now the repetition of such novel pleasures is hardly likely. I wanted to express some of this when I put my arm round your waist. I had not thought of obligations.'

Angela stared at him with the sullen look he remembered from the evening before. 'The last fling of a nostalgic lecher,' she said. 'Well, count me out of all that sweet sadness because I'm not going to be anybody's substitute for adolescent passion, a sort of take you straight back to by-gone vigour. It's now or nothing.'

'Now has a habit of quickly becoming then. It happens every second, every breath we take. You can't experience now till you think about it and by then it's already in the past.'

She got up abruptly. 'I meant I'd rather you thought about me and now, rather than about groping little Annie or Wendy in 1894,' she said angrily.

'It's possible to have more than one thought in one's head at a time. Because of other things I thought of you and because of you I thought of other things. You try and concentrate on a single idea for more than a minute or two.' He started walking back to the car, quite prepared if she did not follow him, to drive off without her. But when it came to it he waited. When she had got in he switched on the engine.

'Turn that bloody thing off.'

Derek did so and sat in silence, waiting. She leant over and kissed him on the cheek. The wind in the telephone wires again. While they had been fucking, a hedgehog had been run over a few yards down the road where it lay crushed and bleeding. Angela studied her knees.

'I've been a bitch, haven't I ?' Derek, correctly assuming the question to be rhetorical, said nothing. She glanced at him defiantly from under slightly lowered eyelids. 'I just couldn't bear you bleating out bogus endearments and telling me lies.' She paused dramatically. 'Do you want to know how many men I've had since I left John?'

Derek felt sick and angry; mostly angry. Perhaps she wanted him to. Perhaps, in spite of all her down-to-earthness, all her sex for now, she felt it was degrading and got her own back by humiliating her humiliators. Perhaps ... God knows what she wanted. Since you're so much in demand I'm extremely grateful that you managed to fit me in at such short notice. She would expect surprise and indignation from him. Derek said in a flat voice, 'Do I get a colour television or a week in Rome if I guess the number?'

'Is it so funny?'

'Remarks intended to hurt people rarely are. Go on, tell me. Enough to form a rugger team or staff a large department store?'

She put her head in her hands and sighed.

'I was trying to tell you why I had to stop you talking about slices out of time and magic moments. I felt guilty, so I tried to make you look insincere.'

'How very precise you are.'

'Somebody who knows what she wants and how to get it.' She shook her head sadly. 'I wish I was. I wasn't happy with John but I wasn't much better when I left him. Promiscuity's a sort of loneliness, didn't you know?'

Marmalade's a sort of jam. He hadn't imagined that a taunt about her numerous affairs would turn into a plea for sympathy. Surprise did not diminish his anger.

'That would make loneliness a sort of promiscuity which might surprise a few old ladies. I'm often lonely too; we all are.'

'I was only trying to explain,' she replied quietly.

'So you did it because you were lonely and apparently I did it because of a few gropes fifty years ago. It levels the score a bit. Wouldn't a few endearments have been better? Isn't the obvious generally right because it's obvious? Your honesty's a waste of time and energy: a hard way to achieve more misunderstanding and new fallacies.'

'Or phalluses.' She smiled apologetically. 'Not much of a joke.'

'Phalli,' he corrected her.

'How very precise you are,' she returned with a bright forced smile.

St Mabyn consisted of a single straggling street. A village with none of Tregeare's picturesque charm. Three small shops, a Methodist chapel with a corrugated iron roof, a garage with two antiquated pumps and the village hall: a green Nissen hut. The Three Pilchards was next to the garage, set back from the road and overlooking a dusty forecourt. No charming little country pub with a thatched roof and low, overhanging eaves, but a very ordinary red-brick building embellished with bright yellow doors and window frames. In the forecourt was a tall white pole and, hanging from it, a painted sign with three silver fishes suspended improbably in mid air above a flat, pale blue sea.

Derek didn't for a moment suppose that his father would be inside the pub but since they had come he decided to look. He would leave a note for him in case he came later in the week. He got out of the car without bothering to ask Angela if she wanted to come too. The Three Pilchards was hardly a place of architectural or historical interest. He was halfway across the forecourt when he saw a bicycle leaning against a tub of tobacco plants to the right of the door. The bicycle looked familiar. A second glance left Derek fairly certain that he had ridden the very same machine into Tregeare earlier in the day. Had it been stolen? Perhaps Charles's gardener had borrowed it. He stopped. His father had arrived at the pub and had phoned Charles's house. Giles had ridden over to meet him. The thought of a pleasant evening drink with Giles, Angela and his father was not immediately attractive. He was about to hurry back to the when he caught sight of his father's face at a ground-floor window. He had heard the car draw up.

Derek went into a cream-painted hall and opened a door to his right with a small notice on it saying *Lounge*. The two of them were sitting over by the window. Gilbert Cushing got up.

'Better late than never. You weren't at the station.'

'You weren't on the train.'

'Which train? I didn't walk.'

Derek imagined the salt water in his watch slowly destroying it.

'I may have been late,' he conceded.

'So I came by bus; just the thing with these high hedges. I could see over them and there are some excellent views.'

Derek imagined a whole busload of people peering over a hedge and seeing himself and Angela setting about each other. But another thought came to him as well: Giles bicycling along the road that led from Tregeare to St Mabyn via Faddon. The boy sees a familiar car parked by the side of the road. He assumes his father to be near at hand and goes in search of him. He climbs over a gate and sees ... Such splendour in the grass. Derek sat down heavily. His legs felt very weak.

'Which way did you come?' he asked Giles.

'There's only one way; or there's only one direct way.'

'Through Faddon?'

The boy nodded. Derek looked at him carefully but could learn nothing from his face. He wanted to ask him how long he had been at the pub but thought better of it. If he'd seen anything he wouldn't be able to conceal it. A sensitive boy of barely thirteen unmoved by the sight of his father's naked body spread-eagled on the equally naked body of his host's sister? Was that likely? In any case coincidences like that simply didn't happen. Across the table Giles was calmly sipping a coke; no mental anguish there. The extent of Derek's relief made him feel like laughing. He suddenly realized that his father had been telling him something.

'Well, aren't you surprised?' Gilbert asked impatiently.

'I'm sorry, I wasn't listening.'

Gilbert looked at him critically and pursed his lips. 'I said that I left all my notes on the train.'

Derek shut his eyes. 'Do you want me to drive you to Penzance to see if they've been handed in?'

His father pushed away his half-pint of beer and leant forward across the table. He seemed extremely excited.

'No, that's what I was telling you. I don't want them back. I'm going to tell you instead.'

'What? Tell me what?'

'Not now. It'll take a bit of time.'

'I don't doubt it.'

Derek heard the door open and turned to see Angela come in. Gilbert was saying, 'I was distressed at first but then I realized that it was intended.'

'What was intended?' asked Derek absently, as he saw Angela joining them.

'That I should tell you in person.'

Derek got up. 'This is my father. This is Angela, Charles's sister.'

Angela came forward smiling. 'Derek's told me so much about you.'

Gilbert Cushing cleared his throat. 'I can't imagine why,' he replied with sudden annoyance.

Angela sat down beside Giles and said, 'Because I asked him. How's your history of the Malayan campaign going?'

'It's gone,' cut in Derek. 'He left it on the train.'

Angela tried to look sympathetic but then she started laughing helplessly.

'If I'd been able to make young women laugh so easily when I was younger, I should have led an interesting life,' put in Gilbert drily.

Angela dabbed at her eyes. 'You're very kind not to be cross. I apologize.'

'Since I have no idea what amused you I can hardly feel offended. Perhaps I could buy you a drink?'

Derek laughed with unashamed relief; his father was not pleasant company when angered.

'The mellowness of age,' he said with a chuckle.

'Mellowness nothing,' retorted Gilbert. 'A general softening of the critical faculties; that's why old men are so affable. Nothing to do with mellowness. What's so mellow about spindly legs, deafness and incontinence?'

'I didn't know you were incontinent,' said Giles.

'I'm not. Good God, Derek, you want to teach your son some manners.' He winked at Giles and returned to Angela. 'I offered you a drink before I was so rudely interrupted.'

Angela asked for a whisky and Derek allowed his father to buy him a pint of beer. The loss of his notes had certainly had a startling effect on the old man. Confused already, Derek became more so when he tried to imagine what his father wanted to tell him. In spite of, or possibly because of, Angela's unexpected laughter, he seemed determined to be jovial. Derek wondered whether, when he was bald, beads of perspiration would stand out on his head with the same beautiful pearl-like definition as they did on his father's shiny skull. Gilbert bowed slightly to Angela as he handed her her drink. He was clearly going to treat her to a dose of old-world gallantry. Derek returned to scrutinizing his son's face.

Gilbert sipped his drink delicately. 'I came up with an excellent man in my compartment,' he said. 'Good in every sense of the word. Runs boys' clubs in the East End, that sort of thing, builds adventure playgrounds with his own hands.' He shook his head and compressed his lips. 'He was vile. Rude, short-tempered, and bitter. Poor chap had an in-growing toenail. All those years of goodness up the spout because of that. Incredible.'

'He probably hadn't cut it right,' said Giles. 'toenails should be cut straight and not shaped like fingernails.'

Gilbert made a fine show of perturbation and slapped his leg energetically.

'Damn it. I didn't tell him that. There he'll be limping about in Penzance not knowing how to cut his nails.'

'He'll probably have to have the nail off in any case. That's what happened to a friend of mine when his toe went septic,' replied an unsmiling Giles.

Hadn't he normally realized when his grandfather was joking? Derek said, 'He was being funny, Giles.'

'Lattimer didn't laugh when they took his nail off.'

Angela was trying to stop herself laughing when she caught Gilbert's eye and burst out afresh. Giles was looking at her with a mixture of incomprehension and hostility. Because she'd laughed at him or because ... Impossible, Derek reassured himself as he took a gulp of beer. He thought of Giles spending hours at home learning jokes to amuse his friends. The memory made him suddenly feel close to tears. Was it his fault for being too serious? Had he killed the boy's sense of humour? Or had Diana done it by laughing at his stones and fossils? He imagined his son as the geologist on an earnest mining engineering project, on some uninhabited Pacific island, telling the drilling consultant the one about the old lady's embarrassing moment with the plumber. Angela was saying, 'Three generations of Cushings and it's hard to tell which is the funnier.'

Derek winced. An interesting competition to be sure. Should the winner be the elderly obsessive with false teeth and two dead wives, or his son, a middle-aged cuckold with piles and an identity crisis? Or should neither of them win the comic accolade? There was a third competitor: the intense and insecure adolescent with adulterous parents and no sense of humour. A real fun family.

'Laughter's usually at somebody's expense,' Gilbert said, 'but I don't really care if it's at mine.'

'How uncommonly wise and mature,' muttered Derek. But if I poured my beer over your head or pulled the chair from under you, would you still be so detached? At ten years old he had locked his father out of his flat in his pyjamas on a January morning. Gilbert had gone out for the milk and Derek had slammed the door on him. He had been angry enough to wrench off the knocker and seriously bruise his shoulder in an attempt to break down the door.

When they had finished their drinks Derek raised the matter of where his father should stay. After some persuasion, which Angela supported enthusiastically, he agreed to come and stay with the rest of them at Charles's house. Having squared things with the publican, they left. Outside Derek suggested that Giles should put his bicycle on the roof-rack and come with them.

'I'd rather ride back.'

'Wouldn't it be easier if you came with us?'

Giles didn't answer but swung his leg over the crossbar and started to pedal away. In spite of the beer Derek's mouth felt dry. He turned to his father: 'Was he upset when he arrived?'

Gilbert thought a moment and shrugged his shoulders. 'He's not very communicative; not with me at any rate. They caught some fish he said, but not much else.'

'Had he expected a whale?' asked Angela as they got into the car. She gave Derek a conspiratorial smile as she flopped down into the back seat. No worries for her. She'd got rid of her irritation, recovered her detachment and ironic sense of humour, and was ready to enjoy anything that Cushing and son had to say. Derek could see her face in the mirror as he drove off. She was blowing him an insolent kiss and half-closing her eyes in a fine imitation of passion. Such fun, such naughtiness when at any moment the one-time Protector of Chinese, Straits Settlement, might turn round and see. Perhaps she would undo her shirt

101

again. Derek narrowly avoided driving into the ditch. Ahead of him Giles was careering downhill, his hair streaming and his shirt flapping. Derek tooted as he passed but the boy ignored him. Derek felt alarmed again. True, Giles had been calm enough, but hadn't he been almost too calm? He'd been very silent in the pub and unusually humourless even for him. Then that emphatic refusal to come in the car and not even a nod or a wave as they passed. Derek changed down too fast as they approached a corner and grated the gears badly.

'The only thing that bothers me,' Gilbert was saying, 'is that Diana may not be too pleased to see me.'

There had been a clock over the bar. It had showed six or a few minutes after when they'd arrived at the pub. Derek remembered noting this when his father had accused him of not meeting the train. Mounting panic was stopping him thinking clearly.

'Well?' said his father.

'I'm sorry,' muttered Derek.

'I said Diana wouldn't be too pleased.'

'She'll be delighted.'

So if it had been six then, how long before had Giles set out? St Mabyn was roughly five miles from Tregeare. Half-an-hour on a bike? About that; it was quite hilly. Giles had arrived just before them. So? He was breathing faster.

'I don't think that's very likely,' Gilbert murmured. He turned to Angela. 'There are some people, and I'm afraid my daughter-in-law is one of them, who find the elderly slightly repellent because they're old. I have false teeth; I don't know whether you noticed, but I have. I'm not ashamed to admit that I make a noise while eating. Diana doesn't like this noise; in fact it irritates her a great deal.'

Derek longed to shout at him to shut up. He felt so confused that he couldn't work out whether precise times mattered. And such a beautiful evening. The golden warmth of the evening sun on trees and fields; the bright red-and-purple splashes of fuchsias in the hedgerows; insects floating in the air, small specks of gold caught by the sun.

They were passing through Tregeare when Derek realized

without a shadow of doubt that the precise time Giles had left was irrelevant. He had arrived a few minutes before them and the field had only been a couple of miles out of St Mabyn. He had to have passed the car, absolutely had to have done. For a moment Derek thought that he was going to be sick but the spasm passed and was succeeded by a feeling of complete helplessness. And now? he asked himself. And now?

Derek could not remember any occasion during the past ten years when he had deliberately set about making himself drunk; but the moment he got back to the house he poured himself half a tumblerful of whisky. By the time Charles offered everybody drinks, Derek had already tipped back the best part of a quarter of a bottle; and, although he was still aware of his problems, they seemed rather less pressing. As dinner progressed and brandy followed wine he attained what he had sought: an irresponsible sense of detachment. There was no doubt at all that Diana was responding unfavourably to her father-in-law but there was equally no doubt that Derek didn't care—didn't even mind too much when Giles went to his room immediately after dinner was over. The others were discussing aesthetic taste. Gilbert and Diana were as usual at odds. Charles was in his element at last.

'Of course,' he was saying, 'because art reflects social conflict and dissonance these have become fairly central elements in our aesthetic experience. Art isn't escapism, and modern realities have led to a rejection of precious tonal harmonies and delicate enamel surfaces.'

'Art's just a social and economic reflex?' asked Gilbert with pretended horror.

'Far from it,' returned Charles with a chuckle. 'The *quality* of art's not something to be confused with the means of expression. On a different tack one could say that because many of the great Renaissance artists worked to commission they were just social tools. Utter rubbish. Or is Mozart's music negligible because it was for a confined society?'

A short silence. 'Sod quality and taste,' Derek announced. 'If somebody gets pleasure from what the cognoscenti call ugly, what use taste? In the eye of the beholder, as the expression goes. How can you say I don't feel the same emotion looking at a pavement artist's work that you feel peering at a masterpiece?'

'You'd have to be rather more precise,' replied Charles.

'Precision's grossly overrated,' cut in Gilbert, who had also drunk a fair amount.

'To people who make generalizations like that, perhaps,' said Diana.

Gilbert smiled affably.

'Take my suit,' he said.

'Not on your life,' chipped in Diana.

Derek clapped appreciatively. Gilbert shrugged his shoulders.

'My suit,' he went on, 'would be essentially the same suit if it was ironed, pressed, altered here and there. You get me? Still inherently the same suit. Detail can become a fetish. Diana may be distressed by a hem a quarter of an inch too high or too low, she may be offended by wallpaper that doesn't quite match or a slight crease below the collar of a coat; but does it matter? Who can say whether a suit should be cut in a certain way when fashions change as they do? My suit looks like a shower curtain, a relic of less scrawny days, but it may be very fashionable in a year or two.' He smiled complacently at Diana.

Derek couldn't help noticing the way his father's adam's apple bobbed up and down when he talked. He wondered whether Diana had seen. He felt inclined to point it out to her but didn't because she was talking again.

'I don't mind people who are casually unkempt, but the borderline between that and looking down-at-heel and seedy is a narrow one.'

'And the borderline between blatant rudeness and friendly argument?' asked Gilbert. Derek stopped listening to them; instead he found himself scrutinizing Angela. She was sitting lengthwise on the sofa with her feet up. Sometimes she smiled and little brackets formed at the corners of her mouth, but throughout the evening she had taken care not to get involved in any acrimony. Derek realized that he was smiling at her. He looked away at once. The way she was sitting stretched her trousers tightly over her thighs. With sudden pleasure Derek recalled the precise sensation of her stomach against his, recalled how he had been convinced for a moment that they were breathing together, that while they held each other's gaze neither could look away. In retrospect, even in his drunkenness he was almost as surprised as he had been when it had all happened.

After the unpleasantness between Gilbert and Diana, the evening broke up quickly. When everybody went up to bed Derek remained in the empty room. He poured himself a final brandy and walked uncertainly back to his chair. The irony of it, the ludicrous irony. He took a sip of brandy and rolled it round his mouth, enjoying the warm sensation in his throat after he had swallowed. To think that for thirteen years he had lived virtuously, drearily, mechanically; had pursued his studies conscientiously, been a dutiful father if not a good one; had, it was true, hankered from time to time but had never attempted to convert his wishes into reality. Then, one summer afternoon because of a few drops of salt water in a watch, he had arrived late at a railway station and because of that he had fornicated in a field and because his father had not been met at the station, Giles had cycled to the pub and because of that . . . ? Derek shook his head and made a plopping noise with his tongue. There had been thousands, no hundreds of thousands of hours of decent clean living and only twenty minutes of indiscretion but it would have to be those twenty minutes that proved significant. Significant! A smashing fuck. Derek managed a wry smile; his head had started to throb unpleasantly but he felt no less detached. The nagging ache behind his eyes grew slightly worse. He started to feel indignant. Why me? Why should fate have singled me out? If Giles had caught Charles and Diana that would have been justice of a sort.

Derek shut his eyes and tried to visualize the sex talks Giles had attended at school. What had that gruesome school doctor told them? The usual stuff designed to keep them off it: the meaning of sex and love, the spiritual and the physical both playing their parts in equal doses. Lust never brings any kind of satisfaction, desire without love brutalises rather than transfigures. Sex was degraded without mutual respect. Derek thought of Angela and sighed. The merging of sex and love? Nothing like that, but at the time better. Unexpected, unpremeditated and even now almost unbelievable. A fantasy fuck made real. A miracle of a sort, pagan perhaps but still miraculous. Was that something to be ashamed of? Should he feel obliged to beg Giles to forgive him? Your mother's flagrant carryings on gave me no right to pursue lecherous liasons on my own account; far from it; two wrongs never made a right. Forgive me for I knew not what I did and wish I hadn't; I have erred and strayed and am no more worthy to be called your father. Why bloody well should I?

Would any self-respecting teenager think twice about the rights and wrongs of a casual lay if it had been fun at the time? Like hell he would, and quite right and proper. With people maiming, killing and exploiting each other all over the world what harm was a bit of fornication? If my only contribution to universal sin is a bit on the side with Angela, I ought to get a first-class ticket to paradise. It'd be worse to drive a car with faulty brakes or to refuse help when it was asked, or to say things intended to wound, than to join genitals with a willing accomplice.

When the missionaries first went to Africa to tell the natives about monogamy they thought it was the best joke they'd ever heard. To be horrified by adultery's about as logical as an African tribesman's fear of bumping into a menstruating woman. Derek gulped down the last mouthful of brandy and rose with dignity. Although they build a fire for me, I shall not recant, I shall not. He stared defiance at the empty chairs as though facing a hostile mob and then turned disdainfully towards the door. He managed to climb the stairs without falling.

Chapter 8

When Derek woke up, Diana's bed was empty; the curtains were half-drawn and invading blades of sunlight stabbed his eyes. He buried his face in the pillow and groaned. Waves of shame and self-disgust flowed through him making him squirm like a pinioned insect. His mouth felt like a decaying fungus and his skull seemed to have shrunk during the night, but his physical discomfort was as nothing compared with the leaden emptiness that filled and enveloped him when he remembered the day before. It wasn't the alcohol in his blood that made his limbs feel like plasticine but the thought that he had deliberately made himself drunk rather than face his son. What could Giles have thought seeing his father soaking himself in drink after the events of earlier in the day? Must talk to him, must explain. Derek rolled over and fumbled about on the floor for his glasses. But say what? He cradled his head in his hands and rocked himself back and forth. Say what? Too soon to think. Wash, dress, have breakfast and then think.

When Derek arrived in the dining-room breakfast was all but over. To his relief Angela and Giles weren't there. With studied composure he helped himself to a congealed egg from a dish on the sideboard and sat down. The sight of the egg made him feel sick. Nor did his father's recollection of visits to out-stations in Perak make him feel any better. Gilbert was describing how his cook would always bring along several live chickens for each meal.

'Fresher, you see. Although I never quite got used to the dying convulsions of my lunch when the time came for neck-wringing.' He paused and gave Diana a nostalgic smile. 'But it would have been stupid to get upset about chickens' necks. I had to witness a good many hangings at the time.'

'What a perfectly repulsive analogy,' snapped Diana.

The idea came to Derek shortly after Giles entered the room and its impact was so sudden and forceful that it made him slop coffee into his saucer. Confess. His hand trembled as he put down his cup. Tell him everything. Make no excuses; just give an unvarnished account without false sentiment or exaggerated remorse. After a brief spasm of fear, Derek was overwhelmed by a deliciously warm altruistic feeling. Of course saying anything about Diana's misbehaviour to mitigate his own was out of the question. The object of the confession was to put the boy's mind at rest, not to worry him still further. A moment later the purity of Derek's altruism received a slight check when he reflected that since Giles already knew what had happened with Angela, he would be most unlikely to think worse of his father for confessing to him.

Charles was telling them all about the Penfillian Ox Roast, which was happening later that day at a village several miles away. Derek listened with scant attention as his host described the Penfillian Silver Band, the stalls, rodeo and the ox roast itself. Diana thought it would be a marvellous idea to go. A visit was agreed upon.

After breakfast Derek followed Giles upstairs to his room.

'I'm not going to any rotten ox roast.'

'Why not?' asked Derek.

'I don't like Charles.'

'You needn't be afraid to tell me the real reason,' said Derek gently.

'That is the real reason.'

Derek rested a hand on his son's shoulder.

'I know what you know, Giles. So you needn't invent things to make me feel better. You don't want to go to the ox roast because you think I'll be going too.'

Derek couldn't make out whether his son's expression was one of alarm or puzzlement. He decided it was alarm. Giles said vehemently (too vehemently, thought Derek), 'He shouted at me when we went fishing. I steered through some seaweed and choked up the propeller. He called me a bloody little idiot and then tried to make out he hadn't been cross really. He was as smarmy as hell.'

Derek cleared his throat. 'You mustn't be afraid to talk to me about what you saw. Nothing very terrible happened; you'll realize that when you're a bit older. You saw us and that's that. I'm not going to shrug it off or make excuses.'

Derek saw his son's eyes grow larger behind his glasses.

'I don't understand,' he replied with a slight catch in his voice.

It occurred to Derek that Giles was trying to make things easier by pretending that he had seen nothing. He wanted to take his son in his arms like a little boy. Instead he said very gently, 'There's no need to hold back.'

'I'm not. I don't understand. That's all.'

The apparent sincerity of his son's denial shook Derek for a moment.

'You mean you don't *want* to understand.'

'No, I didn't mean that.' Giles sounded confused and exasperated.

Derek's mouth felt dry. He could still taste the greasiness of the egg.

'Please be straight with me,' he implored.

'I am,' moaned Giles.

Derek could feel his heart banging unpleasantly. Was there really a possibility that Giles was telling the truth and had seen nothing? The idea made his legs feel weak. He sank down on to the bed. Be calm, he told himself.

'I want you to think carefully about your trip to St Mabyn yesterday. You went to Faddon?' Giles nodded. 'Then you cycled out on the St Mabyn road?'

'No.'

'No?' Derek repeated stupidly as his head reeled.

'There's a footpath to St Mabyn from Faddon.'

'You had your bicycle,' Derek protested feebly.

'The footpath cuts off most of the hill.'

'How did you know that? You'd never been there before.'

'I asked somebody. There was a sign anyway.' Giles seemed shaken and alarmed by his father's questions.

'And that's the truth?' asked Derek unable to keep the desperation out of his voice.

'Yes, yes, yes,' shouted Giles.

Derek put his head in his hands. Several drops of water in a watch and a footpath he had never known about. What chance did anybody have of behaving rationally when such trivial things could create such havoc? If the boy really *hadn't* seen, and it now looked very much as though he hadn't, he could hardly have failed to understand what he had been told a few minutes earlier. Derek could feel tears pricking behind his lids.

'You know what I was trying to tell you, don't you?'

Giles looked at him very straight. 'I haven't the foggiest idea.' He moved across to the door but Derek barred his way. 'I want to go out.'

'We've got to talk about it.'

Giles turned on him furiously. 'Talking never makes any difference.'

'So you do know what I meant,' murmured Derek hopelessly.

'Of course I bloody well know.' The boy was trembling with anger. 'You've got what you wanted, now let me go.' Tears had started to flow down his cheeks. Derek tried to hold him but was pushed roughly away.

'You must be very upset,' said Derek quietly.

'About what?' shouted Giles.

'What I told you. I can understand how shocked you must be.'

'Can you? Well I'm not. I'm upset because . . .' he looked away for a moment and then turned on Derek—'Because you're so pathetic.' Derek bowed his head and said nothing. Giles said, 'You told me because *you* wanted to, you forced me to listen when you knew I didn't want to. Do what you want. I don't care.'

'Don't care?' Derek murmured incredulously.

'Sex is a big deal, isn't it? Jabber, jabber about it the whole time at school. How Bowles touched up Mary Stebbings and jerks off into her bra and how Keating went the whole way with Sally Harvey.' He was blushing furiously and looking at the floor.

'You find it disgusting?' asked Derek, when he had recovered from his son's sudden outburst.

'I don't care, that's all. Everybody does it. We're all here because somebody did it. Millions of us, because millions of people did it. What's so rotten special about it?'

'Sex isn't insignificant,' said Derek, still shaken and confused.

'I wouldn't know,' muttered Giles, kicking at his empty suitcase on the floor. 'Gawton, he's in my form, his mother's always doing it with a new bloke. He doesn't come to school weeping. Says he doesn't give a shit.'

'And that's how you feel?'

Giles nodded and started polishing his glasses.

'And would you still not give a shit if your mother and I split up?'

'You wouldn't dare; even if you wanted to.'

'What makes you so sure?' asked Derek, unable to hide his anger.

'You always do what she tells you. You gave up going to Scotland, you wear silly clothes because she buys them, you let her bully you. You don't like Charles but you came here.' Giles looked at his father scornfully as though daring Derek to contradict him.

'Marriage shouldn't be a battle for dominance, Giles. Husbands don't have to beat their wives to prove themselves men.'

A long silence. Giles was biting his lip. Suddenly he blurted out, 'You've never done anything I can be proud of. Never.'

When the boy ran to the door, Derek called after him but Giles didn't look round. Derek felt sure that he was crying and for a moment he wanted to run after his son, but the feeling passed. Giles would merely see that as a further sign of weakness. Self-willed, authoritative fathers do not pursue and plead with their children. A numb empty feeling soon replaced Derek's sense of shock and confusion. He walked over to the window.

Outside, wispy clouds in a blue sky, a light breeze gently ruffling the shimmering sea; butterflies fluttering, grasshoppers chirping: sweet tranquillity. Little spurts of anger made Derek clench his fists and dig his nails into the palms of his hands. Anger with himself rather than with Giles or Diana. Derek imagined himself stepping out onto a perfectly kept tennis court with Charles. Within minutes Charles was sweating and blowing as winner after winner flashed past him. Sitting at the side of the court, Giles was shouting, 'Well played, Daddy.' Giles at school: 'You should see my dad playing tennis. He'd win Wimbledon if he entered, but he's too busy. Did you see the reviews of his latest book? It's been in the best-seller lists for six months.' Derek rested his forehead against the wall and shut his eyes.

To be Samson now, to put his shoulder to the foundations of the house and shake it like a toy, to speak wrath like a storm, to dispose a mighty army in the field for a just cause. To be Moses turning the sea to blood.

A lovely afternoon ahead, full of cakes and ale and festive village quaintness. Little jokes about the Penfillian Silver Band, witty remarks about the villagers and the side-shows. Confront Diana and Charles with what he knew. Tell them at the ox roast while the band played on. Throw in the story of his coupling with Angela for good measure. A moment of decision: Caesar at the Rubicon, Napoleon at Waterloo, Derek Cushing at the Penfillian Ox Roast; that old self-mockery, that trusty and well-tried preventative of any action likely to lead to extravagant or immoderate behaviour. To hell with it now; to hell with proportion. What price his existence if he went on feeling obliged to laugh at his anger and his sorrow?

Did a fall hurt less because caused by a banana skin? Because he had confessed unnecessarily to his son, because it had been pathetic and absurd, did that make it any more acceptable? To go on smiling stoically in the face of every new insult would be to acknowledge his life as no more than a farce with moments of pathos. How convenient to plead ironic detachment and acquiescence: a fine excuse for those too lazy and fastidious to risk

112

active participation in the lives chance had allotted to them. Tell them, muttered Derek. Tell them.

They had made his life a farce but they would be repaid more generously—a fine corrective comedy, aimed at their heads rather than their armpits or their groins. Farce would be too blunt an instrument; their forfeit had to be more than a kick on the rump or a lost pair of trousers. If there were to be laughter, it should hurt and humiliate; without pain there would be no purging. Familiar themes in this comedy: lust, betrayal, jealousy, deceit. At first the audience feels secure; Charles smiles, Diana laughs, but not too loudly; impersonal laughter, without malice. Such emotions exist, *we* know that, *we* worldly, civilized, urbane people know it all; *we* are never shocked or censorious; occasionally we feel diffidently compassionate. But soon smiles cease and silence comes to the auditorium. Something is wrong with the lights and with the seats; something is very badly wrong. Suddenly they know that all the time they have been sitting on the stage. *Their* faults, *their* weaknesses have been exposed and now they see them clearly, now at last they see themselves.

Chapter 9

A silver-grey Lancia speeding along the narrow Cornish lanes, a glittering metal dart parting the warm hazy air; in front Charles and Gilbert, and behind, Derek, the jam at the centre of a tight-packed female sandwich made up of Angela and Diana. Get-away people, one and all; Gilbert had got away from his conscience, Charles from his wife, Angela from her husband, Diana was getting away from hers, and the archivist . . . what of him? Derek frowned. Was his not a subtler, rarer escape? It is not given to many to contemplate calmly the surrender of security, decorum, forbearance and acquiescence all on a single summer day. Nor is it usual for scholarly men to travel in the back of fast and expensive cars wedged between a wife and a mistress. Stranger still in such company to include for good measure a wife's lover and a parent. At times Derek felt solemn about the task ahead, at others he wanted to laugh to relieve his nerves; apprehension struggled with tense excitement. Music filled the car: a cassette of Mozart's quintet for clarinet and strings.

Diana turned to Derek and said for Charles's benefit, 'I really can't think why Giles wouldn't come with us. I'd have thought he'd have been delighted to, but when I suggested it, he virtually told me to go to hell. It's most unlike him, don't you think?' Derek said nothing. He knew that she expected him to make some light remarks about Giles's serious nature and his frequent self-absorption. Then they could all laugh and not feel guilty about having left the boy behind. When a sharp nudge failed to make Derek say what was expected, Diana added brightly, 'Of course thirteen's such a difficult age.'

114

A brief silence, then Charles saying in a concerned voice, 'Any idea why he didn't want to come?'

'None at all,' answered Diana. 'He ought to realize how rude and inconsiderate it is to go off on his own all the time when he's staying with people.'

Derek concealed his anger and said with a smile, 'I'm quite sure Charles doesn't expect Giles to do things simply to please his host. By that token we'd all have to watch what we said and did. Nobody likes having grateful and grovelling guests to stay.'

'Of course not,' laughed Charles as the clarinet quintet came gracefully to an end. A pleasantly cooling breeze blew in through the open windows of the car. They slowed down to go through a shallow ford.

'If I hated Mozart,' went on Derek affably, addressing the back of Charles's neck, 'you wouldn't expect me to say I liked it. When I'm lucky enough to be asked to your London flat, I don't admire your new de Kooning or your Magrittes because I feel I've got to. I never make cooing noises about your Frink bronzes because I'm indebted to you for the food and drink I'm about to consume.' Derek caught a glimpse of Charles's slightly disconcerted face in the mirror; at the same time he felt Diana give him a warning pinch. He gave her a pinch in return and continued, 'I wouldn't insult anybody by admiring their taste, their money and their possessions out of gratitude.' Derek noticed that Angela was trying hard not to laugh.

'It's just coincidental that your taste's exactly the same as my brother's.'

'Absolutely,' agreed Derek. 'Charles likes *interesting* people, and so do I. He hates the dull and second-rate. I do too. We both find that a rich merchant banker, a scholar manqué, a theatrical impresario, a painter and a well-known columnist provide just the right balance for a successful dinner party.'

'You'd be lucky if anybody at all came to dinner with you in your present form,' cut in Diana hastily.

'Just as well Charles finds academic failures like me amusing,' replied Derek with a grin. 'Nobody ought to confine their acquaintance to the successful; a failure or two gives a far better blend. Less vulgar somehow.'

'I like people for themselves,' said Charles abruptly; making it quite clear that he had had enough of the present topic of conversation. Diana gave Derek a furious look. They drove on in silence. A little later Angela tried to slip a hand into Derek's pocket and giggled when he repulsed her.

On the far side of the crowded village square, against the church-yard wall, the ox was being roasted on a spit over a large smoking fire. From a hundred yards away they could smell a powerful aroma of burning fat. In the centre, clustered round the war memorial, sat the band, dressed in wine-coloured uniforms. The youngest musician was about ten, the eldest in his late seventies. They were playing a medley of hits from *South Pacific*. *Some Enchanted Evening* had just finished, and they were now attacking *I'm in Love with a Wonderful Guy*. Bunting and coloured streamers fluttered overhead, and in front of the shops stalls had been set up: lucky dips, hit a coconut, fortune telling, buy some local jam, try your strength. Signs pointed the way to a large tent where several hundred hens and rabbits were shortly to be judged. Gilbert wandered off on his own to get his fortune told.

The rest of them were walking past the coconut shy when Charles said in a joking voice, 'A fiver if you hit one.'

'Fine,' said Derek, handing Diana his striped jacket.

'Don't be a fool, Derek. He didn't mean it. It'll cost you a fiver if you miss.'

Derek said nothing but started rolling up his sleeves carefully. He paid the boy and was handed six wooden balls. Angela watched him with amusement as he examined the balls know-ledgeably as though he spent much of his life in fairgrounds. The first three balls went hopelessly wide of any of the twelve coco-nuts. Each time there was a dull thud as the ball hit the canvas screen at the back of the stand.

'Scrub the bet if you like,' laughed Charles.

'I'd like to double it,' Derek replied calmly.

'For God's sake,' cut in Diana. 'You can make a fool of yourself any day of the week without making a special effort.'

Derek threw carefully but his fourth ball missed. With the next throw he took no trouble at all, just tossing it at random. The ball went nowhere near any of the coconuts but hit the base of one of the wooden stands. The movement was just enough to topple his prize onto the matting.

'Bravo,' shouted Charles. 'Do I get a chance to win it back?'

'Sure,' replied Derek.

Diana said, 'You're not going to take his money, are you?'

'It'd be rather insulting if I didn't,' came back Derek.

Derek watched the intense concentration that Charles gave to each throw. His aim was far more accurate than Derek's, but all six balls missed; two of them very narrowly. Charles pulled out his wallet and handed two five-pound notes to Derek, who stuffed them into his trouser pocket. Then he took his coconut from the boy and handed it to Charles. Angela clapped loudly. Diana took Derek by the arm.

'You know quite well he meant it all as a joke.'

'He should have told me then.' Derek turned to Charles. 'Was it a joke?'

'Of course not,' said Charles with a forced laugh.

'The least you can do is buy us all lunch,' snapped Diana.

'Why should I?' asked Derek mildly. 'Charles lost the bet and I won. He wouldn't expect me to feel obliged to part with all my winnings.'

'*I* expect you to,' returned Diana loudly.

'You're in no position to expect anything,' said Derek in a level voice.

The band had started to play *If You Knew Susie*. A man with a megaphone was announcing that the best cuts of the ox were about to be auctioned.

'Far too nice a day to quarrel,' said Charles.

'I can't see that the weather's got anything to do with it,' Derek replied.

Charles took his arm. 'Come on, Derek. Enough said.'

Derek pulled his arm away so violently that Charles dropped

117

his coconut. The shell split and milk dribbled out on to the ground.

'Why did you do that?' asked Charles with a mixture of surprise and anger.

'Why did you fuck my wife?' said Derek.

A long time, as it seemed to Derek, before Charles murmured, 'Do *what*?'

The band still playing, the sun shining as before. A small boy nibbling some candy-floss wandered between them.

'Fuck my wife,' Derek repeated obligingly in a controlled voice.

Charles started to laugh. Then Diana shouted at Derek, 'I'll never forgive you.'

'Forgive *me*?' Derek shouted back.

Charles was still laughing. 'He's joking again. Got to be,' he spluttered.

'He'd better be,' said Diana.

'Didn't sound like it to me,' cut in Angela.

'Not joking?' Charles's laughter evaporated. He now looked indignant but too surprised to be angry. 'You can't be serious, Derek. I mean it's absurd.'

'I rather thought you'd react like this,' said Derek, unable to stop his voice shaking with rage. 'Worked it out, did you? If he ever finds out, laugh at him and then be righteously offended. What kind of a moron do you take me for? Bogus dentists, fictitious furniture courses, her in her dressing-gown in the middle of the afternoon.'

'You're raving,' muttered Charles.

'Trying to shoot Giles off with the Scouts, fixing up her time here for the only two weeks I'd be bound to refuse.' Derek was breathing heavily. He could hear the blood surging in his ears. 'Raving, am I?' He was dimly aware of a crowd forming round them. 'Mad Derek who thought his wife was screwing away when she'd just been given a certificate of virginity by the pope. Quite a laugh for you to visit me in my padded cell.'

A very different Charles now; his face red and his right eye twitching. His expression a parody of outraged innocence.

'You could have chosen a better place to make these ludicrous accusations,' he managed to choke out. The look of wounded reproach which he gave Derek proved too much to bear.

'Your wife left you because you fucked around so why stand there looking at me as though I've just pissed on one of your art treasures. Adultery. That's all I said. Nice and easy; an ideal game for two people of opposite sexes. Only rule is, they've got to be married to somebody who isn't playing. You've played it before and I'm sure you'll play it again.' As Derek heard people behind him starting to laugh, he saw Diana cover her face with her hands as though trying to hide herself from a photographer. His attention focused on a throbbing vein in Charles's neck. The sharp flash of light which Derek saw a split second later was not caused by a flash-bulb but the impact of Charles's clenched fist on the side of his face. For several seconds Derek could see nothing at all, just blackness and then a few popping flashes of light. He heard scuffling around him and a long way off a man shouting, 'What am I bid for this lovely cut of meat? Do I hear three? Four from the gentleman in the straw hat . . .' Somebody was helping him to his feet. Derek realized that he could see again, only his vision seemed to have been affected by the blow; everything was blurred. A man was trying to give him something. A moment later he recognized his glasses in the man's hand. Being plastic, neither lens had broken.

A few yards away Charles stood pinioned by two men. His jacket had been ripped badly and his mouth was bleeding. Diana was sobbing. The man who had given him his glasses asked Derek if he wanted a policeman. He couldn't think clearly.

'For adultery?' he asked incoherently.

The man stared at him with bewilderment. He had moist-looking eyes, a neatly cut moustache, and was wearing a regimental tie.

'For assault,' he replied impatiently.

Fucked the wife and assaulted the husband. Derek smiled but quickly relaxed his face. Any movement of his mouth hurt him. Diana's sobbing was getting on his nerves.

'Let him go,' he muttered, pointing in Charles's direction. The two men reluctantly did what he asked. They were clearly disappointed. Without saying a word Charles took Diana by the arm and led her away.

Derek felt slightly sick; he started walking aimlessly towards the centre of the square. The band were having a break for drinks so he was able to sit down on one of their seats. A minute or so later Angela sat down next to him.

'How do you feel?' she asked, handing him a handkerchief which she had just dipped in water. 'For your cheek,' she explained.

'All right,' replied Derek, dabbing at his face with the handkerchief.

'I don't suppose you'll be asked to stay again.'

'It seems unlikely,' he admitted.

The bidding for slices of ox went on.

'Are you going to leave her now?' Angela said.

'Depends on her.'

'What do *you* feel about it?' she asked with unconcealed surprise.

'I don't know.' He paused a moment. 'Nothing. I feel nothing.'

Derek wanted her to go away but the effort of asking her seemed more than that required to sit listening and occasionally answering.

'That's how I felt when I left John. It made leaving him a lot easier.'

'A bang on the head doesn't make much difference,' he said. 'No reason to leave her.'

'And what you *said* to them?' she asked with amazement.

'They know what I know. That's all.'

'All?' she repeated quietly. 'It'd be enough for me. I left John because of a suit I hadn't sent to the dry cleaners.' Derek didn't bother to reply. 'No, really . . . he'd been about to go to a conference and was cursing away about his special suit not being there. He had six or seven others but it had to be the one I'd forgotten about.'

'Tell me another time,' he begged her.

'I'd rather tell you now.' She gave him an understanding smile

120

and went on, 'When he was stumping about in the bedroom, I went down to the garage and smacked a nail into one of the car's tyres. I'd lost the key to the boot a couple of days before, and the spare tyre was in the boot. Are you listening?' She fixed him with her cornflower-blue eyes. He nodded wearily. 'I suggested he caught a taxi, but no, he was going to fix the tyre if it killed him. To get at the spare tyre he had to dismantle the rear seat and crawl into the boot; then he had to free the spare and crawl out with it. I watched him tearing at the seat and trying to wrench it out by brute force. He was scarlet in the face and gibbering like an ape. Have you ever seen anybody really gibbering?' He shook his head. 'Well I have.' The memory made her laugh. She had put an arm round him and he could feel her long blonde hair against his uninjured cheek. The sight of her face so close to his brought back memories of the day before. He felt his penis stirring. 'He was wearing his best suit; or it *was* his best suit when he started on the car. By the time he got the tyre out, he was soaked with sweat and had torn his trousers across the bum. Before he'd jacked the car up and taken off the bad tyre, he was sobbing with rage and exhaustion. It came to me on the spur of the moment that I never wanted to see him again; so when I'd got him some clean clothes, I went to the kitchen and left him a note: "You'll find some lamb and some chicken in the fridge. Have the lamb this evening (twenty minutes a pound and twenty over) and don't forget your mother's birthday on Monday week." Then I added that I was leaving him. When I'd woken up that morning I hadn't any idea that I was going to walk out. I didn't think about it. I just did it.'

She was smiling at him encouragingly. Go, and do thou likewise. The band was returning. Derek got up. She took his hand and said casually, 'You could stay at my place for a bit.'

A peculiar falling sensation in his stomach, dread, sickness and expectation jumbled together. A frightening desire to say the *right* words while the flags fluttered and the sun shone. I'll come, to hell with Giles, to hell with Diana. I'll be out on my ear in a week or two, but what the hell? Easy come, easy go. Fuck the future while I can fuck you. She smiled at him.

'There can't be too many women who'd fancy your peculiarities.'

A silence. Members of the band were picking up their instruments and tipping spittle out of them.

'Can I tell you tomorrow?' he asked.

'I doubt it,' she replied softly.

'But I can't just go without a word,' he protested.

' 'Phone them from the station. Send a wire.' She let his hand drop and shook her head slowly. 'You won't, will you?'

'I have certain problems,' he murmured apologetically.

'Don't we all,' she said, turning away. As the band started playing again, he watched her disappear into the crowd.

Derek was in the pub trying to find out where he could get hold of a taxi when he saw Gilbert coming towards him.

'I've been looking for you.' The old man frowned. 'What happened to your face?'

'A ball intended for a coconut.' Gilbert did not look convinced, but he seemed preoccupied with other thoughts.

'I've been sitting in the church,' he said. 'Thinking.' A slight pause before he added, 'You ought to go in there. A good mural of St Sebastian's martyrdom. So many spears in him he looks like a hedgehog.'

'I had a slight altercation with Charles. Nothing very dramatic; but I think it'd be as well if we were moving on. You wouldn't mind a few days in a hotel?'

To Derek's surprise his father showed no curiosity at all. He seemed relieved rather than put out.

'Actually I was thinking of going back to London anyway.' Gilbert smiled sadly. 'The fact is I haven't been entirely happy. A certain atmosphere from time to time.' Derek nodded. He noticed that his father seemed uneasy and was fiddling with one of his coat buttons. They were standing just outside the main bar and people were pushing past them. Beside them was a phone on the wall. Derek, who had been looking through the classified phone directory for taxi numbers before his father's arrival, resumed his search. Then he heard his father saying urgently, 'I want to talk to you.'

'Can't it wait?'

'I was planning to go back to London this evening.' Gilbert sounded contrite but determined.

'All right, talk,' replied Derek with an irritated shrug.

'Somewhere rather quieter?' suggested Gilbert.

'Anywhere you like, but quickly,' moaned Derek.

He followed his father along a narrow cinder path that skirted the north side of the church. To their right was a large stone cross. Gilbert sat down on the plinth and beckoned to Derek to do the same. An inscription read: 'This monument was erected to the memory of the officers and men of HMS *Primrose*, lost with all hands off the Lizard 12 March 1892.' Derek rested the back of his head against the rough granite and shut his eyes. He could still hear the band playing in the square. Gilbert coughed delicately to get his son's attention.

'Those notes; the ones I lost on the train.'

Derek looked at him despairingly. Today of all days his father felt impelled to tell him things about events of thirty years before.

'Yes,' groaned Derek, opening his eyes.

'I didn't lose them at all.'

'Does it matter?' cried Derek, getting up.

'I'd only been writing it all down to postpone telling you.' The look of anguish on his father's face made Derek relent. He sat down again.

'I'm listening.'

Derek found himself watching his father's adam's apple moving as he swallowed. The old man was obviously nervous.

'The fact is I met Margaret months before I arranged for you and your mother to go back to Singapore.'

'Did what?' gasped Derek, all traces of weariness gone.

Gilbert wiped away sweat from his forehead with the back of his hand and added hastily, 'When I said I thought you'd be safer away from England and the bombing, I wasn't exactly lying.'

123

'You just wanted us out of the way,' returned Derek, as a cold numb feeling grew in his chest.

Gilbert looked down at the cinder path, where a straggling line of ants was crossing it.

'When you'd both gone, Margaret moved in with me. That was before the trouble started in Malaya. When the Japs attacked Indo-China I sent warning telegrams. Did all I could, you understand.'

A sudden spasm of anger as Derek asked, 'Couldn't you have gone on keeping it to yourself? Was that too much to ask?'

'Why does anybody want to confess anything? I needed to.'

A strange booming noise had started, like distant guns.

'We passed some granite quarries in the car. That'll be blasting,' explained Derek, seeing his father's bewilderment. The explosions died away. 'Just a point of interest,' he went on in a flat unemotional voice, 'when you sent me away to school, did Margaret move in again in my absence?'

Gilbert nodded solemnly.

'It was a long time ago,' said Derek, staring out across the jumble of headstones. His anger had gone and now only the numbness remained. He remembered going to their local church with his father and praying together for his mother's safety. Another occasion; a station platform, a woman who from a distance looked his mother's double. He started to run only to see her turn towards him with surprise; a complete stranger.

Gilbert got up from the plinth and said, 'I'd rather you didn't tell the others I'm going until I've gone. I'll get a taxi back to the house and ask the driver to wait till I pack my things.'

Derek expected him to go at once, but he stood where he was in the middle of the cinder path as if waiting for something. Derek waited too. At last Gilbert said awkwardly, 'There's something else. I meant to tell it you first but didn't, and now it'll sound utterly wrong.' The church clock was striking the quarter. 'Margaret's affairs have been finally sorted out and it seems she was a good deal richer than I thought. I'd like to make over most of it to you, death duty being what it is. I had to tell you now because my solicitor will be writing to you in a week or so.' He paused and went on quietly, 'I intended to do this whether I told you about the other business or not.'

Gilbert seemed to be waiting for Derek to release him with a forgiving remark. But by the time he could think of anything to say, his father had started off down the path; a badly dressed, stooping old man walking despondently away. Why, why did he have to tell me? Why when there was so little to be gained and a lot to be lost? But Derek knew the answer almost at the time the questions formed. That warm sense of altruism, that lovely contrite self-abasement that had urged him to confess, urged him to force what he had to say on Giles, whether the boy wished to hear or not, and he had made it very clear that he had not wanted to listen. Other memories; old, old memories. The moment his father had told him that he was going to marry Margaret. His reaction had been anger for a while, refusal to listen and then, very soon, acceptance. Acquiescence through fear: a conscious attempt to persuade his father that he didn't care, and all because he feared rejection. And now, like some gruesome text-book case history, it was happening again. Giles refusing to listen, Giles angry and then saying he didn't care what his father did. And Derek had sucked it up just as his own father had done those years before.

Gilbert had reached the lich-gate. Derek called out to him to stop.

'We'll share a taxi,' he yelled.

Derek took his father's arm as they walked across the square.

Chapter 10

After Gilbert's departure, Derek tried to find Giles, but, seeing no sign of him in the garden or anywhere near the house, he went inside with the intention of packing. Since Charles's car was not parked in the drive, Derek assumed that neither his wife nor his host had yet returned. He was therefore surprised, on opening his bedroom door, to see Diana hurriedly packing their cases. Derek said nothing, and stood waiting for her to speak, but she went on folding shirts as though he was not there. At last he asked quite casually, 'Where's Charles?'

'Having his chin stitched up,' she replied with exaggerated calmness.

'I'm sorry,' murmured Derek.

'Oh you are, are you?' she returned with bitter sarcasm.

'I'm certainly not glad, if that's what you're implying.'

Diana didn't reply, but folded a final shirt and began straining to shut the bulging case.

'Let me,' he said, bending down and trying to flatten down the clothes in the case before attempting to close it. Without warning, she brought down the lid on his hands with all her strength, trapping his fingers. He let out a gasp of pain as she gave one last push before relaxing the pressure.

'You could have broken them,' he cried, rubbing his bruised fingers and then shaking his hands to get rid of the sharp throbbing pain.

'I wouldn't have been sorry,' she returned, getting up and walking over to the window. A moment later she turned and said, in a voice shaking with suppressed anger, 'I don't give a fart for your idiotic suspicions, but as for blurting them out in front of everybody . . . I don't suppose it ever occurred to you to mention them to me first before making fools of all of us?'

Derek had expected grief, contrition, maybe humiliated anger, but certainly not this righteous rage.

'You owe me no explanations, I suppose?' he asked icily, sitting down on the bed. 'Hurling accusations around isn't going to help us understand each other.'

'Do you think I *want* to understand you after the way you've behaved?' She tossed back her head in derision and said in a simpering voice, 'My wife doesn't understand me. Just a bad gag, Derek; and, after what's happened, worse than that.'

'Do you deny it?' he shouted.

'My affair with Charles?' She looked up at the ceiling, as though imploring help from above; then she sighed and shook her head slowly. The sudden and unexpected disappearance of her anger alarmed Derek. Now her expression was almost one of compassion. 'My poor Derek. There was no affair.' She let her hands drop to her sides and looked down at the floor. 'I wanted a change, a fling, whatever one calls it, but he didn't.' Derek watched her with mounting anger as she took a cigarette from a packet on the dressing-table and lit it. She blew out a thin stream of grey smoke. Her look of self-absorbed sadness maddened him.

'You're an accomplished liar, Diana, but you don't begin to fool me. Clever saying *you* made the running and *he* turned you down. Nobody likes admitting to that kind of failure and you particularly hate seeming pathetic.'

She looked at him with the kind of sympathy he imagined the owners of dogs might show their pets when they had decided to have them destroyed.

'But can't you see, Derek, if I'd wanted to lie to you, I'd have made a proper job of it. *Trying* to be unfaithful's not much better than *being* unfaithful.'

'I used to fancy ladies in a certain kind of black lingerie but I didn't rush out and lift skirts in the street.'

She gave him a puzzled frown.

'I don't quite see the relevance,' she said gently.

'It doesn't matter,' he replied brusquely. 'If he turned you down, what the hell were you doing arranging a holiday for your-self here?'

'A last try.' She shrugged her shoulders and looked away. 'But you put paid to that by coming. Charles wanted you to come, so he wasn't sorry.'

Derek came up close to her. 'Let's try something a bit more tangible.'

'There's no point,' she whispered with desperate sympathy.

'I think I can judge that.' He paused and went on sharply. 'When he came to the flat that afternoon, you were in your dressing-gown.'

She gave him a sad ironic smile and said slowly, as though explaining to a difficult child, 'I'd been in bed with a headache. Remember? I hadn't got dressed. I'd also had a bath.'

'I'll get the truth out of you. Your headache went pretty quickly after he'd gone.'

'I'd been in bed most of the day; taken some pills. Headaches come and go. So?' Her calmness seemed too calculated to be genu-ine. Normally Diana would have told him to go to hell and leave her alone.

'You didn't answer the phone when I rang,' he said.

She raised her hands and replied with the hint of a smile, 'Do *you* get out of the bath to answer it?'

'I phoned several times.'

She sat down on a case and put her head in her hands. Then she looked up wearily. 'It's weeks ago, Derek. I slept most of the morning. I must have turned off the extension by the bed. I can't remember turning it off, but I obviously did. If I'd heard the bell why on earth would I have let it ring?'

'You had an appointment at the dentist,' said Derek forcefully, sensing that he had trapped her. 'If you answered the phone your bogus Indian dentist went up the spout. That's why you let it ring.'

'But I had a headache,' she cried, with real irritation. 'Can't you listen?'

'And on the day you had a headache, you happened to have a

128

dental appointment and Charles happened to drop by. It also just *happened* to be the day Giles usually went swimming after school.'

'So bloody what?' She stubbed out her cigarette in the washbasin and added, 'Coincidences do just *happen*.' A slight pause before she said, 'In any case, even if I'd expected Charles, why did I need you to think I'd gone to the dentist? I could have answered the phone with him on top of me.'

'You told me you'd be at the dentist to rule out any chance of my coming back from work early.'

She shook her head as though trying to clear it.

'I'm sorry, but I don't have to be in the flat for you to come back early.' She gave him a mocking smile and added, 'Would you have been lonely without me?'

'I'd lost my key. I asked you to get me another but you didn't.' He paused to emphasize the point. 'I couldn't have got in, if you'd been out, so I wouldn't have come back early.' He stared at her triumphantly.

Diana looked confused for a moment, but then suddenly she gave a little gasp of comprehension, as though some profound mystery had been revealed to her. Her eyes were sparkling with excitement.

'It all goes back to that bloody dentist. Well, doesn't it?'

'You made him up, like other things.'

'But the dentist really matters. Right?'

Derek did not deny it. Diana had reached for her handbag and had soon emptied its contents onto the bed. Derek saw her purse, keys, compact, lipstick and a mess of letters and paper. After hastily sorting through it all, she turned the bag upside down and shook out a couple of envelopes from a side-pocket. Derek watched her impassively. Just another pantomime to convince him that she had really made an appointment and had been unlucky enough to mislay her vital appointment card. She looked around the room, as if hoping that some object or garment might give her a clue.

'What coat was I wearing when I went to see him last?' Her

excitement was still as intense. The effort she was putting into her act brought back Derek's anger.

'It's summer; are you likely to have worn a coat?'

She went over to the fitted cupboards and slid back the doors. He saw her pull out her red raincoat and start turning out the pockets; a handkerchief and a few bus tickets. From the other pocket she produced an empty packet of cigarettes, the programme for Giles's Open Day, several scraps of paper, receipts they looked like, and something else: a small white card. She handed it to Derek with a cry of triumph. He turned it over in his hand and read: 'Dr H. M. Dulfakir, BDS, DOrthRCS, Dental Surgeon, 37a Onslow Crescent, London, S.W.7.'

Derek's head was throbbing painfully; he could hear the blood thundering in his ears. Diana was looking at him with concern.

'Are you all right?'

'No,' he shouted. 'Of course I'm not all right.'

'Now do you believe me?' she whispered.

Derek covered his ears with his hands and tried to think. Anything that would catch her out, anything.

'Your face,' he blurted out suddenly. 'How come you had make-up on your face?'

'What?' She sounded frightened by the intensity of the question.

'When Charles came to the flat. How come you had make-up on your face when he arrived? You didn't know he was coming; that's what you said. People in bed with headaches don't put on make-up.'

'I must have put it on when I went out to get him tea.'

'You keep your make-up in the teapot?'

'I must have gone to the bedroom. I told you, it was weeks ago. Do you remember every time you clean your teeth?' She sounded more alarmed than angry.

Derek had jumped up excitedly.

'I'd remember if my mistress suddenly arrived and I hadn't shaved. I'd remember shaving in those circumstances.'

'Your memory may be better than mine, it doesn't prove anything more than that.' Her alarm was giving way to exasperation.

'Another thing,' Derek went on wildly, 'because you made an appointment doesn't mean that you intended keeping it. You did it all to fool me.'

'Ring him,' she shouted, shoving the card in his face.

Derek shook his head and let out a long sigh. Already he had forgotten the sense of his last remark. He walked over to the window and rested his weight on the ledge. Far across the bay the evening sun picked out the white sails of a yacht heading for the open sea. For a moment he imagined himself on board, watching the land slipping away and hearing the slight thud of the waves against the hull. He felt Diana's hand on his shoulder and turned to see her looking at him strangely.

'You're mad,' she said. 'I've only just seen it. You *want* me to have had an affair. You pretended to be upset about Charles and me, then when I prove you're wrong, you treat it as a tragedy. You ought to be jumping for joy; instead you look at me as though I've shot you.'

Derek could think of nothing to say. He was still too shocked to be able to collect his thoughts.

'I'm right, aren't I?' she asked with a mixture of exultation and incredulity.

'Probably,' he conceded in a stifled voice. 'Turn a man's house upside down and don't be surprised to see him walking on his head.' The desperation in his voice got through to her at once and she took his hands in hers.

'But why didn't you tell me about your fears? Why did you have to wait till you couldn't cope any more?'

'You wanted a different person,' he said, 'that's why. Good God, didn't you make that clear enough when you stopped doing anything to the flat? You despised me enough already without my going to you and whining about whether you were having an affair.' She took his head in her hands and cradled it as she might have done a child's. 'I was afraid that if I told you what I suspected you might feel forced to leave me.' He took a deep breath and sobbed, 'I thought that I'd go mad if you left me. I believed I wouldn't exist.' As he finished speaking he felt her freeze for a moment before she pushed him away. She was staring at him coldly, every vestige of tenderness gone.

'If that's true what does it make me?' she demanded emotionally.

Derek looked at her in astonishment. Seconds before he had felt relief, peace and love. His confession had brought him such a sense of well-being and tranquillity that at first he wasn't able to take in what had happened to change her mood so thoroughly.

'Perhaps I'd better tell you what it makes me then, since you've evidently lost your tongue as well as your wits.' She paused dramatically before shouting, 'A monster. A woman who bullied and degraded her husband so much that she destroyed him; making him her helpless shadow.' She became calmer and asked him quietly, 'Isn't that what you implied?'

'I didn't mean to,' he whispered.

'That's very decent of you. The fact is you like humiliating yourself. A great joke to begin with, the scholarly sage deferring to the wishes of his half-wit wife.' She sat down on the edge of the bed and folded her arms. 'A pity it became a habit; a pity for me at least. Fine for you. It saved you the bother of having to think about what you said to me. When in doubt agree.'

'That isn't quite fair,' he protested.

'Is it *fair* to tell your wife you'll go mad if she misbehaves?'

'A moment ago you were blaming me because I didn't tell you sooner.'

She didn't bother to answer him, but went over to the dressing table and started to brush her hair with brisk businesslike movements. Then she turned and said impatiently, 'If we're going tonight, you'd better start looking for your cat and getting Giles's bicycle onto the car.'

'When in doubt agree,' he replied under his breath, and then out loud: 'You wouldn't like it if I refused, would you?'

She got up and came over to him and rested her hands on his shoulders. 'You know, Derek, I've just been thinking.' She narrowed her eyes slightly and shook her head. 'You thought I was having an affair. So instead of mentioning it to me, you arrange to come and stay with me and my supposed lover. Not only that,

132

you ask your father along and bring your son and your cat.' She raised her eyebrows and let her hands fall from his shoulders. 'If's that's an example of sane Derek, mad Derek might be an improvement.' She walked to the door and looked back at him more with pity than anger. 'The car won't pack itself,' she said.

For almost an hour after leaving the house, Derek felt nothing at all except emptiness, as though every thought, feeling or emotion had been sucked out of him. The sky was a paler blue and towards the horizon he could see a slightly green tinge. The sun was a lot lower now and the air was cooler; but what would it matter if the grass changed to purple and the trees spouted orange leaves? Nothing would blot out the past few hours. Derek had walked about a mile down the road before turning back. Walking was better than sitting; walking was doing something after all, even if his feet seemed as remote and distant as the trees and the sky.

When he got back to the house Derek saw his car in the drive. Better find that bicycle. He began looking without putting much effort into it. Ten minutes later, having found no trace of the missing machine, he realized with a jarring shock that although subsequent events had stretched time unnaturally, his last conversation with Giles had actually taken place earlier that day. He went into the hall and was shocked to see that the clock showed eight o'clock. No trace of his earlier despairing detachment was left as he ran into the kitchen in search of Mrs Hocking. With an unpleasant falling sensation in his stomach, he learned that Giles had left just before ten and had not returned to lunch, nor had he taken any food with him.

The boy's deliberate indifference came back to him with painful clarity. Giles had *seemed* stable enough, but it was quite possible that he had concealed his real feelings, that the whole act of not caring had been no more than a mask. Easy to forget that even trivial disasters are felt so keenly in childhood; and an unwanted and unnecessary confession of adultery was hardly trivial. Derek had a sudden vision of Giles riding his bicycle with deliberate carelessness; saw him drifting round a sharp bend on the wrong side of the road into the path of an oncoming lorry. Or was he floating face downwards in the sea, or lying crumpled at the foot of a rocky cliff?

Derek was standing staring at the phone in the hall when Diana came up to him. All her cool detachment had gone; she looked pale and shaken.

'You can't find him either? It's so unlike him going off.'

Derek took her arm gently. Then he gave her a comforting smile.

'He'll be back soon. Boys are like that. They get carried away and can't imagine their parents might worry. When I was his age I went off to Brighton for the day and didn't get back till after midnight. I was amazed when my father sent me to bed in disgrace.'

Diana was tugging at her hair distractedly.

'Why the hell did we leave him? Why?'

'If he's not back by nine, we'll ring the police.'

'Is it our fault?' she cried suddenly.

'Perhaps,' he replied, wondering how he could have let the boy go off on his own earlier in the day. Waves of shame flooded through him.

'I never showed enough interest,' she moaned. 'You were so much better, Derek.'

If she knew about the morning, thought Derek; if she ever knew ... Giles, aged four: freckled face, snub nose, hair a redder red, no glasses. An eager, inventive child with so many private words. Potato was tubby, oranges ornies, chutney chucketty. Diana saying: He's far too old for that baby talk, and: It's ridiculous a boy his age having to sleep with his baby blanket. Derek the one who understood. Good Daddy, bad Mummy. Diana saying angrily: You keep on undermining me. Always Mummy who has to say no to him. Derek felt tears forming. He put his arms round Diana and they held each other.

When Charles returned from the doctor's, with four stitches in his chin, he seemed surprised to see his guests still in the house. At first he was angry but when he heard about Giles a temporary truce was patched up. Mrs Hocking was told to provide a cold supper.

They ate in the kitchen, mostly in silence. Derek only picked at his food and Diana seemed equally lacking in appetite. Charles didn't open any wine but fetched some brandy afterwards. When his thoughts became too disturbing, Derek studied the plates on the heavy mahogany dresser and vainly tried not to hear the hollow ticking of the large Victorian wall-clock. Charles poured out three glasses of brandy and then started to peal a peach with meticulous care. Diana suddenly pushed back her chair with a harsh scraping noise on the flags.

'I'm sorry but I can't just sit here. We ought to ring the police now.'

Charles put down his knife and said gently, 'It might be worth trying the hospitals first. There aren't many. If he hasn't been admitted we'll be able to discount the idea of a road accident.'

A quarter of an hour later Charles came back. It occurred to Derek that he was enjoying his rôle of capable man of action. Maligned by his ungrateful guests, he was still enough of a good samaritan to do all he could for them.

'Well, no news at any of the hospitals. I'm on the phone to the police in Penzance. I've given them a description and they'll circulate it.' He turned to Diana. 'What was he wearing this morning?'

Diana's lips were trembling. She screwed up her eyes as though desperately trying to remember and then shook her head.

'It's awful. I'm not sure. Jeans, I think, and a yellow sweater.'

'Navy jeans, a pale blue T-shirt and a fawn jersey,' muttered Derek. 'I think he was wearing sandals.'

'Anything to identify him? Name-tags on his clothes?'

Diana let out a loud sob that seemed to surprise her. Her eyes were quite dry.

'He only has name-tapes on his school clothes. These were holiday things.'

When Charles had gone back to the phone she started crying uncontrollably. Long low sobs that came from the pit of her stomach and shook her with each spasm. Derek came and put his arms round her. After a minute or two she dried her eyes with her sleeve, smearing mascara across her cheek.

Before Charles returned, Angela came in looking hot and angry. She glanced at Derek and then started to eat what was left of her brother's helping of chicken.

'I had to walk back,' she complained with her mouth full. 'Somebody might have waited for me.'

'Giles is missing,' said Derek quietly.

'God, I'm sorry.'

For a moment Derek was frightened that she was going to say more, but, before she could, Charles came in again.

'The police are going to contact the local coast guard. He may have been cut off by the tide or got himself stuck up a cliff. If there's no sign by morning they'll get a naval helicopter out to look for him.'

'It isn't happening,' moaned Diana.

'No need to get worried till midnight,' said Charles soothingly. 'To tell the truth the police thought we were a bit over-anxious getting them in this early. But better safe than sorry.'

A little later Charles and Diana went down to Tregeare to ask in the pub if anybody had seen Giles; Angela would stay in the house in case he phoned or turned up in person, and Derek had made up his mind to go down to the beach and search along the shore for a couple of miles.

When Charles and Diana had gone, Derek went upstairs for an extra sweater. On his way through the hall Angela stopped him and handed him a torch.

'I'm sorry I said what I did this afternoon,' she said quietly.

'You weren't to know.'

She kissed him lightly on the cheek as he walked out into the darkness.

Derek picked his way over the rockery towards the edge of the strip of woodland which separated the grounds of Charles's house from the shore. The yellow beam of his torch stabbed out a narrow field of vision: too narrow, he thought. He switched off the torch to gauge how well he could see by the light of the crescent moon and a sky filled with stars. For a while he stood still and waited for his eyes to acclimatize. Have to go carefully.

Ahead the trees reared up: an unreal black wall like a giant cutout against the paler sky. To the right, where the trees were less dense, he could see the far side of the estuary floating indistinctly like a long dark cloud on the silvery water. As his eyes grew used to the darkness, he was able to pick out more detail. The wall of trees was soon no longer impenetrable, for now amid dark leaves he could glimpse the grey bark of trunk or branch. Just ahead of him to his left he could make out a tangle of brambles; a few moments before it might have been a large holly bush or a dense clump of bamboos. The path too had become clearer and he could see a faint white line where it twisted away until obscured by the dark shadows of the trees.

But as he walked deeper into the wood he could make out very little. The prevailing wind had bent the oak trees so that their branches formed a dense and flattened canopy above him. At times pools of moonlight were so rare that he had to use his torch, and then the utter hopelessness of his search became cruelly obvious. He shouted the boy's name several times and waved the torch above his head but there was no answer, only the whispering of leaves stirred by the slight breeze. Derek trudged on across a small clearing overgrown with straggling elders. As though it was remotely likely that Giles should be sitting in a wood half a mile from the house, as though, if he could light the entire coastline with powerful arc-lights, he would find him. A long way away he thought he heard a fox bark. Occasionally twigs fell and branches creaked. Once, a small animal scuttled past with a rustling scratching sound. Weasel, stoat or rat—he didn't know or care. Stories in the papers came back to him; children who had not been seen for years and parents not knowing all that time whether they were dead or alive. Pathetic yellowing photographs in shop windows: 'If you have seen Christine, Sandra, Clare . . .' Derek imagined himself coming to Cornwall at weekends, wandering through resorts, asking in hotels and beach shops whether Giles had been seen. Could he take a room, get work on a paper round, deliver milk or serve in a store? Would people ask

137

him where he came from or suspect that he'd run away? Wasn't it obvious that they would? And yet children, boys and girls in their early teens did run away and stay away. Visions of Giles being kept by an ageing homosexual, or stealing from shops, or sleeping rough.

Derek was crying as he pressed on through tall ferns towards trees silhouetted against water: the sea. Minutes later he was crunching over shingle.

Moonlight shimmered on rock pools and on wet fronds of seaweed, which the tide had recently exposed. Below the rocks the water was a glassy black, the surface smooth as polished ice; and yet there was movement: a long flat swell moving the sea ever so little like water tilted slightly in a huge bowl.

Derek shouted again but his words died at once without echo and the rhythmic sighing of the sea on the shingle went on. Occasionally pebbles clattered hollowly pulled back gently by the water. The black shape of a tanker lit with pin-points of light slid imperceptibly across the bay. Please, Giles, if you're near or far, please answer, please, if you never answer again, answer now. Memories of hide-and-seek. I'll count fifty, only fifty, mind, so hurry . . . forty-eight, nine, *fifty* . . . Coming to get you. My fault, he moaned aloud. I didn't mean it, Giles; I didn't know how you would feel. From the beginning I never considered you, from the day Charles came to the flat. *My* fears, *my* hopes, *my* marriage. Oh Giles.

The shore was ribbed with ridges of rock running from the land down into the sea; clambering over one such obstacle, Derek slipped and grazed his hands on rough barnacles. Later, looking down from the top of another ledge, he saw a black shape in the water, too far away to see distinctly. He half-ran, half-fell down onto the beach and lunged forward, gasping, until he saw not a body but a large piece of wave-worn driftwood. He sank down onto the wet stones and couldn't go on for several minutes. Each breath came like a small sob, and in his chest the same sickening ache of shock which a motorist feels after narrowly avoiding head-on collision. A little later the same horror when he mistook some heaped seaweed for a pile of clothes. Another quarter of an hour and he had reached Tregeare, but, since Charles and Diana would have searched there, he pressed on along the shore.

Beyond the village a steep cliff prevented him sticking to the sea. The only way was to cut across fields for a while. After a long walk he climbed over a low wall and saw the sea again. This time there was no beach but a desolate scree, littered with boulders tumbled together chaotically: the remains of the cliff worn away to its constituent parts by waves and wind. As he descended nearer these large boulders the ground became boggy and sucked at his shoes, making it hard going. By straining his eyes he could make out a small cow-path that avoided the worst of the mud. The whole area seemed a mass of little streams which cut shallow gullies in the soft ground. When he reached the rocks he could hear the water making strange plopping noises under them. Again he shouted and again there was no answering call. Weariness and fear made him feel very weak. He hadn't done anything so energetic since his early twenties and now his calves and thighs felt so strained and numb that they shook uncontrollably when he braced the muscles. A sudden vision of Giles telling him about the geological history of this wilderness of stones and rocks made him weep. At first he tried to hold back but then allowed deep sobs to shake him.

As he stumbled from rock to rock, jarring each joint with every sudden drop, and scraping the skin on shins and hands with each small ascent, he realized that soon he wouldn't have the strength to go back. He sat down for a while and then, leaving the shore, started back across the boggy ground and began climbing up towards the fields. He reached a small grassy plateau and sat down to rest again. His legs were shaking and when he tried to stand they folded under him. Have to wait longer. He lay back on the grass and looked up at the stars. One side of the sky seemed very slightly lighter than the other now. He didn't know when he started to doze but it must have been soon after he lay down because he seemed to be back at the house and Giles had come back and was eating cold meat in the kitchen. He was explaining how he had spent the day in Birmingham and had then gone on to see the Scouts in the Peak District. Then Charles came in and started kissing Diana which made Derek laugh and a little later Giles joined in. Somehow they had all moved to the Afro-Asian Institute and Derek was showing Giles the archives. They started tossing letters about like confetti. The dream stopped.

When Derek opened his eyes the stars were pale and indistinct. The crescent moon had become a small insignificant half-disc. From the east, light was flowing as if from a screen lit from behind. From the fields around him he could hear birds singing. The land was no longer grey, silver and black, for now the earth was beginning to glow with dark browns and umber. He sat up and rubbed his eyes. The sky was still a pale misty grey but just above the horizon a pink haze was beginning to flush gold. The colour reflected in the sea but still no sun. For a moment Derek forgot why he was sitting where he was, for, as he looked eastwards, a light no bigger than a flaring match had appeared where the sea and sky met. In seconds this tiny area of molten fire was brighter than all the fires he had ever seen. A channel of gold reached from the horizon almost to the shore. A minute it seemed and the top of the sun was distinct and growing all the time, a half-circle and then an orb. He looked away and pulled himself to his feet; light seemed to be flowing past him like something he could touch. When he looked at the sun again it should have been bright but, strangely, although light was growing all around him, the sun itself seemed paler, its fire diminished by its own reflected light.

As he started walking the agony of the night before flooded back. He felt cold and ill; his limbs seemed to have been stretched and twisted out of place. And yet his despair had lessened. The sun rises every day. Should witnessing a sunrise change anything? And yet his growing optimism could not be denied. As he hurried on across the rough grass, the belief became stronger that when he reached the house Giles would be there.

Like a shipwrecked sailor in a bad storm, in sight of land, but still in danger, Derek made vows. If he comes back I will not indulge my indifference and lack of will by allowing Diana to coerce me, nor will I pretend that my laziness with people is really self-effacing reticence. If he comes back, I will never again fool myself into the belief that I am happy because of my cautious lack of expectations. I will hope for more and therefore give more, if he comes back.

When Derek reached the narrow lane that led back to Tregeare he started to run. Ahead of him a lorry had stopped to take a couple of milk churns from a farm gate. A final effort and he reached the vehicle before it moved off. The driver helped him up into the cab.

It was just after six when he jumped down onto the grass verge at the end of Charles's drive.

Chapter 11

The hall door was shut but had not been locked. Derek paused at the bottom of the stairs. If he hasn't come back? For almost a minute he could not bring himself to go up. Around him the stillness of the house, only broken by the distant ticking of the kitchen clock. He started violently as something rubbed against his leg. He looked down to see Kalulu, arching his back and purring. At last he began climbing, slowly at first, but then faster until by the time he reached the landing he was running up three at a time. At the end of the corridor he pushed open Giles's door.

The boy was sleeping with one hand half-covering his face. Derek denied his first impulse to go across and touch him. Instead he leant against the door-frame and looked and looked at the boy as if afraid that if his eyes left him for a moment his son would vanish again. Tears filled his eyes; relief flooded through him, soothing his aching limbs. He let himself slip down to the floor. Never before such relief. The sudden disappearance of fear left a strange vacuum inside him, but soon a great bubble of happiness was expanding. He scrambled to his feet. A desperate desire to shout and sing his happiness. He dashed across the corridor to his own bedroom.

Diana was asleep. She had not drawn the curtains the night before and early morning sunlight filled the room. Derek could hear birds singing in the garden. He sat down on the bed.

'He's back, he's come back.'

Diana stirred a little and buried her face deeper in the pillow. Derek shook her gently.

'When did he get in? Where has he been? I knew he'd come

back. I knew. I sensed it; you won't believe this but I went to sleep by the sea and woke up when the sun was rising. I knew then.' A lump in his throat made him pause. 'I thought I saw him dead on the beach but he's back, he's come back.' Tears were running freely down his cheeks. Diana had turned over and was shielding her eyes against the light. Derek was still too excited to notice the way she was looking at him. 'Where did he go?' he asked again.

'He tried to book in at a hotel in Falmouth with no money and no luggage. The clerk phoned the police.' She raised herself on an elbow. 'They brought him back between two and three.' Derek put down the flat tired way she had told him this to continuing drowsiness.

'You weren't hard on him?' he asked anxiously. 'You're not angry, surely? He's back; that's all that matters.'

Diana shut her eyes and sighed. 'I wish it was.'

'He's not in any kind of trouble?'

She shook her head.

'Well then, smile, for God's sake.' He went up to her and put his arms round her shoulders.

She made no movement at all. Then she looked up at him and said in a dead expressionless voice, 'He told me, Derek.' Seeing his look of incomprehension, she added, 'Giles told me.'

'Told you what?'

'Everything, as the saying goes,' she replied in the same thin lifeless voice.

'About Angela?'

She nodded. For a moment Derek couldn't adjust to the new situation. He still felt elated.

'But can't you see that it doesn't matter?' he cried. 'A few hours ago we thought Giles might be dead. What happened with Angela was nothing, an accident.' He looked at her imploringly. 'Last night changed everything.'

She sat up very straight and said quietly, 'An accident? Copulation by accident. A strange notion.' She shrugged her shoulders and frowned. Her breasts looked very white against the browner skin of her arms and shoulders. 'Actually,' she went on, flicking

143

the hair back out of her eyes, 'I don't care about what you did with each other. It's a bit sad that you had to have your first fling in years with a nymphomaniac, but there it is. You could have left it just a day or two after her bloke had gone, but then they don't exactly throw themselves at you, do they?' She looked at him scornfully.

'It wasn't quite as crude as that,' he said.

'I'm sure the trees caught fire and each blade of grass shone like silver.'

'But we agree about it. It didn't matter much. That's what you've just said.'

She glanced at him sharply. 'Then what do you think I'm so sick about?' he shrugged and raised his hands in supplication. 'You told that boy what you did and then you left him. That's what makes me sick. You fooled around tossing balls at coconuts while all the time you knew what Giles must have been going through.'

'He wouldn't come,' Derek protested. 'Should I have forced him to or followed him about all day?' He looked at her reproach-fully and added, 'Anyway, he didn't seem shaken or upset.'

'It never occurred to you that he might keep his real feelings to himself?'

'Of course it did,' exclaimed Derek. 'But what could I do? Twist his arm till he told me how he really felt? My sin was in telling him what I did, not in leaving him to himself.' He put his head in his hands. 'If only I'd known he hadn't seen us.'

A short silence. Derek thought he detected a hint of sympathy breaking through her contempt as she said, 'He *did* see you.'

'He never saw us. He went on a footpath and not by the road.'

'There was never any footpath,' she said emphatically.

'There was,' he shouted, with sudden anger. 'Isn't it enough for you that he betrayed me? Do you have to pour acid into the wound too?' She was looking at him with the same cool derision. 'Why the hell should he lie about the path? I'd told him by then.'

'Can't you guess?' she asked quietly, with a taunting smile. 'To save your dignity. He didn't want you to think he'd seen his

144

father thrusting away in a field, bottom up, bottom down.' She pushed back the bedclothes and got up briskly. Derek watched her pulling on her pants. For a moment he felt angry enough to hit her, but the feeling passed, as rage gave way to humiliation and shame. Giles had told *her*. Mummy, who never really listened, who couldn't be bothered to read the books he gave her, who made jokes about her studious son at dinner parties. The worst of it was that Derek believed that she had told the truth, that Giles *had* seen them but had pretended not to, simply to save his father's dignity. Derek's limbs had started to ache again and he was overwhelmed by a leaden numbness of spirit.

Diana was making up carefully in front of the mirror, pursing her lips and then opening her mouth a little as she finished with her lipstick; next she set to work with her eye-liner. He watched her methodical movements in the mirror.

'Why bother?' he asked suddenly.

'The heart pumps, the bowels churn. Life goes on.' She dabbed powder on her forehead and then snapped her compact shut. 'The sort of thing you say.' She turned round and faced him again. 'I think I could have forgiven you everything—Giles, your sad little fumble in a field, the lot—if it hadn't been for the way you behaved at the ox roast. Sanctimonious, self-righteous, spotless Derek ranting on about adultery as though he hadn't had a sexual thought for twenty years, while all the time he was wondering when he could get into Angela's pants again.' Outside the birds were singing as loudly as ever; another glorious day ahead. 'Hypocrisy can't be more blatant than that,' she said.

'I'm not all bad.'

'Just bad for me,' she replied.

'All the time?'

She got up from the chair by the dressing table and came and sat down beside him on the bed.

'It'd make you feel better if I said yes, wouldn't it? Help you to dismiss everything else I've said.' A slight pause. She intertwined her fingers and held a knee in her hands. 'No, you're not bad all the time. I liked you more before you got bored; it's hard to get on with people who find one dull, who think they've found out all there is to know about one.' Her tone was reflective; almost like somebody talking in an empty room, he thought bitterly. She gazed at him for a moment. 'I liked you while you tried.'

'Tries hard but could do better if he tried less. You mean *I* bored you.'

'Nothing wrong with trying hard; it's the opposite of indifference, after all.' She was staring ahead of her with a faint smile parting her lips. Diana the wise, the omniscient. 'You knew much more than I did. I liked listening. Sometimes I found you a bit too earnest but you could be funny too. I often thought, how strange that he still wants to impress me. I was flattered that you thought me worth impressing.' She scooped up a red sandal with her toes and started to fasten the strap. The last time you bothered with me was in Greece. Five years ago. Then you got tired of trying.'

'You drained me,' he said, rubbing his eyes. All right for her to be so cogent after six hours' sleep in a comfortable bed; she hadn't spent most of the night stumbling over rocks. She shook her head and gave him a sad, knowing smile.

'Remember telling me that love is really ignorance? Imposing your own fantasy figure onto a real person?'

'That's one kind of love,' he conceded.

'Your kind?' she asked innocently.

'Not now,' he begged. 'I'm very tired.'

'When you got to know me, you stopped bothering. When I tried with you, you said that you were fed up with conversational opinions; just a way of discovering old arguments and fallacies and dressing them up in new clothes. That's what you said.' She bent down and picked up the other sandal. When she had done up the strap, she went on calmly, 'Everybody has his or her limits, so face facts and recognize them. Never expect too much. Don't use any other person to compensate for your own deficiencies. Be bored and be boring with your wife or husband; it's bound to happen and, when it does, accept it.' Her voice had risen slightly while she had been speaking. 'Your arguments, I think,' she concluded sharply.

Derek looked down at his mud-stained trousers and shoes and

saw them blur as his eyes misted with tears. A clinical posthumous résumé of the evidence before passing sentence. Derek Cushing, I find you guilty of the brutal and senseless murder of your own marriage. How do you plead? Diana was looking at him coolly, as though he had already ceased to concern her. He got up and said passionately, 'I stopped trying because *you* stopped wanting me to. My opinions bored you, so I said no opinions mattered. I said everyone was limited, because you found me dull. Excuses to hide the size of your rejection and to reduce the pain.'

'If that's true, it makes your silence at the time all the more unforgivable.'

'It takes two to have a conversation,' he replied.

'Easier to explain years afterwards when it's too late.'

'That's what you're doing,' he came back angrily.

'Why didn't you shout at me, then? Why, if you cared so much? Because it was less trouble to change tactics and say, "If I can't impress, I'll ingratiate, cajole, please." '

'Would you rather I'd insulted and infuriated?' he asked. 'To please demands effort too.'

She raised her eyebrows in mock surprise.

'As much as lying down in the street and letting people walk on one.'

'That's easy?' he cried.

'If you like footprints on the face—very.'

Derek grabbed her by the wrist and pulled her roughly to her feet so that her face was inches from his own.

'Why do people ingratiate themselves?' he asked in a trembling voice.

'You're hurting me,' she said softly.

He let her go and went on intensely, 'They do it to *stop* people walking on them, they bow down so that people won't knock them down. They give a lot, to retain a little.'

She didn't reply at first, and Derek was surprised to notice that she did not seem displeased; it was almost as though she had wanted him to say something of the sort.

'You've had a very hard time.' She spoke with no apparent

sign of sarcasm. Her sympathy made him feel uneasy; nor could he understand the gentle way she took his hand and kissed it—a gesture he remembered well from the early years of their marriage. She was looking at him expectantly as though she wanted an opinion on her last remark. A moment later he realized that he should have argued, should have said that he was happy, that everybody had hard times, but by then she had taken his silence for assent. He heard her say with tragic brightness, 'At least we don't hate each other. Far better to call it a day before that happens, before you can't take my demands any more. Forbearance can't go on for ever.' Her face frozen for a moment, then tremors at the corners of her mouth; her shoulders shaking; tears. What incredible courage she had needed to remain poised so long. How dreadful when the mask of capability slips to reveal a helpless woman's grief. Derek grasped her by the shoulders and shook her hard.

'Stop it,' he shouted.

She sucked in quivering cheeks and looked at him with outrage and incredulity, then drew herself up with dignity and stifled a sob.

'It's no use,' she choked out.

'You tricked me,' he came back furiously. 'You forced me to defend myself by attacking me, forced me to criticize you.' He paused and took a deep breath to control the shakiness of his voice. 'I came in happy, I came in wanting to start again. Of course I argued. Don't we all exaggerate when we argue? How can anybody be logical when they're confused and angry? You made me angry, made me go too far and then you sprung the trap; making it seem that *I* wanted you to leave me.'

'What does it matter who leaves who? Let's both do the leaving if it's so important. *I'll* leave *you* if it makes you feel better.'

As though she were arguing with an unreasonable child. How often had she spoken to him like that when she wanted him to blame himself?

'It matters,' he said, 'because you wanted me to feel responsible. To think that I loused it up. You didn't want my misery on your conscience.'

148

Her green eyes opened very wide with surprise as she said, 'But Derek, it isn't a competition. Let's share responsibility. Nobody's ever entirely to blame where two are concerned.'

'But I want you to stay with me,' he protested.

She gazed at him wistfully, as though their conversation had taken place several months before and she was now trying to remember it. Then she screwed up her eyes as if recalling herself to the present.

'You can't want me to stay,' she replied quietly. 'If you did, you wouldn't have made all that fuss about being misrepresented. You'd have told me you loved me, been tender to me, said you needed me.'

Her tears were completely gone, and now she was looking at him with serene composure. Derek felt a spasm of anger and then a sharp stab of panic, but he was determined not to give in to it. She'd made up her mind to leave him and nothing that he could have said would have altered that. So much he was certain of. He'd happened to make it easier for her by being angry as opposed to pathetic.

'I do care,' he said defiantly, 'enough not to make one last conciliatory gesture only to have it thrown back in my face.'

Dignity restored, the wronged man turns proudly on his heel and leaves without a backward glance. His horse is waiting and he leaps up into the saddle and rides away. The slate wiped clean, he starts life again with renewed optimism and courage. A battle lost, but not the war. Life goes on and the strong man goes out to meet it undismayed. His horse does not shy at the first hedge and toss him into the ditch; no shared possessions, children, mortgages, insurance policies or faint forebodings cause him a moment's unease. He was always a loner, a man with sharp piercing eyes made to scan far horizons and strange new shores, a man never to be caged or tamed.

'Have you told Giles what you're going to do?' Derek asked.

'Yes.'

'What did he think?' Derek was unable to disguise his fear.

A slight pause as she ran a hand through her hair.

'You'd better ask him in case I misrepresent what he said.'

'Tell me,' he shouted.

For the first time she looked guilty and embarrassed.

'Well?' he cut in desperately.

She avoided his gaze and said uneasily, 'I'm sorry. I don't pretend to understand his reasons, but he wants to stay with me.' Derek's legs buckled and unless he had been standing close to the wall, he might have fallen. His face had become ashen. She came towards him but he turned his face to the wall. 'I put no pressure on him,' she said hastily.

Except you cried when he told you about Angela, except you took my part and told him not to be too hard, except you were generous and forgiving in the face of treachery, blinked back your tears and comforted him after the trauma of the departing police car and the emotional impact of reunion; and all the time no faithless father to be seen. Nothing more to say.

A sudden wave of nausea broke in Derek's stomach. He rushed to the bathroom and vomited painfully. Hardly anything came up; he had not eaten since the night before. With his forehead resting against the cold rim of the lavatory bowl, he started to weep. A little later he lay down exhausted on the bathmat and went to sleep.

Chapter 12

Derek sank down onto the lawn and ran a hand across his forehead. He was sweating freely and felt alarmingly weak in spite of several hours' sleep. He had spent the best part of the remainder of the morning searching for Giles, but although he had looked all over the house and the garden and had even gone down to the beach, he had been unsuccessful. Giles's bicycle was leaning against the garage door, so Derek was relatively certain that he had not gone far. That being the case, it seemed likely that the boy was hiding. Can't face me, thought Derek. Because he feels guilty? Or because the thought of seeing me revolts him? Through the trembling heat-haze he saw Charles coming towards him, looking long-faced and sympathetic. Wanting at all costs to avoid a serious conversation, Derek waved cheerily and said, 'I think I shall buy a hat. Next summer I shall buy a nice straw hat to protect my bald patch from the sun. I shall look rather elegant.'

Charles left a discreet pause and then said in a quietly diffident voice, 'Diana tells me she's leaving you.' He gave Derek a surprised questioning look, as though inviting him to deny such improbable news.

'Perhaps she'll buy radio and television time to tell the world,' Derek replied briskly. 'To do her justice she did tell me too, after she'd told Giles, but I was informed.'

Charles was studying the grass uneasily. He coughed.

'She asked me if I'd help her find a flat.' He hesitated. 'Something temporary to tide her over till she gets something permanent.'

'Go ahead,' said Derek.

'You're not going to try to dissuade her?' asked Charles with pained amazement. Derek shook his head emphatically. 'But this is absurd,' Charles exclaimed with a forced laugh. 'She's told me you've accepted that you were mistaken about me and her. Well you have, haven't you?'

Derek lay back on the grass and watched dark clouds beginning to build up above the horizon. The good weather seemed at last to be coming to an end.

'When one's lost all sense of cause and effect, it doesn't much matter what one accepts,' he said reflectively.

'For God's sake, Derek. She's going to leave you. You're going to have to pull yourself together.'

Derek started to laugh.

'I might as well pull myself to pieces for all the difference it would make.' He could see how puzzled and offended Charles looked. 'Really, I mean it,' he went on. 'When anybody starts misinterpreting people as regularly as I've done, he might as well drop the idea that other people's behaviour is governed by ascertainable motives. When that assumption goes, normal life's a thing of the past.'

Charles was looking at him strangely as though he had learned more from Derek's words than their sense. A brief silence before he said with sudden nostalgia, 'Funny, but that's how I remember you talking to me at Oxford. The same sort of ironic hopelessness. You impressed me a lot.'

'Mercifully I can't remember what we used to say. In love with paradox and aphorisms. The easier and more superficial they were, the more we liked them.'

'It never struck me like that,' replied Charles in a wounded voice. 'But then I wasn't as quick as you.'

Derek watched a bee moving from flower to flower. 'How doth the little busy bee improve each shining hour, and gather honey all the day from every opening flower.'

Charles smiled at him affectionately. Derek felt suddenly ashamed. Perhaps he really did like him.

'We had some good times,' conceded Derek. 'Your sports car and your bank balance and your booze. No wonder I sounded amusing. You had a lot to offer.'

'A rich father?'

'No, more than that. A reckless eagerness to enjoy yourself and the cash to make it possible.'

Charles frowned and gave Derek a reproachful look.

'You never cared about my money. If anything you despised it.'

'But I drank your wine and let you pay my bills.'

'Precisely,' cried Charles. 'If you'd cared you wouldn't have let me.' He paused and smiled. 'You threw up that lecturing fellowship as though it were nothing. Started work on your book with a nominal salary. Ten, twenty years but you wouldn't sell out. You came here as a bloody favour because you never gave a damn and still don't about who people are or what they're worth. No book, no reputation, but you don't care.'

'You always overestimated me.' Derek was uncomfortable. He wanted to deny what Charles had said but knew that he couldn't face doing so. Instead he said quietly, 'I'm sorry about everything.'

Charles lifted a hand to his chin and smiled.

'One of those things . . .' A moment later he said awkwardly, 'Diana asked if she could stay on a few days. I said she could.'

'I was going to go today anyway,' said Derek, getting up.

The sun had gone in behind a heavy mass of unbroken cloud.

Diana was lifting her cases down from the roof-rack, while Derek watched.

'I thought you'd better keep the car,' she said.

'I don't want it.'

'You can't want to take the cat back in the train.'

Derek kicked one of the car tyres. 'As if that trivial inconvenience would bother me after what's happened.'

Diana sat down sideways on the passenger seat with her feet resting on the gravel of the drive.

'Your new flat,' enquired Derek in a dull voice, 'how do you intend paying for it?'

'By working.'

'Isn't freelance journalism a little unreliable; unreliable, I mean, for somebody who hasn't worked regularly for three or four years?'

'If I have to, I'll write copy for the trade papers and publicity stuff.'

'You'll like that?' he asked viciously.

'Perhaps you'll send me something for Giles every now and then,' she said, scuffing the gravel with her sandals.

'A birthday cake? A pocket battleship with automatic guns and radio-controlled steering?'

'I meant money, Derek.'

'How stupid of me.' Suddenly he was laughing. The money. His father's gift, as yet unspecified, but possibly considerable and certainly in the order of thousands rather than hundreds. In the normal course of events he would have told her at once, but the past twenty-four hours had been anything but normal. She was looking at him with real bewilderment. Broken men do not laugh.

'Tell you what,' he said breezily, 'I'll set up a trust for him.'

Diana got up and slammed the car door.

'We'd better discuss it when you can manage to be serious.' She turned on her heel and started to walk towards the house. Derek shouted after her:

'Margaret left my father all her money.'

Diana wheeled round and stared at him threateningly.

'So?'

'He's making most of it over to me. Death duty and all that. God's truth, I can assure you.'

'You're lying,' she said in a trembling voice. 'You'd have told me before.'

'I only knew yesterday.'

'Rather a coincidence, wouldn't you say?'

'Not really. Her affairs were complicated. Lawyers always take their time. He told me just before he left. Probably didn't want to say anything earlier because he knew what I thought of Margaret.'

'You rotten sod,' she said in a limp expressionless voice.

'It's hardly my fault,' he returned primly.

154

For several seconds it seemed that she was on the verge of tears. He took her by the arm and said firmly, 'Stay with me.'

She shook her head violently.

'How the hell can I?'

'Pride isn't so important. It won't buy food or heat a room. Ask a starving man what it's worth.' He slipped an arm round her waist and went on gently, 'Don't go and live in some pokey flat. We'll buy a house. To hell with Abercorn Mansions.'

She seemed to consider for a moment before saying bitterly, 'It's too late. Money can't wipe out what's happened.'

'It might help distance things a bit.' Her expression was unchanged. With a final effort, he went on eagerly, 'Let's call it chance. Chance brought her back, not money. Chance had been about to take her away. Chance brought her back. For once coincidence redressed the balance and went in my favour.'

She looked down at her feet and spoke with quiet emphasis. 'When I wanted money, you didn't have it; and now it doesn't matter to me any more.' She shrugged her shoulders and looked at him sadly. 'As simple as that. You had your books and your ideas. I had the tawdriness of the flat. Perhaps you taught me to enjoy renouncing pleasure.'

She blinked away the tears that had started to brim.

'Why are you lying?' he asked tenderly.

'Why do you bloody well think?' she screamed as she ran into the house.

Derek stared at the ground for a time and then picked up her cases and replaced them in the car. Having done so, he took out his own case and Kalulu's basket. A few large but isolated drops of rain had started to fall. He took his case into the porch but didn't go into the house. In spite of the rain he walked out into the garden again. As the falling drops intensified he heard the rumble of distant thunder. He made for a large beech tree near the old tennis court.

He had been sitting on a root for some minutes, watching the falling rain, when he saw a movement in the summer house on the far side of the court.

Only one side of the roof kept out the rain and most of the

floorboards were rotten. Giles was sitting in a splintering cane chair; on the back of the chair, above his head, crouched Kalulu. Derek watched his son hacking at the end of a bamboo cane with his penknife.

What are you making?' he asked.

'A harpoon,' Giles replied, without looking up from his work.

Kalulu jumped down from the chair and rubbed his sides against Derek's leg. The rain was splashing down noisily from the eaves of the summer house. Giles was biting his lip, whether with embarrassment or concentration on the bamboo, Derek could not make out.

'Why did you go off like that?'

The boy looked up and put down his knife on the side of the chair. 'To be alone.'

'But why?'

'To think.'

Silence, except for the noise of the rain.

'What do you think about Mummy leaving?' Derek asked, doing his best to stop his voice shaking.

'You haven't got on for years.' Giles picked up his knife again and started scraping at the bamboo. As he moved the stick, Kalulu dabbed at the end of it playfully with his paws. 'Mum hasn't been happy for ages.' He caught Derek's eye and asked insistently, 'Have *you*?'

Derek sighed and looked away.

'Only children and very silly people are happy most of the time. Happiness is just the absence of unhappiness as often as not.' Giles snapped his knife shut and shook his head. 'You don't think so?' asked his father.

'You might be happier with somebody else,' whispered Giles; almost a question. Derek stared at him open-mouthed. His heart was racing. He wanted to shout but knew that if he did, the boy would tell him nothing else. With difficulty Derek contrived to sound casual as he asked, 'Why did you tell Mummy?'

Giles was looking at him warily.

'You aren't cross?' he asked anxiously.

'No.'

156

Giles shook some bamboo shavings off his knees and looked down at the floor.

'You couldn't have been happy to have done what you did.' He looked at his father as if for some confirmation of this statement. Then he went on nervously, 'You might be better off apart.'

Derek covered his face with his hands. Far from having betrayed him, Derek was now certain that Giles's principal motive for telling Diana had been a simple desire to help his father end a dead marriage and begin again with Angela or another woman. Derek murmured weakly, 'You did it for me.'

Giles said nothing but went on stroking Kalulu, who had just jumped up onto his lap. Derek felt suddenly exasperated by his silence.

'Your feeble father would never have had the guts to leave his wife, so you thought you'd give him a helping hand.' Derek had said this more harshly than he had intended. Still no answer from Giles. 'I'm right, aren't I?' shouted his father.

Giles had gone very red and seemed close to tears. Derek was taken aback when the boy pushed the cat off his knee and jumped up angrily.

'I did it for me,' he blurted out defiantly. 'Not for you or for her, but for me, because I wanted to.'

Derek was too stunned to be angry. The idea that Giles should have acted for personal reasons of his own had never even occurred to him. He heard Giles going on vehemently, 'How could I have come home and seen you both lying to each other? Day after day you saying, "Yes dear, no dear", and all the time her not knowing what I'd seen, and me having to kid you that I didn't care; and you wondering if I'd tell her; and me not knowing if you wanted to go or stay.' He paused and took several deep breaths before shouting, 'That's why I told her.'

Derek found himself staring at his son with stupefaction. Vulnerable he might look with the soft down on his upper lip and the harsh line of his glasses breaking the curve of his cheek; touchingly awkward too—the way he bit his lips when embarrassed and couldn't keep still when talking. But there he was, not just a boy with an erudite hobby, skinny white arms and a freckled face,

157

but Giles, who considered things strictly from his own point of view and made his own plans and decisions. Giles, who thought for himself, and then acted upon his thoughts. His trousers were too short and the top button of his aertex shirt was missing. Derek wanted to embrace him but was afraid to do so in case he was rebuffed. He could feel his eyes filling as he said, 'Are you really going to go with Mummy?'

Derek had expected the question to embarrass the boy, but it didn't. Giles looked at him seriously and replied, 'It wouldn't be fair if I didn't.'

'Because of Angela?' asked Derek bitterly.

Giles seemed surprised by the question. 'Nothing to do with that.' He picked up his harpoon and stabbed at a rotten floorboard, breaking off bits of worm-eaten wood. Water had started to seep through the roof in more places.

'Tell me,' whispered Derek.

'Because I get on best with you.'

Derek was on the point of arguing but then he realized what Giles had meant. For years Diana had known that Giles preferred his father. If the boy stayed with Derek and she went off by herself, she would really be alone in a way that Derek would never be. For, in spite of separation, he would know that Giles would go on caring and that they would often see each other. Diana would have had no such certainty.

'That boy in your class, the one whose parents split up—was he . . .' Derek raised his hands as he searched for the right word. 'I mean, did it take him long to get over it?'

'Timpson,' said Giles thoughtfully. 'He was a bit low for a month or two. His mother married someone else; a travel agent. They get cheap trips all over the place. Timpson's always boasting about going to Egypt and countries like that. He brings back dozens of boring photographs and hands them round.'

Derek wondered for a moment whether Giles was making fun of him, but the boy's seriousness was so obviously sincere that he discounted the idea. Perhaps adults overestimated the effects their behaviour had on their children. Hadn't he read that young children who had been sexually molested usually thought nothing

158

of it until their parents started weeping and tearing their hair?

'We can see each other as often as we want,' Giles said.

Derek nodded helplessly. He wanted to plead with Giles, beg him to stay with him, but the thought of an almost inevitable refusal, probably accompanied by tears on both sides, deterred him. He took his son's hand and squeezed it gently.

'You won't really be leaving home at all,' he said with an attempt at a smile. 'Home will be leaving me.' He'd intended it as a joke, but saw at once that Giles had taken it as a plea for pity. He added hastily, 'I won't be lonely, anyway. I'll have Kalulu for company.' He was afraid that he had made matters worse, but Giles seemed to have taken his remark seriously.

'Poor old Kalulu, he's going to find it a bit strange being alone all day.' Giles picked up the cat from the cane chair and started stroking him under the chin. Derek remembered painfully the day when Kalulu had first arrived as a kitten; how excited Giles had been, and how, three days later, he had wept for hours when they had thought the animal lost. The cat had been shut in the linen cupboard by mistake.

Derek said shakily, 'I suppose it will be a bit dull for him.' He put a hand on Giles's shoulder. 'Look, why don't you keep him? I'm sure he'd be happier.'

Giles considered for a moment, then looked at his father dubiously.

'Are you sure?'

'Certain,' replied Derek.

'How about Mummy?'

'She won't mind.'

'Perhaps it would be best,' said Giles with adult gruffness, and then, with firm reassurance, 'I'll look after him well.'

'I know,' muttered Derek, finding it hard not to cry. Crying over a cat? Your wife leaving you, your son with her; but the cat proves the final straw. He felt water trickling down his back. A drip had been coming down onto his shoulder for several minutes but he hadn't noticed until it had gone through his jacket.

'We'll muddle through, won't we?' he asked, looking away across the rain-sodden tennis court.

159

'You bet,' said Giles, stifling a sob.

'I'll ring you tonight when I get back to the flat.'

'Must you go today?' Derek saw Giles's mouth sag a little.

'It'll be easier if I do.'

Pray God he doesn't weep now, thought Derek, but the boy gave a resigned nod and took his father's hand. A moment later they were walking towards the house together through the slanting rain and the long wet grass. Derek was grateful for the rain, which masked his tears.

Chapter 13

The skeletal trees etched black against a leaden sky, the lake a chill muddy streak in the distance, the deck chairs long since put away for the winter. A hint of fog over Horse Guards Parade. Beside the path the leaves had been swept into large piles and would soon be removed in trucks or burned. St James's Park on an afternoon in early November. Derek and his father, who had both spent several hours with their solicitor, were crossing the park together. During the past two hours Derek had become considerably richer in purely financial terms. They had walked in silence since leaving Birdcage Walk.

If you were with me now, Diana, we would buy something to celebrate our good fortune, we would go out this evening to a restaurant of your choosing, and very likely see a film or a play also of your choice. Since you are no longer with me, I will do none of these things, not because I am incapable of making up my mind where to eat or which entertainment to choose, but because I have no inclination to go anywhere. Since the removals men came four months ago to take away your things, I have done very little. Sometimes I run out of clean shirts and often I wear socks that do not match. I eat scrappy meals and leave books scattered in every room of the flat. But, as we said, life goes on, the heart pumps and the bowels churn. Your going has left a hole in my life and I am unable to fill it, but my fears of personal extinction have faded. I hope you won't think me flippant, but yesterday I bought a brown herringbone suit and two silk ties; I have other purchases in mind. I may well go abroad next year and think it likely that I will have the flat redecorated. Before you went away I was frightened, but you've gone, and I still go on. I

161

have a strange feeling that I ended last summer but I can't have, can I? *Now* has little or no relation to *then*. In anticipation everything is always worse, and, although I do feel a bit like a dead man's toenails growing after their owner's death, I daresay the feeling will pass, or, if it doesn't, I'll get used to it. I hope you won't think me stupidly sentimental if I tell you that three weeks ago I found a hairbrush which you used to use, and, instead of throwing it away, I carefully extracted a number of your hairs and placed them in a match box. Hair is so much more tangible than words or thoughts, don't you think? Then a week ago I broke a cup which you often drank from. I have kept it and intend to glue the pieces together. I don't want to give the impression that I spend my time weeping, but neither do I leap laughing from room to room. So, Diana, when we have been apart for a little longer I shall write and say that if whim, loneliness, or lack of money ever leads you to consider returning to Abercorn Mansions, I would like you to do just that. Things could never be the same, which, I am sure you will agree, is just as well. My best guarantee of better behaviour is the fact that I no longer need you as I thought I did, so please accept my invitation as simple fondness with all old strings cut. There are no debts between us to be paid, which is never a bad basis for partnership.

How it rained last month, the wettest September for years and early on I lost my umbrella. November now and looks more like snow. My father's with me and unwittingly sends you his regards. That's all, I think.

Derek and Gilbert reached the lake and walked along beside it until they reached the bridge; there they stopped and looked at children throwing bread to the ducks in the water below. Derek watched the frantic struggle for crusts impassively. The seagulls undoubtedly were getting more than their fair share, largely because they managed to catch most of the bread in the air.

Please understand that only my fear of being thought guilty of emotional blackmail made me omit mentioning how I miss you in many ways; not just the absence of flowers in the flat, although I admit small things sometimes strike hardest; old shopping-lists found in a drawer ... Gilbert tugged impatiently at his son's sleeve, as they both leant against the metal balustrade of the bridge.

'Well, how do you feel? Not every day you get your hands on sixty thousand pounds.' The old man laughed throatily and made as if to clamber over the railings. 'You'll have to watch me; seven years I've got to live.' Gilbert paused and stared morosely at the muddy water. 'My God, if that money had come my way when I was your age.'

'What would you have done?' asked Derek.

'I'd have left the Malayan Civil Service for a start.'

'And then?'

The old man shrugged his shoulders and sighed. 'It's a bit late now.'

'Only for the more athletic forms of debauchery,' replied Derek with a smile.

'I might have made a passable Chinese scholar. Got together a decent collection of jade.'

Derek had been trying to trace the underwater journey of a tufted duck, but had finally lost track of it. Gilbert was looking at him expectantly.

'You want to know what I'll do with it.' Derek grimaced. 'I'll let you know when I've decided.'

They walked on past an old woman feeding crumbs to the pigeons and sparrows. Derek winked at his father and gave him a gentle nudge in the ribs.

'I'll buy a young Eurasian dirt cheap and use her body to satisfy the most bestial desires that whim can invent and my constitution can stand. Then I'll sell her at a profit and start a brisk business in eighteenth-century sado-masochistic erotica.' As they walked north towards the Mall, Derek told his father that he intended to grow his fingernails to an exorbitant length and disregard all forms of personal hygiene; that he would keep several wild animals in his sitting-room and sell their dung to market gardeners; that he would wear shoes with holes in them, dye his hair grey to get pensioners' rates in cinemas, and force friends to pay all his restaurant bills. He would most certainly die a millionaire and would then leave the money to a fund for destitute ministers of the crown.

Gilbert looked at him more with reproach than amusement. Derek wondered if he had wanted to discuss the best way to invest it and whether to go for annual income or maximum capital growth. It was hardly enough to retire on, whatever he did with it.

They had crossed the Mall and were climbing up Duke of York Steps, heading for Piccadilly Circus and the tube. To their right the office lights in Carlton House Terrace shone yellow in the fading light. Gilbert had to stop at the top of the steps to get his breath back. It was getting colder and their breath came in steamy clouds. Derek took his father's arm.

'I haven't any idea what I'm going to do with it. Diana once said I'd renounced the enjoyment of money. Perhaps I'd better start buying things to see what it feels like. I'll let you know, of course.'

They weren't far from Piccadilly Circus when Gilbert said, 'Not much point, you mean, if there's nobody to give things to.'

'Something like that.' He saw how crushed his father looked and added at once, 'I'm damned glad to have it, though. I don't have to say that, do I? Better to be rich and alone than poor and alone. Nobody to share it with. So? I might have nothing to share with nobody and that'd be a whole lot worse.'

'You're young, too,' put in Gilbert encouragingly.

'That's right. I've probably got another thirty years, so I'll have to do *something* with them. They'll go a bit slower if I don't.'

They were passing the offices of a shipping-line. A large-scale model of a liner, complete with cabins, portholes and lifeboats, took up most of the window. The pavements were crowded now and every so often they were separated.

'You could go round the world,' said Gilbert.

'Several times, I shouldn't wonder. I could spend the next ten years in constant motion. It's a thought.' A steady tide of people was forcing them towards the steps leading down into the tube.

164

Gilbert stepped to the edge of the pavement and asked with an attempt at jocular irony, 'You'll ring me soon?'

'Of course.'

'Two months or three?'

'It'll be soon, I promise.' Derek suddenly took his father by the arm and said, 'Let's go and get some tea somewhere.'

Three days before, a similar scene. Another tube station. Derek had taken Giles to a film. Giles had had to rush back afterwards. A friend dropping in, or so he'd said. Their parting had been so hurried that there had been no time to fix up the next meeting.

'If it isn't too much trouble,' muttered Gilbert.

'Trouble? Sixty thousand's worth a cup of tea, isn't it?' The joke had been intended to cheer up the old man, but it seemed to upset him. Derek suddenly felt guilty. 'We must celebrate. Dinner together. That Greek place near you.' They had reached the top of the steps and Derek was being pushed down by the pressure of numbers towards the ticket machines and the escalators. 'Eight o'clock,' he yelled. When he reached the bottom of the steps he remembered he had done his father out of his cup of tea.

The restaurant had only opened recently and the owner had spared neither time nor treasure when decorating it. Greek fabrics, goatskins, reproduction classical plates, musical instruments, dried gourds of various shapes, and framed travel posters covered every available inch of wall-space. Two tall vases of brightly coloured plastic flowers stood on each side of the entrance. Ironically, although the cook was Greek and the food authentic, the extravagant décor tended to keep away the would-be cognoscenti, who preferred the austerity of 'real' Greek restaurants with rough walls and oilcloth-covered tables.

After several glasses of wine, Gilbert's mood improved and soon he had become mellowly anecdotal, treating Derek to many old favourites. The Raja Bharu's funeral, when the mourners had forgotten which way round he was in his coffin and had had to take him out and unwind his grave clothes to make sure that he was buried facing Mecca. There were the three Javanese murderers who, when taken to execution, on seeing the ropes hanging from the beam, had stood on tiptoe just before the traps opened, since they assumed they would be pulled upwards. Then poor old Fred Dalton who spent an hour every evening writing his epic pornographic verse play with characters like Bollocks: a pair of hangers-on; Scrotum: a wrinkled retainer and his pal Scratchet. Gilbert himself had had his moments, like the time he'd been delirious with malaria and had seen a snake eating a frog on the lawn. With a cry of 'Save the frog', he had snatched up a knife, slipped and cut his hand so badly that it had had to be bandaged for two months. They both laughed a lot and drank more wine and said that it was a pity they didn't see more of each other, past mistakes notwithstanding. Derek felt a warm, self-approving sensation. His own problems were considerable, his life empty, his future uncertain and yet he still had it in him to give his father happiness. He hadn't intended to eat anything else but he changed his mind and ordered a sickly-looking Greek cake. If there was an off-licence open they might buy a bottle of liqueur and take it back to Gilbert's flat.

Gilbert was sipping Turkish coffee and Derek eating his cake, which was covered with a watery syrup. After a long silence Gilbert leant forward and said quietly, 'Not much fun being on one's own.'

'We all are,' Derek replied philosophically. 'In here,' he went on, tapping his skull. 'It's got to be faced.'

'Company can make quite a difference; ask anybody who's been in solitary confinement.'

Derek felt suddenly uneasy and apprehensive about what his father might be getting at.

'Come on,' he said with a laugh. 'Living alone's not solitary confinement. A man can live in an army barracks in the middle of hundreds of other men and still be lonely. So can married people.'

Gilbert put down his coffee cup and pursed his lips.

'You know what I mean. How many people are you seeing these days? A few because of work; but apart from that? You must have shared most of your friends with Diana. Awkward for them now. Asked you round once or twice, did they? Then nothing. I ought to know. When Margaret died I had a few sympathetic callers but sympathy doesn't last very long. I'm old too; a widower, just the sort of jovial fellow to make an evening swing along.'

'Rubbish,' countered Derek with too much emphasis. 'You've done all right this evening. I've hardly said a word and you've had me in stitches.'

'Quite an old card, aren't I? All right once a month for a funny story or two. He *made* their evening and went back to an empty flat.'

'That isn't at all what I meant.' Derek emptied his wine glass and sighed. 'Look, you're right. We don't see each other enough. Couldn't we fix up a regular evening every week?' His father's look of disappointment told Derek all he neeeded to know. Any moment now Gilbert would ask him directly and he knew quite well that he couldn't refuse. Undeniably alone himself, undeniably lonely. Sixty thousand was a fairly generous payment for a room and company. Derek sat back and placed his outstretched hands on the table. 'My flat or yours?' he asked.

'Yours is bigger,' his father replied without any pretence of being surprised or grateful. 'I'll let mine. The people on the ground floor have been trying to get a second-floor flat for years. We should be able to fix things up in a month or so.'

Derek nodded and said nothing. His coffee finished, Gilbert pushed back his chair. Nothing to stay for, thought Derek, as he paid the bill; the old man had got what he'd wanted without too much of a struggle and now he was ready for bed. As Derek was getting into a taxi his father said, 'You'd better come round and see what furniture you want me to bring. Tuesday evening?'

Derek smiled wryly. 'You might have suggested another day as well. No, I shan't be out on Tuesday or Wednesday or Thursday. Tuesday's fine.'

'Till then,' shouted Gilbert as the taxi drove off.

Chapter 14

December 10. Derek flicked the small wheel on his plastic desk calendar and turned winter into summer. Dates had become largely a matter of the past; the calendar itself had been a gift from Diana to insure that her husband never forgot days when she had arranged shopping expeditions, dinners, or other outings or festivities.

He stared across the manuscript room at the empty tables between the tall bookshelves and looked at his watch. Since it was Thursday, Professor Elkin would be arriving soon. There were two new PhDs doing research on the East India Company and the Opium War respectively, and an elderly woman who claimed to be writing a book about Sir Bartle Frere. There were not going to be any other readers in during the day, unless the visiting professor from Madras turned up. Derek wandered round the room, checking that most of the radiators were more or less at blood temperature—the best that could be expected. Having hung up his coat, he returned to his desk. Recently he had been so bored by his days at the Institute that he had contemplated sending a circular to a number of publishing houses suggesting that they drew to the attention of some of their more popular authors the controversial material in the archives. Eye-witness accounts of infanticide, voodoo, sutteeism, ritual murder, and religious excesses of every description, not to mention the odd colonial massacre and missionary scandal.

Derek started opening the day's mail, and quickly glanced through a letter from an American academic wanting to know about possible copyright problems on the Swettenham papers. The next letter was hand-written. 'Here's my address. Come and see me. If you've patched things up with Diana, don't bother. Angela (Vaughan).' Dear Angela, Considering the chaos you have wrought in my formerly predictable and peaceful life, do you think it likely that I should wish to see you? Dear Angela, Your letter came when I was so terribly in need of comfort, both mental, spiritual and sexual ... Derek was still pondering as he opened the next letter: 'Dear Sir, Your adamant refusal to accept the authenticity of my two letters written by Cecil Rhodes is completely at variance with the opinion of Dr Muldoon, whose opinion as you must be aware ..." Derek was re-reading Angela's letter when he heard the door opening and a second later saw Professor Elkin coming towards him. Elkin's normal routine was to hang up his coat, arrange his papers on his usual table and then write out numerous manuscript slips. Today he came straight up to Derek, who noticed that he looked irritable and worried. Derek stuffed Angela's letter into his breast pocket and looked up.

'I must ask you to come down to the archives with me,' the professor demanded authoritatively.

On coming in to the Institute that morning, Derek had been certain that the day would be as drearily predictable as most days were. He would have laughed heartily at the idea that any reader might involve him in any debate that would have more than the most transiently fleeting repercussions; and yet the proximity of Elkin's red and sweating face and his undoubted anger seemed likely to lead to an unusually involving dialogue. Derek smiled affably and said, 'I'm sure you must know, Professor, that no reader is allowed into the archives.'

Elkin rested his hairy hands on the table and looked down at Derek grimly.

'I have reason to believe that you are withholding documents from me.'

'What reason?' asked Derek innocently, knowing perfectly well that this confrontation had been inevitable ever since he had deliberately stopped Elkin getting hold of the private correspondence of the secretary to the Imperial British East Africa Company. Elkin was well aware that Derek was working on the same subject, and had been doing so for several years. For ten months since the donation of these precious documents, the archivist had kept quiet about them. They had been given by an elderly Scottish widow, who rarely visited London on account of steadily deteriorating sight. Derek listened while Elkin explained that on a trip to Edinburgh he had happened to meet a cousin of the lady in question; and this cousin had very understandably expressed surprise that the professor had not heard about the gift to the Afro-Asian Institute.

At first Derek inclined to let the angry scholar have his way, but then he changed his mind. He would lie, lose the key to the chest, fake a letter from the donor, do almost anything in his power to prevent Elkin getting his hands on the letters. Grown men should not be allowed to take such things so seriously. Derek wanted to tell Elkin how his own marriage had been destroyed by his work on East Africa, that the subject was lethal and should be avoided at all costs. The possession of sixty thousand pounds gave him confidence. For a moment he felt inclined to ask the professor offensive questions about his private life, or at least to call him a gorilla and to inform him that the dense hairs in his nostrils moved when he breathed. Instead, he removed his glasses and polished them carefully.

'The letters in question were given on condition that they are not made available until after the death of the donor.'

'You can substantiate this?' asked Elkin, looking momentarily shaken.

'You mean, do I have letters? The answer is no. Mrs Macdonald is nearly blind. When I suggested that she ought to send me a letter or her solicitor's instructions, she refused.'

Elkin nodded knowingly.

'How very convenient.' He paused and smiled unpleasantly. 'I see that I shall have to talk to the lady in person.'

'By all means,' replied Derek. 'I ought perhaps to tell you that she lives in Inverness.'

'If necessary I shall go there,' replied the professor resolutely.

Half-an-hour after Elkin's departure Derek was making notes for his letter to the Director. Then he wrote on another sheet of paper: 'This clock was donated to the Institute by readers of this library as a token of their gratitude for the dedicated services of D. E. Cushing. Chief Archivist 1964-1973.' He screwed up the paper and reapplied himself to his letter of resignation. A few minutes later he brought down his fist on the table and shouted aloud in the empty room, 'I'm damned if I will. They can sack me.'

By midday the three other readers he had expected were all working diligently at different tables, and Derek himself was getting on with the work he had been doing the previous day: explanatory notes to go with a series of letters written by H. M. Stanley between 1875 and 1888. The third in the pile was one written from The Grafton Hotel, St Lawrence-on-Sea, Ramsgate. Headed paper with a very fine picture of the hotel, a vast neo-gothic structure with a tall tower and various minor pinnacles and numerous arched windows. In front of the hotel people were walking on the beach. Beneath the picture, on three separate scrolls, was the following description: 'The climate of St Lawrence is largely recommended by the Medical Profession for its health-giving properties. Famous for its complete system of Baths, comprising Turkish, Ozone (most efficacious in all cases of Rheumatism, Gout &c), Salt Water Plunge, Hot and Cold Sea Water, Sitz, Douche, Electric, &c., &c. A medical rubber in attendance.'

Derek picked up the phone and dialled a number.

'Directory enquiries? Good. I'd like a number for the Grafton Hotel, St Lawrence-on-Sea, Ramsgate.' After a short wait he was surprised to hear that the hotel was still in business. He jotted down the phone number on a scrap of paper and pocketed it. Then he started reading the letter: 'On Saturday the Doctor brought me down here for a change of air—I have made rapid progress but it will be several days yet before the system can be said to have regained its former tone & vigour. . . .'

Derek read on, making occasional notes. He was going through his seventh letter when his phone rang and he heard Giles's voice. His form was being taken to the Science Museum and could Derek meet him somewhere afterwards since the Institute was so close? Derek suggested the Natural History Museum instead of the Institute since he knew how keen Giles had always been to visit the Fossil Rooms. He was a little disappointed when the boy simply asked him to be there at quarter to five and made no comment on the venue. But Derek wasn't depressed for long. He hadn't heard from Giles for almost three weeks, and although he hadn't believed his son had stopped thinking about him, there had been moments of anxiety: visions of Diana ripping the phone from his hands and weeping whenever the boy mentioned seeing his father; Diana suggesting films as a diversion, working slowly but persistently at undermining her son's affection for his absent father. Derek smiled at the folly of such melodramatic thoughts. Giles had simply been waiting for the right time and, as soon as that time had come along, he had got in touch at once. Now there was no question of the embarrassing performance of making a special occasion of it. Derek looked at his watch and willed time onwards. His trouble with Elkin seemed very much less important.

A fine drizzle had misted his glasses by the time Derek reached the imposing wrought-iron gates of the museum. Drops of water fell heavily from the tall plane trees, making the rain seem worse than it was. But neither the darkness, the rain, nor the fumes of the slowly-moving traffic in the Cromwell Road could do anything to reduce Derek's happy anticipation. Several yards from the ornate entrance archway was a notice: 'No ice creams to be taken beyond this point', and near it another sign forbidding the feeding of pigeons. Derek smiled to himself. He would amuse Giles by telling him that the authorities were alarmed by the thought of pigeons becoming the recipients of discarded ice creams.

He looked up at the dark soaring twin towers above the entrance. As a child, the extravagant architecture of the place had overwhelmed and alarmed him; the rows of grotesque animal gargoyles staring out from beneath the upper windows, and, inside, in cold echoing halls, the vast skeletons of dinosaurs, stark against stained-glass windows and gothic arches, had seemed

172

more terrifying than instructive. But with Giles's affection for the museum, Derek had undergone a change of heart. He liked the way the atmosphere of the building could change so suddenly.

When he'd started on his wait he had peered into the main exhibition hall and seen streams of schoolchildren milling about shouting and chattering, giving him the illusion that the museum with its high iron-vaulted roof was a huge Victorian railway station and the children passengers waiting for a long-expected school train. But now, as Derek stood under the archway, the children were leaving, laughing, pushing each other, shoving notepads into pockets, buttoning raincoats as they went. Soon the exhibition halls were quiet and the railway station, with its arches and columns, had become a medieval cathedral filled with strange relics.

Fifteen minutes passed without Derek becoming worried. The master had obviously kept them in the Science Museum longer than Giles had expected. After another five minutes Derek felt momentarily irritated, but to become too concerned about twenty minutes outside a museum in which was recorded the passing of several hundred million years seemed petty. If Giles had been kept waiting he would have gone inside and wandered round the Fossil Rooms. Derek pushed open one of the two doors and went inside. Giles was an intelligent boy; he'd know that rather than do nothing, his father would look at things. The Fossil Rooms were on the ground floor immediately to the right of the entrance. Derek intended to walk round them fairly briskly and then return to the entrance.

As he walked Derek occasionally glanced at an exhibit. 'Lower Jaw Fragment of the Dinosaur Megalosaurus: Middle Jurassic'. The possessor of the jaw had once lived a few miles outside Oxford. A few yards away there was an artist's impression of the London area in the Lower Eocene Period. Wide swamps, interspersed with belts of tropical rain forest, not unlike Malayan jungle. Large reptiles, some with wings, lived in this steaming landscape. Around Bournemouth and Southampton there would have been mangrove swamps. Then there was the elephant found by some Royal Marines near Chatham in 1911—or what was left of the elephant; it had lived and died there a million years before. There was the picture of Mary Anning, a fat middle-aged carpenter's daughter from Lyme Regis who found the first skeleton of an ichthyosaurus. After a cursory glance at the gigantic skeleton of Diplodocus Carnegii, eighty-four feet long and with a brain estimated to have been no larger than a hen's egg, Derek headed back for the entrance.

Still no Giles and the rain had become harder, slanting in under the archway and running in rivulets down the steps. The notice about ice creams, the animal gargoyles and the scale of the building all seemed less amusing. It was half-past five and in another fifteen minutes the staff would be ushering members of the public out into the rain. The large lamps above the gates picked out the bare branches of the overhanging trees and cast reflections on the wet pavingstones. Derek felt bitter and lonely. The traffic flowed westwards; people returning to warm, well-lit homes and happy families. He had decided to wait five minutes more when he saw Giles hurrying towards him up the steps. Only pride made him look sternly at his son; in fact Derek's anger had gone and all he felt was affection and relief: humiliating happiness. He was touched to notice how flustered and disconcerted his son seemed to be. No point in making a thing of his lateness. Derek smiled and said, 'Come on. We'd better get going. They'll be turfing everyone out in a quarter of an hour.'

Giles looked down at the steps. He hadn't come in out of the rain.

'I can't,' he stammered.

'That's absurd.' Derek took his son's arm and guided him under the shelter of the archway. 'Would you rather go somewhere else?'

'I meant I can't stay to do anything.'

'That's a bit much, Giles. I hadn't meant to say anything about it but I have been standing here getting on for an hour.'

'I know. I feel awful. Mummy came to the Science Museum. She hadn't told me she was coming to collect me. She's got tickets

174

for some Christmas show. A musical, I think; and if I don't go now we'll be late. I'd forgotten.'

'Damn the bloody show. Tell her you don't want to go. I'll take you another time.'

Giles looked desperate.

'I can't tell her that. She's bought the tickets and lined up supper somewhere. Everything's arranged.'

'It can be unarranged.'

Giles started running down the steps but Derek caught him at the bottom and held him firmly by the hand.

'Please don't go,' he whispered, regretting the pleading tone at once. Giles paused for a second or two as if undecided but then pulled away his hand and hurried through the gates. It was a moment before Derek realized he was holding one of the boy's gloves. He ran after him but there was no sign on the pavement. A large car was pulling away; a large opulent car. Derek looked around in case he had missed his old familiar saloon but there was no car like it to be seen. The rain had already plastered down his hair and soon he could feel water dripping down behind his collar. He started walking to the tube. There would be little point waiting for a taxi on such a rainy night.

The lights were on in Derek's flat in Abercorn Mansions, so he knew that his father was in. Gilbert had moved in at the end of the previous week. Derek had lent his father his key so he had to ring the bell.

'Good God, you're wet,' said Gilbert, throwing open the door.

'It's raining,' said Derek.

'That's a relief anyway,' chuckled the old man. 'I shouldn't have liked to think of you swimming in your clothes.'

Derek dumped his coat on the back of a chair and went into the sitting-room where he flopped onto the sofa. Gilbert had followed him into the room. Derek noticed that his father was wearing a green apron, his cooking uniform.

'I'd expected you back earlier. Been anywhere?'

'The Natural History Museum.'

'Skeletons and stones,' said Gilbert after a pause.

'That's the place.'

'Not for me. At my age skeletons are a bit near the bone, if you'll excuse the expression.' He waited for Derek to react but when his joke was greeted with silence he left the room. A minute or so later he returned with a towel.

'Thought you might like to dry your hair.'

'It can dry itself.'

'Up to you.' Gilbert paused and then went on briskly, 'I've bought you a present. It was your birthday last Thursday but I forgot it.'

'That makes two of us.'

'*Made* two of us. I've remembered now.' Gilbert fetched an oblong box from the sideboard and handed it to Derek. 'I thought it'd be a bit much to wrap it up specially since it isn't your birthday.'

'Very sensible.' Derek opened the box and saw an electric carving-knife. He wanted to put it on the floor and stamp on it. Instead he put the lid on again and said, 'I'm sure we'll find it most useful.'

'Of course it's a bit gadgety but it works incredibly well. I've tried it out on that cold beef. Sliced it up like butter. Amazing, considering how jagged the blades are. Surprisingly enough it can't cope with cake. I bought a fruit cake and it made an awful hash of it. I expect it needs grease to lubricate it.'

'I expect you're right.'

'You can have a shot with it yourself later on. I've got a duck.'

Derek imagined carving up furniture with it, slicing through floors, walls and window frames. A present from my father. Goes through anything except fruit cake. He picked up the towel and started to dry his hair. When he'd finished he got up and poured two glasses of whisky. Gilbert took his and said, 'Many happy returns of last Thursday.'

When they had toasted Derek's forgotten birthday, Gilbert said, 'You seem a bit down. What sort of a day have you had?'

'I've almost certainly lost my job; my son's rejected me. Otherwise it's been an average sort of day, wetter than some and not as wet as others.' He saw the sympathy in his father's face and ended simply, 'About as bad as it could have been. Being ironic at your expense won't make it much better. I'm sorry.'

Gilbert looked at the floor. 'I wish you'd told me straight away and hadn't let me go on about that stupid knife.'

'Well, I didn't.' He got up and poured himself another drink. 'I was going to meet Giles at the museum, and while I waited with the fossils, the banal but comforting thought occurred to me that my job didn't matter at all, that my work was utterly without importance, that most work is the same and that men are not remembered for the numerous ball-bearings they produce or even for the erudite articles they write. My graveside won't be lined with weeping archivists and lecturers; there may be a friend or two, there may not, but one person will be there: my son, whom I love. So what sort of a father I am means a thousand times more than what sort of a scholar. And so I waited for Giles with optimism. I didn't feel oppressed by the knowledge of my tiny life-span in the vast wastes of time. With love the lamp that lights us through the darkness of countless millennia, why should I be afraid? Fossils may come and go but love endures.' Derek took a gulp of whisky. 'That was roughly how I reasoned it out in the Fossil Rooms of the Natural History Museum. And then Giles came and said that his mother had arranged some show and he was sorry to have kept me waiting for nothing and off he went.' Derek put down his glass on the table and smiled at Gilbert. 'It was a bit worse than that really because, you see, I begged him not to go, and when I'd begged him, he went; went quickly too, leaving his glove in my hand. What could I tell the fossils after that? Love endures?'

Gilbert rested a hand on Derek's shoulder.

'Giles can't know what life's like for you at the moment. All he knew was that if he didn't go to the show with his mother she'd be cross for weeks. Since he lives with her and not with you, he made the easiest choice. You might have done the same.'

'Whether I've been temporarily stood up or thoroughly rejected, I *feel* rejected and you can be as sensible as a sensible man can on a sensible day but it won't make the blindest bit of difference.'

They didn't use the electric knife to carve with, and although the duck was good they didn't enjoy supper much, which was a pity because Gilbert had gone to a lot of trouble preparing it and had made old-fashioned syllabub for pudding.

Later in the evening, when looking for a biro, Derek pulled Angela's letter out of his pocket and with it a folded piece of paper with the telephone number of The Grafton Hotel, Ramsgate. He examined both for several minutes and then went out to the phone. Having booked a double room at The Grafton for the following Saturday, now only two days off, Derek sat down to write to Angela.

> Dear Angela,
>
> Perhaps instead of my coming to see you at your flat, you could come to the sea with me on Saturday (the day this letter reaches you)? The Grafton Hotel, Victoria Parade, Ramsgate is palatial in appearance and was, when Henry Stanley stayed there, eighty-six years ago, very well equipped. I'm afraid I rather childishly booked a room for us in Mr Stanley's name. (By the way he went there to get rid of an attack of gastritis: inflammation of the walls of the stomach.) The trains to Ramsgate are frequent and if you could send a telegram (Mr Stanley) about which train you'll be on, I'll meet you at the station. This is an arbitrary invitation given at short notice, but time gives too much opportunity for thinking which I have done a lot of in the past to no good effect. I shall go in any case since I need a change of everything.　　　　　　　　　　　　　　　　Derek.

After placing his letter in an envelope, Derek went to bed. His unhappiness had lifted a little. During the night he dreamed that he shot Professor Elkin while they were both on the Emin Pasha Relief Expedition.

Chapter 15

Apart from knowledge of its position on Kent's eastern extremity, Derek's information about Ramsgate was based on three facts: Victoria, Princess Victoria at the time, had caught typhoid on a holiday there in 1835; Frith had painted his minutely detailed picture of the crowds on Ramsgate Sands some years later; and H. M. Stanley had stayed there on doctor's orders in 1886.

From these facts taken together, Derek concluded that Ramsgate had been a sought-after resort throughout the Victorian Age. Taken individually, the facts made others seem likely. Victoria's illness was proof that local sanitation had been bad in the 1830s; but since the Prince Consort had been killed by the drains at Windsor Castle thirty years later, conditions at Ramsgate were unlikely to have been exceptionally bad at the time of the royal visit. The fact of the royal visit was evidence, drains notwithstanding, that Ramsgate had been popular for many years before that, probably since the turn of the century. This made the existence of Georgian and Regency houses likely. Frith's picture, unless inaccurately named *Ramsgate Sands*, led Derek to discount a rocky or pebbly beach. Since Stanley was sent to Ramsgate to get rid of a gastric complaint, it was almost certain that the Ramsgate drains had been much improved during the fifty years since Victoria's attack of typhoid. *Sewage Disposal in Victorian Seaside Towns: A Deductive History* by D. Cushing MA, PhD. With such thoughts Derek amused himself in the train.

Other thoughts called for attention. There was the question of what to say to Angela and how to behave towards her. How had she interpreted his letter? A great many interpretations seemed possible. Deserted by his wife, half-witted with lust and tormented by night-starvation, Derek suggests instant intercourse but dresses it up as a pretentious seaside fantasy. Derek, a lonely and embittered man, wishes to remind the girl whom he blames for his marital rupture that she has wrecked his life; to drive home the pathos of his story, he dreams up the backcloth of an out-of-season resort. Made thoroughly irresponsible and whimsical by repeated traumas, Derek wants me to go to the sea for no better reason than the arrival of my letter while he is reading an item about a murder in Ramsgate. Derek wants me to help him re-create a touching love affair, which blossomed on a childhood holiday at Ramsgate. His wife gone, the archivist consoles himself with his work and burrows deeper and deeper into the past. Convinced at last that he is a well-known nineteenth-century explorer, he writes unstable letters to numerous women and begins a compulsive series of journeys to hotels and houses where the explorer stayed.

Derek obviously likes me a lot and wants to start a permanent relationship in a memorable way. I have no idea what's going on in his head, but unless he's raving, it could be an amusing weekend. Derek is witty, courageous and sexy and I love him enormously. If he asked me to meet him in Botswana I would go at once. On the whole Derek believed that she would come. He had, after all, left her little opportunity for refusal. During the morning, before his departure, he had left the phone off the hook.

When he saw the harbour, Derek paid off the taxi driver and got out. Apparently he was now less than half a mile from the hotel. It was nearly four o'clock. Across the wide bay to the west of the town, he could see, rising from the isolated chimneys of a power station, smoke delicately tinted pink by the sinking sun. A slight mist was forming over the sea.

He walked up from the twin quays of the harbour and soon found himself in a perfect Regency crescent. The paint was flaking but the porches and balconies were almost all intact. He passed along several similar streets and decided that he liked Ramsgate. A little farther on he reached a long elevated esplanade and looked down sixty or seventy feet to a muddle of amusement arcades strung out along the beach. In the distance, above the roofs of the deserted fun land, a sign in dead neon letters caught his eye: *Nero's Casino.*

From a distance the gigantic silhouette of the Grafton looked strikingly like the picture on the writing paper. The tower was still standing, the spiky line of pinnacles and pointed roofs was still the same, so too the long first-floor conservatory. Yet almost from the moment he saw the place, Derek felt uneasy. There were lights in a number of windows, so it wasn't deserted, but something was definitely wrong. Drawing closer, he saw that on the ground floor, where dining-rooms, ballrooms and bars should have been brightly lit, there was almost total darkness.

When he reached the main doors, nicely polished doors with solid brass handles, he peered into a large panelled hall lit by a single dim bulb. He walked between white columns to the foot of the stairs and saw a large board: GRAFTON HOUSE, *156 Residential Service Flats*, and below a list of names.

Derek walked outside again. To the right of Grafton House, built onto the side of the tower, and set back several yards, was a modern building. Derek had no difficulty making out the illuminated sign over the wide plate-glass doors: THE GRAFTON HOTEL. He was still feeling irritated and disappointed when he started laughing. Standing by himself in the growing darkness, he went on laughing for several minutes. It had been outrageous to suppose that a place the size of Grafton House could have kept going in a small resort like Ramsgate. Derek had imagined being shown the old steam rooms and ozone baths, had seen himself eating thin slices of bread and butter in a forest of aspidistras and palms, had almost heard the large brass gong summoning the handful of guests to dinner. And all of it pure fantasy. The steam baths would be used as storage cellars, the piping and boilers would have been ripped out and sold long before the last war. There was no call for feeling maudlin about what had been inevitable from the moment the upper-middle class had taken to continental travel between the wars.

A small nylon Christmas tree was shimmering on the receptionist's desk. Muted music filled the room. The walls were strik-

ingly papered with a red and black abstract design which con-
trasted with the plain grey carpet. The chairs and sofas were
upholstered in navy blue. But although the red on the walls was
still a strong red and the navy of the chairs true navy, the place
looked tired already. Here and there the wallpaper was coming
away, and the backs of the chairs looked a little too shiny.

Behind the desk the girl was reading a book.

'I booked a room. Name of Stanley.'

The girl flicked over the pages of a large diary.

'Number seven, Mr Stanley. Would you like to see it now?'

The girl was worried that he had no case. He could see her
looking over his shoulder to see whether he had parked a car
outside.

'I may go out for a bit first. I don't need to see the room.'

'Most people like to.' She sounded suspicious. Possibly
suicides were the only guests uninterested in their rooms. A full
orchestra had started *Moon River*. Derek couldn't see any of the
speakers. The noise seemed to come from overhead.

'Have there been any messages for me?'

'I've just come on.'

'Could you look?'

She searched through some papers on a shelf under the desk
and lifted up a telegram. Her eyes narrowed and she went red.

'Yes?' said Derek.

'Sir Henry Stanley KCB?'

'GCB.'

'Sorry?'

'It's much the same sort of thing.'

She handed him the telegram and he ripped it open.

IF KNIGHTHOOD PREMATURE SORRY MR
STANLEY STOP YOUR PHONE DEAD STOP
IMPOSSIBLE COME GOOD REASON HONEST STOP
WANTED TO BE WITH MR STANLEY AT THE
SEA STOP

The girl had watched him while he read the telegram and was

looking at him expectantly. Derek folded the paper carefully and placed it in his pocket. He inclined his head a little and murmured, 'I have to be elsewhere.'

On the esplanade the words of a telegram which he wouldn't send came to him: BECAUSE IT COULDN'T BE AS IT SHOULD HAVE BEEN—BETTER THAT IT NEVER WAS STOP

Derek felt deep disappointment but would not dignify it with self-pity and unhappiness. Doubtless her reason for refusing was good: a dying mother, father, uncle, granny, dog, cat, or other domestic companion. A swollen ovary or foot. An infectious skin disease or long-awaited evening with a favourite Nobel prize winner. Perhaps a combination of such reasons. No cause for wounded pride; she'd wanted to come. No rejection after all; just inconvenience and bathos. The actor enters with rhetoric and flourish and the lights fuse. Under the scrutiny of television cameras the scalpel melts like heated plastic as the famous surgeon prepares to make his first incision. The concert pianist plays the opening notes with artistic gusto and finds his fingers firmly stuck to the keys. Those long familiar with such things do not laugh but look away and pass on by. Derek began to walk. Only a quarter to five and already it was dark.

In a small garden in front of Grafton House Derek made out the outline of a statue. He went to examine it. A. W. N. Pugin 1812-1852. The famous architect's hair was snow white with accumulated seagull's droppings. His sightless eyes stared out through the thickening mist towards the French coast. Derek set out for the station.

Alone in his compartment Derek watched the lights of Ramsgate, Broadstairs and Margate grow indistinct. A bend in the track extinguished them. Derek imagined Professor Elkin on the night-train on his way to Inverness. He imagined Giles and Diana playing an intimate game of chess. If Angela had come, the following day would have brought back the old problems. But respite, however brief, was not negligible. And if here and now had lived vividly enough to shut out tomorrow, that would have meant more achieved than a weekend's anaesthetic. A precedent for other isolated days when past regrets and future wishes could be thrown out of doors.

It would have been so right if she had come; so easy and so right. A special time made by circumstances and not by effort. The mist, the residential service flats, the new hotel and white-haired Mr Pugin overlooking *Nero's Casino*. Nor did such randomly engineered chances come often. Without that picture of the hotel there would have been no invitation. Possibly he would never again achieve such planned lack of planning. He had probably been as surprised by his invitation as she had. And yet an hour and a half after his arrival he was on his way home.

There hadn't been many special times for years now. Ten years ago they'd happened every now and then, fifteen and twenty quite frequently. One or two even happened with Charles, when they'd been friends and not long-standing acquaintances. They'd been twenty or twenty-one. Charles had borrowed a friend's father's cottage for a weekend. Two girls with them. A bright January morning in a Norfolk market town. Sex still as new and intriguing as Charles's first car. The plastic washing-up basin at the cottage had perished, so they chose another. Derek had just bought a frozen chicken. He had started tossing it high in the air, catching it in the basin. A crash as the rock-hard bird smashed through the blue plastic like a stone through glass. The most perfectly funny thing that had ever happened, at the time.

The train was crossing the bridge over the Medway; the lights of Rochester reflected in the black water. Derek took the telegram from his pocket and read it again. He paused over the last sentence. WANTED TO BE WITH MR STANLEY AT THE SEA. Derek had brought photostat copies of several letters written by Stanley during 1886, the year in which he had spent his brief stay at Ramsgate. He had intended showing them to Angela. Now as the train sped on, he pulled them from his overcoat pocket and read them by himself. Poor Stanley, back from the Congo and waiting in vain for Leopold of Belgium to offer new work. In 1887 he would find a different challenge but no

184

help to him the year before in London or resting by the sea. He wanted marriage, but the man who'd founded the Congo Free State and traced that river from its upper reaches to the sea didn't dare ask any woman in case he was refused. A workhouse childhood lived with him still, with all its humiliations. At seventeen he'd slept several nights with a girl in New Orleans. She'd been scruffy and had short hair. He'd thought she was a boy. When he'd seen her breasts he'd become confused. Weren't they painful? he asked. They seemed to be swollen and inflamed by boils. His own chest was not like that.

And at forty-five Stanley had got no further with women to judge from the letter Derek was reading. 'I have found a young lady whom I can appreciate, but whether she can win me over & above Conventional Platonism is very doubtful. I don't believe she exists who can do that.' Another letter written three months before: 'My timidity is unconquerable. To propose and be refused would be my death. Were I assisted by a good friend to push me forward at the back I might venture. I am rich enough to keep half-a-dozen economically—I am in perfect despair. There is one I know that I should be tempted to propose to, but my timidity will prevent it.' At fifty, after the end of the Emin Pasha Expedition which brought Stanley more fame than his meeting with Livingstone, he at last found the courage to propose. He was surprised to be accepted.

Derek stuffed the letters back into his pocket. They were passing through South London now. He shut his eyes and saw Stanley sitting despondently by himself eating his lunch in Grafton House. Afterwards an hour in the ozone bath and then a walk down the esplanade under a cold March sky before coming back for a solitary tea.

In the tube on his way home to Abercorn Mansions, Derek realized that he no longer felt depressed. He would be jolly with his father and tell him the air had done him good. You didn't stay long. Anything go wrong? Nothing at all. I drank in the essence of the place and left. Could any man have done more? Very likely his father would tell him the story about his aunt Nadine who had been driving in an open car on a road skirting the Sandwich

Golf Club when a golf ball unexpectedly removed the tip of her nose. She held it in place and it was stitched on later. In cold weather a thin blue line showed where the skin had been broken. You went to Ramsgate? Really. Well, my aunt Nadine lost her nose in Sandwich just along the coast. As the tube came into Marble Arch, Derek surprised his fellow passengers with a sudden fit of laughter.

Chapter 16

Although the shops were filled with turkeys, Father Christmases, and many seasonal gifts and greeting cards, Professor Elkin was unhappy. He sat at his table in the Institute on the Tuesday before Christmas and informed Derek with appropriate gloom that Alice Macdonald had died three days earlier in an Inverness nursing-home. At first Derek had been unable to think who Alice Macdonald was and why Elkin should have been telling him about her demise, but then he remembered. The professor was unhappy, not because he had any personal feelings about the late Mrs Macdonald, but because her death put Derek in the clear. It would now be impossible to determine whether the deceased had intended, during her lifetime, to deny readers of the Afro-Asian Institute a sight of the letters she had donated. On the credit side, Derek would keep his job; on the debit side, Elkin would have to see the letters. There would now be no point in trying to outdo the professor in a purely scholarly work on the same period of East African history.

Some minutes later Derek became excited. He would write a popular book around five of the more dramatic protagonists: Stanley, Lugard, de Winton, MacKinnon and Johnston. Call it something like *The Imperial Adventure* or *British, Christian and White*. Away with the careful drudgery of a serious analysis of cultural differences, social, political and economic conditions in Europe and Africa and enter with flourish five men in a new continent. At once an introduction calculated to madden all his colleagues was forming in Derek's brain. He would start with Marx's famous statement: 'History does nothing, it possesses no immense wealth, fights no battles. It is rather man, real living man who does everything, who possesses and fights.' This book is an examination of the impact of a few men on a vast and little-known continent and an attempt to understand how they felt and why they acted as they did. I shall not insist on calling it history but will leave my readers to apply whatever label they like. Labels do not interest me much and I will waste no time in speculating about the degree to which individuals can be seen as distinct from groups or classes. Such distinctions on journeys of exploration become largely academic.

The book should be lavishly illustrated and glossily produced. Possibly it would become a best-seller. Derek was still exultant and enthusiastic when he rang Diana later that morning to suggest a meeting over the holiday. Something he jokingly compared with the brief Christmas truce of 1914; jokingly, so that he would not be forced to take offence if she refused.

'Why not both come over?' he said. 'If that's no good, we could go out somewhere, or if you don't want to come yourself, perhaps Giles could come on his own.'

Silence on the line for a little and then Diana's voice, flattened and depersonalized by the wires and the receiver, saying, 'We're going abroad. Turkey. Giles is looking forward to it.' A pause while she waited for his objection; he made none. 'I'm not being unreasonable. Now I'm working I can only get away at holiday time.'

'Since he's with you all the time, I thought he might come and be with me at Christmas.'

'Wouldn't the following weekend be as good?'

'No.'

'Why?'

'It isn't Christmas.' No answer from Diana, although Derek could imagine her expression. 'On the subject of Christmas,' he went on, 'what should I do with Christmas cards sent to both of us? I had thought of cutting them in half and sending you one of the bits. I suppose I could send every other card.'

'I can understand how you feel, Derek, but you really ought to have said something earlier about wanting to have Giles with you. I'm not telepathic.'

188

After a silence Derek said, 'Are things all right?'

'Yes. How about you?'

'I'm going to have that operation for piles. In February. The hospital sent me a letter.'

'I'll come and see you.'

'Not before that?'

'I'd like to leave it a bit.'

'That's that, then,' he replied emphatically.

'You do understand how I feel?' she asked gently.

'No I don't,' he shouted. 'I don't understand at all,' and he slammed down the receiver. Just a phone call, he told himself, but all his earlier exultation had gone. The time to have written a popular book would have been when she was still with him. Now the idea seemed trivial and useless. If he wanted to show historians like Elkin what he thought of them, there were easier and less time-consuming ways than writing a monumentally unprofessional book. Send them obscene letters, dance naked round the manuscript room on a crowded day on the pretext of re-creating a Papuan fertility ceremony; simple too to make an indecent suggestion to the young woman working on the Dutch East India Company. Let me fondle your folios, as the archivist said to the actress.

Derek was still depressed when he met his father for tea in an ABC off the Bayswater Road. Gilbert was sitting on the far side of the room at a table by himself. Derek passed along the self-service counter and selected a packet of biscuits and a glass of milk. Coming up to his father's table, he noticed that the old man was sitting next to a small Christmas tree; since it was resting on a chair and was without any decorations, Derek assumed that Gilbert had bought it. Before he could make sure of this, an elderly couple two tables away started shouting at each other. The man was well dressed and had a venerable white beard.

'You're coming home,' the woman was bellowing.

'I'm not. No, I'm not. I'm never coming home,' he yelled back.

The woman started poking at him with her blunt stumpy little umbrella but he stayed where he was, shouting, 'Never, never, never.'

Gilbert went on eating a sausage roll while he watched. The manageress came up and talked quietly to the old man, who stopped shouting. Then his wife—Derek thought she was his wife—told the manageress that the old fool couldn't control his bladder.

'Sometimes he does it in the street; goes out into the Fulham Road in his nightshirt and does it against trees like a dog.'

A little later the man started moaning and allowed his wife to lead him out. Derek, who felt slightly sick, was surprised to see that his father was quite unaffected.

'They ought to live in the country,' Gilbert said unemotionally. 'More trees and fewer passers-by.'

'Talking about trees,' said Derek, pointing at the Christmas tree next to Gilbert, 'is that yours?'

'It is.'

'Why did you buy it?' asked Derek quietly, opening his packet of biscuits. He imagined travelling home in the tube with his father; saw branches of the tree sticking in people's eyes, getting caught in the doors, causing all manner of trouble.

'I wanted it. Don't you ever want things?'

'Of course.'

'It's important to do things, however routine they may be. We couldn't have ignored the time of year, sat in the flat refusing to admit that it's Christmas because of how things are.'

'We could have listened to the carols on the radio.'

'Not the same at all.' Gilbert paused to sip lukewarm tea. 'A tree demands attention. I've bought bells and bobbles to hang on it. You can help me if you like.'

Derek finished his milk and stared at the stained table-top. I shall never forget the simple pleasure he got out of that last Christmas; I can see him so clearly standing back with sparkling eyes to admire his finished work. Father and son together again for a family Christmas like Christmases of long ago. The happiness recaptured, the past living in the present in a way that brought tears to the eyes. Over the turkey they discuss the step-mother who brought them to blows and the unhappiness they caused each other. By the time the spry septuagenarian has placed a flaming helping of Christmas pudding before his son of nearly forty summers, they have arrived, via paper hats and crackers, at a deeper understanding of themselves and others, a greater compassion for mutual failings and a determination to bring to the coming year the fruits of their new awareness. The Christmas spirit has come to 36 Abercorn Mansions.

Gilbert had opened a small box and taken out a silver bell which he held up between finger and thumb. He looked at Derek for some sign of approval and getting none replaced it with a sigh. Sour, ungenerous Derek, lifeless loveless Derek, sitting in an ABC eating biscuits and drinking milk.

'Let's look at them,' he said, taking the box and pretending interest. That's what should be done: the stubborn assertion of zest for life in the face of a wife's desertion and a son's forgetfulness. Why, on the way here I picked up a glove in the gutter and so great was my curiosity and interest that I was able to re-create the owner almost as though I knew her, age, sex, income, married or single. I do it the whole time in tubes and buses; observe people and lovingly note their little mannerisms and gestures. Just the same in the country; as I walk through fields my wide interest in birds, insects, grasses, herbs and trees makes each path and track a potential delight. Derek turned over a green ball in his hand, seeing the distorted reflection of the tea-room mirrored on its shining surface. He laid out other bells, bobbles and balls on the table.

'They'll look splendid. Splendid.'

Gilbert seemed pleased; so pleased that he produced a carrier-bag and fished out a yellow sweater.

'I bought you this. Not really a proper present, so you might as well have it now.'

Derek took it and held it up against his chest. Then he took off his coat and jacket and put the sweater on.

'Not a bad fit,' said Gilbert.

'Excellent,' replied Derek, thinking of another Christmas nearly thirty years earlier; himself unwrapping a red Indian suit with an

191

animal's head on the chest; a pink flap of material for the tongue and sequins for the eyes. Derek with a feathered head-dress on, standing in front of a mirror, flipping the tongue up and down. Then running whooping from room to room. Sudden vision of Derek now, singing like a canary in his yellow sweater to the amazement of other tea-eaters. Other Christmases: 'D. Cushing made the best Virgin Mary for years, although his halo was a little too large.' Derek discovered by Margaret rifling his stocking the day before Father Christmas was due to deliver it. He must have jogged the table, because a moment later one of the bells fell on the floor and smashed.

Back at the flat Gilbert looked for and failed to find a reel of cotton to tie on the decorations with. Later Derek went out for a walk.

The shops were still open and the pavements were crowded with people returning from work. Derek passed the phone box where he had sweated so profusely while waiting for Diana to make a journey which she never made. He sat down on the bench where he had eaten his lunch on that same day. In spite of his yellow sweater he felt cold. Many lights shone warmly in Abercorn Mansions as Derek recalled returning from work on a multitude of similar winter evenings. With a conscious effort he stopped remembering and tried to think of the future, but the more he tried the less clearly he felt able to construct anything or even to imagine a time several months ahead. A summer holiday with his father? Another year in the Institute? His father's question came back to him: Don't you *want* anything? Without wishes there could be no future, no possibility of change.

He got up and started walking, making deliberate efforts to avoid the cracks between the paving stones; that was an aim after all. If I avoid the cracks for a hundred yards my rectum will be cured spontaneously without the aid of surgery. A wish too, an expression of superstitious faith; faith of a sort. The same old game, rationalize everything and so deny that anything can touch one; defuse emotions and fears like dangerous bombs. Distance the world and it has no effect upon one; but distance the world and one has no impact on it either; and with no impact, no

192

reality; reducing present and future to a dream without shape or content. Too much power politics, too much bureaucracy, too much psychology, too much passivity and bang goes will power; far easier to become grovelling worshippers of determinism.

Avoiding the cracks between the paving-stones involved a careful scrutiny of the pavement, which in turn brought into focus discarded bus tickets, sweet papers, and a varied range of dog shit. A man wishing to avoid the cracks between paving stones views a street in a particular way, a man wishing to buy a shop in that same street sees it in quite another manner, a man shopping regards it differently again, so too anybody driving along it on their way home. Vision is just a matter of intention or preoccupation; change the intention, change the view, change, change.

A man without immediate aims is like a watch without hands. A man without hope of change is like a day without night. *Cushing's Collected Clichés* for the feeble-minded, bound in tooled leather and twenty-five copies signed by the author.

Past a baker's and a jeweller's Derek came to an estate agent's. He stopped and looked at photographs of houses for sale. Flats for sale too. Comprising nine rooms ... in need of some modernization ... bathroom 6 x 8 ... small patio at rear ... central heating ... elderly sitting tenant. Derek pushed open the door.

The secretary was putting on her coat. The man behind an adjacent desk was tidying and sorting papers; he had a flabby yellowish face and a roll of flesh under his chin, which moved as he said, 'We're closed.'

Derek sat down and folded his arms.

'I want to sell my flat.' The man was flicking cigarette ash off his lapels. '36 Abercorn Mansions.'

The man said, 'Your name?'

Derek watched him writing down details. Name, address, phone number. Another flat to be sold; one of many. Derek said casually, 'I'm leaving London to start a market garden. Mushrooms and chrysanthemums.'

The man expressed polite interest and looked at his watch.

People left London every day, by road, rail and air, some by crematoriums.

The man said, 'Would Thursday morning be all right?' Measurements and other details for a description of the flat, he explained. Yes, Thursday morning would be fine. The Institute shut four days before Christmas.

On his way home Derek bought a reel of green cotton for his father. Aims were of the essence; aims immediate and distant. Derek decided to visit Angela and stay the night. He would take books out of the local library about market gardening. Discover in action what cannot be discovered in the head. Margaret saying: But, Derek, how can you say you don't like artichokes when you won't try them.

In the hall of the flat Derek prepared to tell his father about his visit to the estate agent's. As he walked towards Gilbert's room, Derek heard the sound of gentle snoring; the old man was having a late afternoon sleep.

Derek lay down on the sofa in the sitting-room and tried to imagine what he might say. Dear father, in a life too exclusively mental, without sufficient immediate contact with the earth from which all our nourishment is drawn, I have decided to make amends, to be precise I intend to begin a small market garden; this will mean selling this flat. I made the decision with the same ease, or difficulty, as I have when forcing myself to get out of a bath on a cold morning. I was unaware of the precise moment of choice and do not intend to make myself aware of it, just as I am never aware of making the decision to get out of the bath. I am not being flippant, or if I am, I consider it essential. I intend to *construct* a future for myself, since I have recently found it impossible to see one coming in the normal way. The ebb and flow of the seasons and the part played by them in vegetable production attract me, since in them quiescence is as important as growth. You will say that it is typical of me that, at a time when even the most unimaginative farm worker will do anything in his power to get into the nearest town on his day off, I should be thinking of going to live in the country. I shall not argue with you, nor will I do so if you say that my new venture is no more

194

likely to succeed than my earlier attempt to become interested in stamp collecting. For my immediate purposes it is enough to have set in motion a series of events likely to change almost everything I do. By choosing one course, I am refusing others; and the rejections may be as important as the acceptance. Only a fool would consider East African history to be more important than vegetables. But such comparisons, as I am sure you understand, are beside the point. Did you know that many explorers discovered that natives thought they had no feet? The reason was of course their boots, which being non-existent in most tribes, were hard to 'see'. Having no foreknowledge of my vegetable life I will not attempt to form an idea of it with words and symbols from my past. The prosecution of such substantial change demands this caution.

Over an hour later, Derek was aware that he had gone to sleep; aware because the room was dark and the bell was ringing.

When Derek opened the door there was nobody outside. A moment later he heard a cat crying and looked down to see Kalulu's basket on the landing. Kneeling, he could see the cat through the gaps in the cane-work. Then, a few feet in front of him, he saw Giles's face rise slowly above the brown carpet as the lift clanked and juddered to a stop. The boy was holding a suit-case.

'I thought you'd gone to Turkey,' said Derek, feeling a strange weakness in his legs.

'We weren't going till tomorrow,' replied Giles, picking up Kalulu's basket and taking it into the flat.

'Are you going to go?' asked Derek, following his son and shutting the door behind them. Giles bent down and unfastened the straps of the basket.

'No,' he said after a pause.

The cat jumped out and began prowling and sniffing; moving stealthily along the skirting-board.

'The taxi driver didn't want to take Kalulu so I had to give him more. It cost over a pound.' Giles walked into the sitting-room and saw the Christmas tree. 'Did you get it just for yourself?' he asked.

'Your grandfather bought it.'

'Where's the stuff to go on it?'

'In that box.'

Giles examined the decorations in silence and then turned abruptly.

'Aren't you going to ask why I'm here?'

'If you want to tell me.' Derek was afraid to assume that the boy had come back to him, scared of possible disappointment, unwilling to jump to the emotional conclusion that Giles had selflessly returned to brighten his lonely father's Christmas.

Giles sat down in a chair and moved around as though unable to make himself comfortable. At last he said hurriedly, 'You'll probably find it hard to believe, but this morning she said we weren't going to Turkey on our own and that it would be a good opportunity to get to know the person, because we'd be going to live with him when we got back.'

'A bit sudden, wasn't it? What did you say?'

'Asked her who it was, of course. I wouldn't have minded somebody else coming if they'd been all right.' Giles sounded angry and upset. 'You'll never bloody well guess who she's fallen for.'

'I may not know him.' Derek was surprised to feel so detached; as though he were listening to the doings of a stranger.

'You know him. We only stayed with him. Smoothy Charles. Incredible, isn't it?'

'Yes, I suppose it is,' replied Derek.

'Aren't you angry?' asked Giles indignantly; he seemed genuinely shocked by his father's passivity.

'I don't think so. I don't know what I feel.'

'You ought to smash his teeth in,' said Giles.

For a moment Derek felt relief rather than anger or sorrow; relief that he hadn't been so entirely deluded. His timing had been at fault but not his general thesis. Several seconds later he jumped to his feet with sudden horror. His timing *might* have been correct, she might have been having her affair right from the beginning just as he had thought, every word that she had uttered to convince him that he had been wrong could have been a lie.

'Are you OK?' asked an anxious Giles.

'I want you to think hard,' said Derek intently. 'I want you to think when it started. In Cornwall? Before I left? After I left? In London? When, Giles, when?'

Giles screwed up his face with perplexity.

'What the hell does it matter? She's moving in with him. Isn't that what counts?'

'I want to know,' shouted Derek.

'He started being all mushy and sympathetic after you'd gone. How awful for her, such a shock and lots of sentimental muck like that. Never said how awful it was for me or you or anybody else. Then when he found the flat for us, Mum was always droning on about how kind and good he was.' Giles twisted his fingers together and frowned. 'That evening I dashed off—he'd arranged tickets for a musical and we had to go because of all he'd done; paid the deposit on the flat, lent Mum his car, things like that.'

Derek sat hunched on the arm of his son's chair and shut his eyes. She'd not asked *him* for the deposit but had gone to Charles; the helpless woman in distress out to arouse Charles's chivalrous instincts, making him plume himself with protective importance. It occurred to Derek that Diana had left him simply to improve her chances with Charles. And in the end, as Giles had said, what did it matter *when* it had started? What indeed, since it was now perfectly clear that his attempt to stop their affair had merely brought about what he had hoped to prevent. If he hadn't argued with Charles, Diana wouldn't have had a chance. Charles had been a model of loyalty until accused of the very sin which he had in fact so virtuously avoided.

'Do you think they'll get married?' asked Giles in a flat un-emotional voice.

'Possibly.'

'Will you try and stop them?'

To Giles's amazement Derek started laughing uncontrollably until tears brimmed over his lids. When he could speak, Derek murmured weakly, 'I would have tried once. But not now, dear God, not now.' He took off his glasses and dabbed at his eyes with the corner of his unbuttoned cuff. 'They can commit bigamy or live in a polygamous commune for all I care.' As he stopped speaking he realized that he had meant precisely what he had said; there had been no posturing bravado, no dignified stoicism about it, no self-deceiving attempt to stave off possible bitterness or panic. Whether he had been cured of his chronic acquiescence when Diana left, or when he went to Ramsgate, or in the tearoom watching the old man dragged out by his wife, or in the instant that he entered the estate agents, he had no idea, but cured he must have been; that was a certain fact. It was not a method for resolving personal problems that ought to be recommended to many marital appeasers, too violent a therapy for most, but in his case, and with hindsight, apparently effective.

Giles looked as confused as ever when Derek said, 'Do you think they'll ask me to be the best man?'

Giles didn't smile but bit his lower lip. 'Nothing she did ever made you angry, she could have . . .'

'Hit me on the head with a frying-pan?' cut in Derek.

'Worse than that; tried to poison you, cut off your nose.' The glumness with which the boy said this made Derek want to laugh again, but he managed to say calmly, 'I was angry once; very angry. About a dentist she went to.'

'What?' came back Giles angrily, suspecting he was being made fun of.

'I know it sounds stupid now. But *then* it was different.'

Derek was smiling to himself until he saw the tears glistening on Giles's cheeks.

'She doesn't know I'm here. . . . I don't even know if you want me here, you seem so strange. I can't live in Charles's flat. I won't.'

Shame engulfed Derek like a breaking wave. 'But of course I want you here,' he said, taking his son's hands and squeezing them. 'She can't force you to go back. Nobody can.'

Giles began fumbling in his pockets for a handkerchief.

'I do hate crying too,' he said, drying his eyes and breathing deeply to stop his chest and diaphragm trembling.

'You'll have to get used to me again,' said Derek softly. 'I'm going to be a lot more selfish now. I want you to make demands too, we've all got to make demands, lots of demands, understand.' Giles sniffed a couple of times and smiled weakly as he nodded assent. 'People who don't get angry aren't really such saints. They may be no better than ivy clinging to a tree; parasites using other people's feelings and emotions because they're too apathetic or tired to have their own; because it's always easier to say yes than no, because they're frightened for no good reason. Then it becomes a habit and *no* becomes impossible and so there's no alternative but agreement.'

Giles looked away and whispered, 'Please can you ring Mummy when she gets in? She should be back in half an hour.'

'Of course I will.'

'We've been doing parasites in biology, but I can't think straight today.'

'Why should you?' asked Derek. 'Think crooked. Think any way you like.'

Giles smiled gratefully and said, as though it were the first thing that came into his head, 'Isn't your sweater a bit bright?'

'Should I wear drab and dirty colours? I like it; makes me look like a canary.'

'Rubbish.'

'Is it?' asked Derek flapping his arms and executing little jumps, in imitation of a bird about to take off. Giles broke out laughing, and, encouraged, Derek flapped harder and jumped higher. He turned to see Gilbert standing in the doorway nodding in his direction and tapping his head with a resigned expression. The cotton Derek had bought on his way back from the estate agent's must have fallen out while he had been leaping, because Gilbert bent down and picked up a reel of green thread. He examined it in the palm of his hand and then said in a slow thoughtful voice, 'Do you know, that is exactly what I was looking for.'

Gilbert broke off a length of thread and picked up a silver bell from the box on the table. As the old man moved towards the

Christmas tree, Derek knew that his father had never made a better purchase than his small and derided tree. Gilbert paused for several seconds as though on the verge of a momentous decision, and then, like an artist making the first mark on a virgin canvas, he leant forward and tied the bell to one of the lower branches. Moving back a couple of steps to admire the effect, he said with quiet confidence, 'I have a feeling I am going to do this uncommonly well.'

Giles caught Derek's eye and they smiled at each other, but neither laughed or contradicted Gilbert. Of course he would do it well. It went without saying. There was no reason to suppose him capable of doing it badly; no reason at all.